FILLINGS

FILLINGS

DAVE GARLOCK

The People's Ink
http://peoples-ink.com
Copyright © 2013 Dave Garlock
All rights reserved.

ISBN: 0989889742
ISBN-13: 978-0-9898897-4-2

Text set in Crimson
Printed in the USA

For Melissa

ONE

As Lee stretched over the edge of the dumpster with his feet dangling inches from the ground, reaching out for a sack of carrots he saw nestled under withered flowers, a burning pain erupted in the back of his mouth. It felt as if someone had stabbed a knitting needle up through his chin into a molar and was twisting it around. "Fuck!" Lee cried out, and dropped back to the concrete of the Trader Joe's parking lot, clutching his jaw.

"Are you ok? I knew this wasn't a good idea," Patrick said, looking out across the wide empty sea of concrete, its darkness pocked here and there by high lampposts, to 39th and the occasional car rushing there through the night.

"It's not the dumpster," Lee said, "it's my tooth. Shit, it hurts!"

"Has this happened before?"

"No, this is exciting and new," he said, sarcasm a slight distraction from the pain, which was like a small flame blazing at the base of one of his lower teeth. Lee pressed his hands against his mouth, not knowing what that might do, but pressing in hard. He was glad he hadn't dirtied his gloves much.

"Well, let's go home and get you some Advil."

"God yes. Or Vicodin, morphine maybe. Whatever you have."

"Advil."

"If you don't mind me taking the whole bottle. Wait..." The pain, as suddenly as it had arrived, was gone, leaving a vast cold emptiness in his tooth. His whole body shivered. "It doesn't hurt anymore," Lee said, amazement in his voice.

"Really?"

"I know, weird, right? It was killing me and now, nothing."

"You still want to go, take some pills in case it comes back?"

"No, I'm fine for now, I think. You want to give this a try?" Lee nodded his head at the large green dumpster that waited patiently, its black lid thrown open against a chain link fence.

"Anything I got would probably kill us. You're the expert; if anyone's pulling something we're going to eat from the trash, it's going to be you."

"Ok. Keep looking out for cops." Lee was taller than his compact, sandy-headed friend anyway, so it would be easier for him. The pain seemed already like something he'd dreamed, so he clambered back up the side of the dumpster, gaining a tentative balance with his stomach pressed into the lip. As he stretched out again he felt his jaw clench with the anticipation of agony, but it didn't return.

Most of the carrots in the red mesh bag seemed fine in the dim light, so Lee called out to Patrick and passed them down. More rooting around uncovered tons of plastic bags full of packing material, paper towels, coffee grounds and wadded up napkins. He pulled each one into the light, tore it open and sifted through, but found nothing worthwhile. The next bag his digging hand grabbed, however, had a promising heft. It was full of food. A bonanza of cheeses, a glass jug full of apple cider, some onions, a bag of tomatoes, a steak in cellophane and a dinged can of black beans. "We're in luck," he said.

"Wonderful," Patrick replied dryly. Lee started handing things down to him, leaving the steak because he wasn't that brave, the tomatoes because his hand squished through one when he went to grab it and some of the cheese because he didn't need that much and maybe some other dumpster diver would find it later that night. This was a popular spot.

Near where he'd found the first bag, Lee saw another that looked promising. It was just out of reach. He was scooting further over the edge of the dumpster when he felt his phone vibrate against his hip. His first thought was to ignore it. But Patrick, he could tell, was getting antsy and he didn't want to push his luck; he'd gotten plenty already. So he dropped back to the ground, peeled off his trash-smeared gloves and pulled out his phone. The screen showed his parents' number, which was odd since it was almost midnight. He answered.

"Hi, son, this is your father." Lee envisioned him clutching the old clunky phone to his bald head. He'd be sitting at the scarred wooden kitchen table in the home Lee'd grown up in, right above their general store in the tiny town outside of Eugene.

"I know, Dad. Why are you calling so late?"

"We were just wondering if you'd heard any-thing from Paul. He was supposed to meet us for din-ner tonight on his way back from the coast, but he never showed up."

Paul was Lee's older brother, who Lee had fol-lowed the hundred miles up I-5 to Portland. "No, I haven't," Lee said. "We were supposed to be camping together this weekend, but the person who was cov-ering my shift bailed. Did you try calling?"

"Of course," Lee's dad said. "He didn't answer."

"Well, maybe his Jeep broke down, or he decided to stay out there another night somewhere there's no cell reception. Or maybe he's just running really late. Paul's not the most prompt person in the world." Still, a little tinge of worry washed darkly over the back of Lee's mind.

From the background Lee's mother, who must have been standing close enough to hear both sides of the conversation from the loud phone, added, "That's what I said. There was no need to bother Lee, no need to worry anyone."

"I just wanted to see if Lee had heard anything, is all," Lee's dad said, defensively.

"I haven't, but I bet he'll wake you both up later tonight with some kind of excuse."

"That's what I said," his mom said again. Lee no-ticed that Patrick had put away their finds in his backpack and was gesturing with his head in the di-rection of his house. Guessing it didn't make sense to hang around the scene of the crime any longer, Lee started walking with him, the phone still pressed to his ear.

"You're both probably right. Sorry to bother you, Lee," his dad said. "I hope you weren't asleep."

"No, I'm hanging out with Patrick. Say hi to my parents, Patrick."

Patrick waved in the direction of the cellphone. He'd grown up with Lee and was his oldest friend besides Paul.

"Hello, Patrick," his dad said while his mom gave an enthusiastic "Hi!" They'd both always liked him, more than they liked Lee himself, he sometimes thought. Patrick had a real job as an electrician, for one thing, unlike Lee's four days a week at the liquor store and his insistence that painting was what he really did.

"Anyway, it's late. We should be going," Lee's father said. "Keep in touch, Lee, and we'll let you know when we hear from your brother. We love you."

"Alright, Dad. I love both of you, too. Goodnight."

"You didn't mention that we'd been digging around in dumpsters," Patrick said with a smile.

"Yeah, imagine that." They dashed across 39th and made their way east through quiet residential streets lined with looming dark Craftsmen houses towards Patrick's place. The late summer night air was warm and both wore shorts and a tee-shirt. Lee's shorts were black jeans from a thrift store he'd raggedly cut off when holes had enveloped the knees, his shirt from a free box. Patrick's were from the mall.

"Anyway, what was that all about? It's kind of late, isn't it?"

"I guess Paul was supposed to meet them for dinner on his way back from the coast, but he hasn't shown up yet. The whole thing is weird, because I thought he was going up near Astoria, not down south. I told my parents it was nothing, but it doesn't feel right. The whole night's been strange, though: my tooth, somehow convincing you to finally go dumpster diving? That's some once in a blue moon kind of shit."

"Don't worry about it. Paul's Jeep probably just broke down and he's walking along the highway with his thumb out, cursing the whole way." That was it, or something like it, Lee thought. It had to be.

TWO

A few minutes later they reached Patrick's house. It was a low fifties bungalow he rented with his fiancée, Cindy. She was visiting her parents in California for the weekend. Most of the furniture was from the closest IKEA, up in Seattle. Framed Matisse and Monet prints hung on the walls and the living room was dominated by a big entertainment center with its wires tucked neatly out of sight. Lee and Patrick spread the bag of dumpstered food out on a wide granite countertop in the gleaming kitchen.

"It looks like a good haul," Patrick said. "You were right, that was fun. I guess I don't get enough illicit thrills these days. It reminded me of coming home drunk on beers your brother bought us and hoping my parents didn't smell it on my breath, or sneaking into those crazy hippie parties at the Country Fair when we were sixteen. Now comes the hard part, though; convincing me that I'm not going to get food poisoning if I eat any of it."

"I never have."

"And how many times have you done this disgusting, illegal thing?" Patrick asked with a grin.

"Quite a few. Elly knows a bunch of good spots up north and I go with her. She'd be jealous of all this, though," he said, indicating their spread. "Well, except the cheese." Elly was vegan. She was one of Lee's housemates and his other best friend.

"Yeah, well, Elly's tougher than both of us combined," Patrick said. "Germs wouldn't dare mess with her. And vegetables must be safer than meat and dairy. Who knows how long that cheese has been out of the refrigerator? You don't want to add stomach cramps and nausea to tooth pain on you list of ailments for the night, do you?"

Lee didn't, and though his tooth felt fine now, mention of it brought back the ghostly memory of the pain and he shuddered. But he was confident. "Fine, don't eat the cheese; more for me. But the beans? They just threw those out because someone knocked the can off the shelf and it got dinged, the cider's a day past its sell-by date and, as for the onions and carrots, one probably went a little bad so they had to throw the whole bag away."

"We can start with the cider. If I don't die from that, maybe we'll move on. Though we could just buy non-poisonous cider in the morning."

"Yeah, but what if I couldn't?"

"Can't you?"

"Well, I probably could, though that stuff isn't cheap. But why waste your money when it's free, when it's just going to go into the landfill if we don't eat it?"

"Oh, why didn't you tell me it was about saving the planet?" Patrick joked, opening the cider and pouring it into two matching pint glasses. He raised his in cheers and they clinked glasses. "To drinking trash."

"To drinking trash," Lee seconded. They both took big swallows.

Patrick clutched his throat and bugged out his eyes for a second, then smiled.

"And to Paul," Lee called out, "having so much fun in the woods without me he lost track of time."

"To Paul," echoed Patrick. "Though we should be cheersing him with beer, not cider. You don't have anything to do tomorrow morning, do you?"

"Do I ever have anything to do on Mondays?"

"Lucky bastard. And my only job isn't 'til two. So we could definitely have some beers."

"I'm not going to say no."

They finished their cider, then Patrick pulled two Bridgeport IPAs from the fridge and they went to sit out on the wooden rocking chairs on the front porch. The street was quiet except for the rustle of leaves on the huge oaks and elms planted alongside the road. Lee leaned back and took a sip. It was icy, bitter and much more delicious than the swill he usually drank. "Thanks," he said. He took another swallow and yelled, "Crap!" dropping the beer, which twirled across the porch spewing a spiral of white foam and clutching at his jaw.

"Your tooth again?"

"No shit my tooth. Fuck!"

"I'll get the Advil." Patrick got up and ran towards the bathroom. Lee sat in the chair, pressing into his face with both hands, continuously cursing, tears in his eyes. Finally Patrick was back. "How many?" he asked.

"The whole goddamn bottle!"

Patrick shook out five orange pills, put them in Lee's hand and passed him his beer. Lee jammed them in his mouth and washed them back. Nothing, of course, happened. It still hurt like hell. It was going to hurt for a half hour or however long the painkillers took to work, if they were going to work, if Advil stood a chance against this agony. He got up and started pacing, clenching his jaw.

"Is there anything I can do?" Patrick asked, sitting back down and staring at Lee worriedly.

"Kill me, put me out of my misery."

"Cindy doesn't let me have guns. Anything else?"

Lee stopped his pacing and leaned up against the wall, staring at his friend. "Fuck if I know. Make it stop hurting. Find me a free dentist."

"Who is your dentist?"

"I don't have one. I haven't been in years."

"That's not good," Patrick said, getting up and putting a hand on Lee's shoulder.

"No shit. But everything's been fine until now. Jesus Christ it hurts!" Lee pulled away and resumed pacing like a caged tiger from one end of the small porch to the other.

"Well, OHSU, where Cindy works, has a dental school that's supposed to be really good. Maybe they can help you out for cheap."

"At midnight on a Sunday?"

"No, probably not, but we can go there first thing tomorrow morning. I'll give you a ride from here, since you're in no shape to be biking home tonight."

"Thanks. Maybe Cindy can call and pull some favors, get me a discount."

"She's a receptionist in the pediatrics department, but, sure, maybe."

"It's worth a shot, huh? Hopefully it's something that they can fix easily."

"Yeah, hopefully."

"You don't sound very optimistic."

"I'm not."

"Neither am I. Anything that hurts like this can't be cheap or easy to fix."

"Probably not."

"Fuck."

Eventually the Advil kicked in and the pain went from a sharp stabbing to a dull steady ache, like Lee's tooth was in a vice that was continuously squeezing and grinding. He took a few more pills and went to lie down on the couch in the room Cindy and Patrick used as an office, hoping to be unconscious as soon as possible. Patrick promised to look into OHSU.

Lee lay face down so the pillow pressed up against his mouth, which was somehow comforting and stared at the green and yellow lights of the computer. The couch was leather and felt sticky on his skin but was otherwise comfortable. Soon, somehow, despite the pain or maybe because of it, he was asleep.

Lee woke from a dream in which he, or maybe it was his brother, had been teetering on the edge of a deep dark pit, swaying, unable to get firm footing. He found himself in strange blackness, knowing nothing but pain. Some animal part of him had curled his long thin body into a ball, his head under his arms to protect it from harm though it was his head that was causing the misery. His mind was filled with panic. Then, slowly, dimly, he remembered who and where he was and then that the bottle of Advil was on the desk. He found it by the faint light of the electronics, poured out a small palmful and forced them down his dry throat.

Lee tried to lie back down but the pain was too intense. He pulled out his phone to check the time. It was only 4:23, still hours until dawn and the hope of relief. Too early to wake Patrick, who was already doing so much. So he paced back and forth, cursing softly under his breath, not knowing how he could live with this. I get it, he told his body, I understand there's a problem, I'm going to get it fixed soon, you don't have to do this to me. His body didn't listen, sending pain that seemed to lap over him like waves and made him want to take pliers and rip the tooth from his mouth himself.

When the medicine started to kick in and the pain subsided, slowly, to something that he would be yelling about normally but seemed blissful by comparison, he set an alarm for two and a half hours later, so he could take more drugs before these wore off. He'd rather overdose on Advil, fuck up his liver or whatever that did, than feel that pain ever again.

THREE

In the low glare of the morning sun, hours earlier than Lee ever got up, he settled himself in the passenger seat of Patrick's old truck. They headed west down Powell, the least Portland street in Portland: tangles of over and underpasses, the blazing neon of fast food restaurants and stunted trees. They went over the Ross Island Bridge, the Willamette River gleaming wide and placid below, the island the bridge was named for a patch of bright green to their left. After skirting downtown, its small cluster of skyscrapers reflecting back the morning light, their route twisted upwards through tall evergreens.

They didn't say much, both yawning a lot. Patrick sipped coffee from a shiny silver mug; Lee had declined, feeling that it might make his tooth, which throbbed still with just-bearable pain, worse. He kept wondering if his parents were going to call to say that Paul had turned up and pulled his phone out several times to check, but told himself they'd wait until a time he'd usually be awake.

Lee had never been to OHSU, though he'd often seen its white buildings perched on a hill south of downtown. Now they emerged from trees and it seemed like they'd entered a completely different, futuristic city. Tall buildings with sweeping arcs of concrete and glass jutted out of the hillside everywhere, slender walkways far overhead stretching between them. They found a space in the dental school parking lot and Patrick turned off the engine. "Do you want me to come in?" he asked.

"That's ok. You've got to work later and you've already helped me out a ton. Hopefully they can fix me up soon and I can try to forget about that shitty, shitty night. But thanks, man."

"Don't worry about it. What are friends for, right, other than giving their friends painkillers when they need them?"

"I couldn't have said it any better myself." Lee shook Patrick's hand hard, then turned away.

There was a short line at the check-in window; he was there right at eight o'clock when they opened. When it was his turn a matronly lady with thick black hair covered by a brightly patterned cloth asked if he had an appointment.

"No, sorry. My tooth started killing me late last night, so I didn't have time."

"Are you in pain now?"

"Yeah, but not as bad. I took a lot of Advil."

"That's good, hun. This place is really busy, but hopefully we can get to you today since it's urgent care." She handed him a clipboard with a thick stack of papers. Lee found a chair and started filling out questions about his insurance (none) and his social security number, which he'd memorized applying for various jobs, most of which he didn't get, over the last four years. Next came page after page on which he got to say he didn't have every medical condition known to man, that he didn't smoke, that he had five to seven alcoholic drinks a week (or so) and that the only medication he was on was Advil. The receptionist thanked him when he handed it back and said, "It might be a while, honey. As in any time between now and when we close at five. So just make yourself comfortable."

The waiting room was huge, with most of its seats filled. Along one wall stood a short line of what Lee assumed must be the dentists or dental students, dressed in either blue or purple smocks, chatting quietly, preparing to drag their patients back to whatever mysteries awaited. Lee's fellow patients seemed older and more diverse than an average Portland crowd. The lady across from him grinned, her face lined with wrinkles like the veins in a leaf, revealing perfectly white teeth. He wondered what she was doing here. Stifling a yawn, Lee smiled back. Some of these people were clearly worth painting; he wished he'd brought a sketchpad. He expected to hear the sound of drills and grunts of pain with all the dentistry no doubt going on, but there were no noises other than soft coughs, low conversations and the rustling of magazine pages being flipped.

The next hours were filled with stale magazines, dozing and staring into space. When the pain started moving from bass to alto, Lee rattled dusky orange Advil into his palm and gulped them back with sips from the drinking fountain. He was wondering which would drive him insane first, boredom or pain, when his phone buzzed. Glancing at it, he saw that it was his parents. "Hi," he said, relieved that they'd finally called.

"Lee, we still haven't heard from your brother." It was his mom this time.

Shit. "He still hasn't called, let you know why he's so late?"

"No. We haven't heard anything and your dad's starting to get very worried. Probably it's nothing, Paul just forgot he was going to stop by and went home and his phone's out of batteries from his trip. But we were wondering if you could go over to his house to make sure he got back safely."

"I'm at the dentist now, but I can go afterwards."

"Why are you at the dentist? Is something wrong?"

"My tooth's been hurting ever since last night."

"I'm sorry. Do they know what the problem is?"

"Not yet. I'm at the dental school, actually, and I've been waiting forever for someone to see me. But at least it's going to be cheaper than a regular dentist."

"If you need to go to a real dentist, we can help you pay. But hopefully it's something they can take care of there quickly."

"That's the goal."

"Anyway, a customer just walked in so I have to go. Make sure you check on Paul's house and let us know that he's back. I love you."

Would his brother really forget to stop by his parents'? Maybe. And his phone certainly could have died. Or his car could have broken down somewhere in the middle of nowhere and he hadn't gotten help yet. There were lots of possibilities. But it really seemed like he should have called by now.

Lee opened another magazine to distract himself from his worries, but before he could read a word he finally heard his name. His eyes met those of the girl who'd called for him and she smiled. It was a lovely absentminded half smile, slightly lopsided, maybe a little too big for her rounded nose and her small pointed chin. Lee grinned back, forgetting about his pain for a second.

He half raised his hand, but instantly felt foolish, like he was answering a question in class, and lowered it. Rising, he walked forward. Her green-brown eyes focused on him again and she smiled wide this time, showing a gleaming row of small perfectly white straight teeth. Maybe her first smile was for him then, not him as her patient? "I'm Lee," he said with a grin.

"Valerie Brooks. Nice to meet you, Lee." She held out her hand and it was warm, soft and dry in his, her grip firm. His palm tingled when she let it go.

"It's good to meet you, too." It was quite an understatement. She was stunning, even in her loose blue gown and with a scrunched cap covering her hair. It was mostly her smile, he thought, the slightly crooked smile that seemed to light her face and eyes. Of all the hundreds of students in this place, she was going to be his.

"What brings you in today, Lee?" she asked, looking at him, not at the clipboard in her hand.

"I thought, what could I do for fun today? And sitting in a waiting room for five or six hours reading ancient AARP magazines was the best I could come up with."

She laughed, a lovely trill.

"Actually, I wish that were it. Starting last night I've felt horrible pain in my tooth, towards the back, bottom left."

"Does it hurt now?" she asked with concern in her eyes.

"Yeah, but not as terribly. A lot of Advil helps a tiny bit."

"Ok. We'll do a few tests to find out which tooth is bothering you, then we're going to take some X-rays to pinpoint the problem. Does that sound ok?"

"Sure."

"Great. Follow me, then, and we'll get started on you right away so we can get you feeling better as soon as possible." She placed her hand on his back as she walked past, a light quick pat, and his skin shivered with her touch through his thin tee-shirt. Shit, what was he wearing? Actually it was one of his favorite shirts, black with a stylized turntable in white on the chest. He'd found it at a thrift shop, like most of his clothes. And he had on gray shorts that didn't have any paint splatters that he could see in a quick glance down. But it didn't matter, this was stupid. She was going to be his dentist.

They headed out a back passageway from the waiting area to a small bare room with a dental chair. "Take a seat, please," Valerie said.

Lee sat back in the enveloping chair, remembering the last time he'd been in one of these. It was towards the end of high school, back when his black hair, growing out from a buzz cut now, had been down to his shoulders. He'd gotten a cleaning and, for once, everything had been fine. The elderly Eugene dentist he'd had for most of his life had congratulated him and shaken his hand. His parents had taken him there about once a year. Since he'd moved to Portland four years ago, he'd never gone. Never thought to, couldn't afford it if he had. He'd never had a job with medical insurance, let alone dental.

Lee felt the chair lower and Valerie positioned the flexible light to shine into his mouth. He closed his eyes. "Open wide, please. Now I'm going to tap on your teeth, to find out which one is sensitive. Ok?"

Starting on the opposite side of the mouth from where the pain was, Valerie went around, tapping sharply and asking if it hurt. Lee said no, or a little, or just shook his head. As she worked her way towards the throbbing tooth Lee tensed, preparing himself. But he wasn't anywhere close to ready for the tap that sent pain blossoming like an action movie explosion through his head. His whole body curled and he made some kind of animal noise.

"Oh, God, I'm sorry," Valerie said. "That must be the one. But I have to do the rest to make sure." More taps, causing nothing like that pain, which was slowing draining away.

"I'm really sorry about that, Lee. Anyway, we can skip the other tests for now. Let's go get you X-rayed and then we can get started fixing up that tooth for you." He hoped it was that easy.

FOUR

Valerie left Lee alone, his mouth aching from all the slides she'd stuffed in there, while they were waiting for the X-rays to develop. Lee stared at the little rolling table topped with various picks and mirrors and other contraptions she would soon be jamming into his mouth. He thought about his brother. What if everything wasn't fine? What if he'd broken a leg somewhere out on the trail, or gotten hopelessly lost? Lee shouldn't worry, though; his brother went hiking and backpacking all the time, plus kayaking, cycling and rock climbing. He knew first aid. No, he was fine. He had to be.

Valerie came back and put developed X-rays down on a light box. Lee could see teeth and the bone of his jaw with various darker and lighter spots. While she examined the X-rays without a word, he examined her out of the corner of his eye. A wisp of hair had freed itself from her cap and nestled, a soft brown, on the achingly kissable pale back of her neck. Her lips were a light rose color. It didn't look like she used lipstick, or any makeup but he couldn't really tell. He couldn't tell how old she was, either: between twenty-two, Lee's age, and twenty-six, maybe. Her skin was smooth, unmarked. Her ears were adorable little whorls.

Finally she put her clipboard down and turned to Lee with a serious expression.

"Well, what's wrong?" he asked.

"It's not good news, unfortunately," Valerie said. "First, you've got a large caries, that's a cavity, which has reached down into the root. That's what's hurting you, and you're going to need a root canal. We'll start on that today and end the pain. But there are also two or three other cavities that need filling just on the few teeth we X-rayed here. Which makes it likely that there's more in the rest of your mouth. Sorry." She put her hand lightly on his shoulder for a second. Was it better or worse to get terrible news from a beautiful girl? Lee couldn't decide.

"How much is this going to cost?" he asked, wishing he didn't need to.

"I can't do an estimate for all the other work yet, but the root canal's going to be about three-fifty and the crown you'll need after that maybe another four hundred. You'll pay after each step of the treatment is done."

"Seven hundred and fifty dollars for one tooth?" Lee asked.

"I know. It would easily be over a thousand at a normal dentist, not that that'll make you feel much better."

"Not really. And I have to do this, right? Or I'm going to keep feeling this pain?" Lee could probably afford that, just barely. But could he pay for however much all those extra fillings might be?

"Right. There's a hole into your pulp, where your nerves are, and it's infected and inflamed, which can be incredibly painful."

"That's about how I'd describe it, yeah."

She grimaced sympathetically.

A professor checked Valerie's assessment of the situation then told her to get the tooth opened up. A needle gleamed then pricked lightly, again and again. Lee felt his lips begin to tingle and swell, then his cheeks. The sensation spread slowly down the left side of his tongue, which felt like a balloon. The pain that had been in his tooth since the beer last night slipped away somewhere and he breathed out a huge sigh, felt his shoulders relax a little. Valerie took impressions that dribbled pink goo down his chin and put on a dental dam that kept his mouth yanked open and covered it with a blue film. A trickle of saliva leaked from the corner. It wasn't really how he'd want a cute girl seeing him.

"Now we're going to drill your decayed tooth away so we can access the roots and clean them out. If you feel any pain, raise your right hand, ok?"

Lee nodded. There was no way he'd be able to talk with this contraption on his mouth. He closed his eyes when he heard the whir of the drill.

At first he felt nothing. The drill buzzed, Valerie sprayed water on the tooth, then sucked everything up. Lee stared up at a strange device with antennas on the paneled ceiling and decided it was probably for wireless internet. That or mind-control.

And then there was the first hint that drilling into a tooth that had been on fire earlier was maybe not such a great idea. Just a brief shimmer of faint discomfort, gone as soon as it registered. He didn't want to look like a wimp, so he didn't raise his hand.

Valerie wasn't saying anything while she worked, which Lee appreciated. There was another twinge, this one seemingly closer, a little more urgent. Still not what he'd describe as pain, but the worry of pain, its shadow.

"Almost there," Valerie said. The drill whirred again. Lee's hand shot up as agony raced through his mouth, rocking his body.

"Oh, no, you felt that?" Valerie asked. Lee could just nod, a tear running down his cheek.

"I'm sorry. We're almost done with the drilling. Was the pain bad?"

Lee nodded vigorously.

"Let me get a professor. Hold on."

Staring at the ceiling as the pain drained away, Lee wondered if his brother had called his parents or showed up yet.

The professor finally came, a rounded balding man who introduced himself as Dr. Gunder. Peering into Lee's mouth, he said, "Looking good, Valerie. The access is almost there."

"I know, but he's still feeling pain and I'm pretty sure he was completely anesthetized."

"Let me give it a try."

So the Professor stuck needles into his mouth, grabbed his cheek and shook it like Lee's grandma had done when he was a kid, then gave some technical advice to Valerie about where to inject Novocain that Lee couldn't follow. He hoped it was very good advice.

After a few minutes Dr. Gunder asked, "Are you feeling numb now?"

Lee tried to figure this out. It wasn't easy. There was tingling all over his mouth and the throbbing was gone, as was anything that could easily be described as pain. But there was still something there, some subtle signal of disquiet his body was sending. "Ahm not thuur. Thorry." He was a little proud he'd managed to get even that out around the numbness of his mouth and tongue.

"Well, let's do a little test," Dr. Gunder said. He picked up one of the tools on Valerie's tray. Lee opened reluctantly. The Professor rapped sharply on a tooth and asked, "Did that hurt?"

Relieved, Lee shook his head. Another rap. "No." Another. And there was maybe a shiver up his body, but it didn't hurt. "No."

"Good," Dr. Gunder said. "You should be ok now. Finish up the prep, Valerie, but call me over if there's any more pain."

So the dental dam went back on and the drill came out again. And, thank God, he didn't feel anything. Eventually Valerie stopped and said, "Now we're going to open up the roots so we can clean them out. There's a chance this might hurt, but hopefully things will keep going fine."

The drill whirred to life. And, as best he could through the dental dam covering his mouth, blocking his tongue, Lee screamed out in pain.

When the world came back into focus, Valerie was gone. She was back with Dr. Gunder in a minute. "So it was fine until you accessed the pulp?"

"Yes, Professor."

"Well, it's very possible that the tooth is so infected that no amount of Novocain is going to keep the patient from feeling pain. Now, Lee, we could take the dental dam off and inject more anesthetic, which would take more time and very well might not help, since you were, I'm almost positive, completely anesthetized before. Another option is to give you antibiotics and wait a few days while you continued to feel this pain. That may or may not work. Or, what I think is the best option, we could just do this quickly and get it over with. Only one of the roots should be inflamed and once we get in we can inject the anesthetic directly into the nerve, which should make the pain vanish instantly. However, it's going to hurt like hell, twice. So, what do you think?"

Lee wished he could talk, ask questions. That had hurt so much. But to get it over with rather than waiting, wasting more time? He had to go check on his brother, so he nodded.

Dr. Gunder took up the drill. "Valerie did a great job opening you up, but I'll do this part. Now, Lee, I want you to grab onto the arms of the chair and squeeze when it starts hurting."

It sounded like they were going to give him a shot of whiskey then amputate his leg. Jesus. He nodded again. At least it was the professor, a professional dentist, doing it now.

The drill whirred. Pain tore through him. Lee grasped the arms of the chair, felt them digging deep into his palms. His vision went red. Then it stopped. Lee felt his body shaking, his hands slowly unclasp. There was still pain, but it was like a candle compared to the blazing sun of what he'd just felt.

"Ok, we're in," Dr. Gunder said. "You're doing great. Now we just need to do the injection. So, I'm really sorry, Lee, but this is going to hurt again. But it'll work almost instantly and then you'll be fine."

Lee kept his eyes closed, concentrating on the fact that soon he should feel no more pain, trying to ready himself. It didn't work. More waves of agony, the chair arms digging into his hands, the world fading away or his tooth growing to encompass it all. He was gone. He didn't really know who he was anymore, he just knew misery. And then, just as the doctor said, "Ah-ha," the pain went off like a light burning out, leaving his head dark and empty. His body was covered in cold sweat and he shivered. Lee opened his eyes, looked at his hands; a red line ran through the center of each from where the chair had pressed in. Tears filled his eyes and the world became blurred and wavery. Valerie was looking at him with concern.

"Is that better?" Dr. Gunder asked.

Lee nodded. It was all he could manage.

When the professor was gone Valerie said, "God, Lee, I'm so sorry, that was terrible. I've never caused anyone pain like that. But you did great with it, you were very brave. And it should be easier from here on out." She'd called him brave. Which was what you'd say to a five-year-old.

The rest of the appointment was painless. Valerie scooped out the dying, infected pulp that had been making his life hell then stuck tiny round files down into Lee's tooth one after the other, enlarging and smoothing out the canal so they could fill it later.

Lee couldn't stop shivering, his body utterly drained and exhausted.

Valerie didn't have enough time to finish, so they put in a temporary filling and a temporary crown. This was a little whitish bit of resin she glued down on top of what he imagined to be the remaining stump of his infected tooth. It didn't fit right at first so she had to keep adjusting it. Finally Valerie said, "That looks like it'll work. Just don't eat anything too sticky or it'll pop right out."

They made another appointment and Lee was given a few extra-strength ibuprofen, just in case the pain came back. He thought he deserved much stronger painkillers, but didn't say anything. Then Valerie said, "Ok, we're done here for today. I'm so sorry you had to go through that, Lee, but you did great." She held out her hand and he shook it, trying to keep himself from trembling. The warmth of her touch comforted him.

Outside Lee found green manicured lawns and huge trees, fresh air and sunlight. The world seemed both alien and hyper-real after all those hours under fluorescents. He couldn't believe it was over, that he was free, that his tooth wasn't in agony anymore. He breathed in deeply.

And then he remembered that he had to go check on his brother.

FIVE

Lee approached his brother's home cautiously, as if it were a coiled snake. It had taken an hour and a half and two buses to get here, Lee's anxiety building the whole time. The ranch style house was surrounded by and partially engulfed in a beautiful garden of native plants and wildflowers that Paul, a landscaper, had done himself. No lights were on, but the sun was still shining strong so that didn't mean anything. He got close enough to see that the Jeep wasn't in the driveway. Maybe Paul had come home and gone back out.

Lee went to peer in the windows, but the glare from the sun made it hard to see through the gaps between the drawn curtains. There was no answer to his knocks so he went around into the sunny backyard. It was mostly taken up by planter boxes full of vegetables and herbs, the tomatoes heavy with red and yellow fruits, the squash huge-leaved and tropical. Lee walked up to a basement window. Looking around, he decided it was safe; he was blocked from view by trees and the house. He yanked on the window handle. Nothing. He got down on his knees and put his weight into it, pulling backwards. It swung up

28

and outward with a creak and Lee almost fell back. He'd gone in this way before at the end of a long night out drinking with Paul, who, after they'd stumbled home singing Beck songs at the top of their lungs, had no idea where his keys were. He'd said the other windows were locked but this one just stuck, so it would seem like it was locked if anyone tried it.

After another look around for nosy neighbors, Lee lowered himself feet first into the dark basement. He turned and pulled the window shut behind him. Dusty light fell from the windows to partially illuminate rows of shelves. They were filled with climbing gear, basketballs and baseball bats, life vests, paddles and much more gear, carefully arranged. A kayak and two bicycles hung from hooks. Lee walked to the center of the room and pulled the chain on the lightbulb hanging from the ceiling then yelled out, "Hey, Paul? Are you home? It's me, Lee. I'm in the basement!"

No answer. Lee went over to where the backpacking equipment was kept. The orange North Face pack, the one Paul took everywhere, was missing, as was some other stuff that wasn't so immediately identifiable but left gaps among the rest of the gear.

Lee walked past the washer and drier to the stairs. At the top he knocked on the door then pushed it partway open, saying, "Paul? Hello?"

He cautiously entered the house. There was no noise, no light except what came through gaps in the window curtains, painting golden patches on the hardwood floor. Lee went from room to room, looking for signs of recent habitation. There were no dirty dishes in the sink, no clothes strewn on the floor, nothing out of place. On the desk was a neat stack of unopened mail; bills from PGE and the water department, a letter, probably asking for money, from the Oregon Natural Resources Council and an advertisement with coupons for oil changes. The bed was made, its brown sheets pulled tight. Lee had known his brother was neat, but not that he went that far. Everything was perfect, maybe too perfect. It was hard to say, though, because he'd never really spent much time in here. Most of the time with his brother they'd been outdoors, hiking to lakes on Mt. Hood, laughing over a whiskey bottle around a campfire, riding bikes down sunny streets.

The bright orange backpack was nowhere. Paul hadn't returned from his trip. He was almost a full day late, he wasn't answering his phone and he hadn't contacted anyone.

Lee sank into a long green couch. For the first time since he'd heard about Paul he felt true worry, which quickly rose to near-panic, a queasiness in his stomach. Something was deeply wrong. The closed up house was foreboding, terrifying. Paul could have crashed his car, fallen off a cliff, been mauled by a mountain lion, been murdered if he'd tried to hitch-hike. Anything could have happened as he was out hiking alone. Lee should have been with him. He should have fucking been with him but instead he'd been at work selling Bombay Sapphire to soulless yuppies. As Lee sat there he noticed that his tongue was playing over and over the temporary crown Valerie had put over his destroyed tooth, feeling a slight difference from the original, a rough unevenness.

After a few minutes Lee took a deep breath and forced himself up. He went back into the basement and climbed out the window, shutting it behind him with a strong push. As he started walking towards the bus stop he got out his phone. He had to call his parents, though he really, really didn't want to. Didn't want to make this real.

"Garrett Country Store."

"Hi, Dad."

"Hello, Lee." Lee wished it were his mom who'd answered. She was usually the more reasonable one.

"Dad," Lee said, then took a deep breath. "Paul hasn't been home."

After a slight moan his dad said, "I didn't think he had, somehow. I'd hoped I was wrong. I guess, I guess we're going to have to do something now, start searching for him somehow. Maybe call the police. I don't know, I don't know anything about this, how it works. Hopefully he'll just show up. Of course he will. It's only been a day. Should we really call the police?"

"I don't know. There's just so much that could have happened, so many places that he could be. I don't even know who we'd call. The state troopers?"

"Maybe. Your mom and I will figure it out. We'll call after I talk to her. I just pray this is some kind of mistake and that he'll show up, or at least call, any minute now."

"Me too, Dad."

Lee wondered how he and his dad had remained so calm in that conversation. Probably because none of it seemed real. And it wasn't, it wouldn't be, once his brother showed up.

SIX

Lee raced up Patrick's steps, eager to talk to his friend about all the shit he'd gone through that day, hoping it would get his mind off his fears, but no one answered his knocks. He pulled out his phone to call and saw that his battery was almost dead. In case any important calls about Paul came in he decided to save what charge was left. Around the side of the house Lee unlocked his beloved bike, an old black and silver Peugeot, from the fence it had been chained to.

A twenty minute cruise took Lee through Patrick's quiet residential neighborhood then through a fancier one with curving streets, massive trees and big houses presiding over immaculate lawns. Lastly he rolled into his own, a bit more run down, more diverse, livelier.

Lee pulled up in front of his house, an old Victorian, the lawn overgrown with weeds and spotted with patches of dead grass, its tan paint peeling in strips. He rolled to a stop and jumped off, feeling sweat on his back and under his armpits from the ride in the warm evening. After unlocking the garage he wheeled his Peugeot into its spot among the metallic tangle of other bikes, some working, some under repair or disassembled for parts.

The porch was littered with empty Pabst cans and overflowing ashtrays. "Anyone home?" Lee called into the dim house. He wanted to find Elly, but her job as a caretaker for various elderly and ill people made her schedule unpredictable.

No one answered, so he walked through the living room with its thrift store and side-of-the-road furniture, its Ramones and Clash posters, then up the stairs. The soft strumming of a guitar came from behind Elly's door; he couldn't tell if it was her playing or recorded. Her usual instrument was the mandolin, but she could play just about anything with strings. Lee knocked softly.

"Yeah?" Elly asked.

"It's Lee. Can I come in?"

"Sure thing."

Elly was sitting on her unmade bed cradling an acoustic guitar. She was a short, broad girl with hair chopped close and dyed black, a ring in her lip and three studs in her nose. She wore black torn and patched clothing, had blue eyes and a wonderful smile.

She was grinning at first, but it faded quickly and she asked, "What's wrong, dude?"

"What isn't? My brother went to the coast this weekend and hasn't come back yet, no one's heard from him and he was supposed to be home last night. And I just went through the most goddamn agonizing day of my life. My tooth started killing me and I went to get a root canal but they couldn't totally numb it and it went on for fucking ever. Holy shit, it hurt.

And it's going to cost me basically all the money I have then there's probably lots more work to do after that. Plus the girl who drilled into my rotten tooth was beautiful and I think she smiled at me before anything that could have happened between us was ruined by her being my dentist." He realized he'd been grasping the frame of her door hard while he'd been talking.

"Shit, man."

"Yeah. So much shit."

She put down the guitar, held out her arms and said, "Here." He went into her embrace and she held him warmly for a minute. Then she asked if he needed a beer. She was great. If she weren't a lesbian and if she were more his type he'd probably marry her.

Elly handed him a Pabst from her mini-fridge that was always stocked with them and various weird vegan snacks. He took a small sip with trepidation, remembering the pain that his last beer had caused, but nothing happened. It tasted familiar, mediocre, just fine. He put the cool bottle to his forehead, then took a longer drink.

"Do you want to talk about any of that crap, man? Does anyone have any idea where your brother might be?"

"I don't think I want to talk about him. No, no one knows anything, but he'll probably get home soon, his car'll have just broken down or something, right? But, fuck, my tooth. I went to the dental school up at OHSU, that place is like the Jetsons. And they said this might hurt a bit and then they stuck a flaming spear into my jaw and twisted it around. They told me to hold the chair tightly, like they were about to saw off my leg or some shit. And I had to wait forever..."

Elly listened patiently while he told his rambling, disjointed story of all the pain he'd felt, laughing at the appropriate parts, expressing sympathy when it was needed, which, Lee thought, was just about the whole time.

When he was done she said, "Well, fuck, man. Good luck with everything, and let me know what I can do to help. And don't worry too much about your brother, I'm sure he'll be fine. He seems like a really competent guy."

"Yeah, he is. Thank you."

"Want another beer?"

"No, that's ok." He'd felt maybe the shimmering of discomfort from his tooth while he'd been drinking, though it was very possible it was just his imagination. He pulled out a packet of the extra strength Ibuprofen they'd given him and downed one with his last sip.

"So, what are you up to tonight?" Lee asked Elly.

"Well, I kind of have a date, actually."

"Who with? That same girl from last time?"

"Yeah. Steph."

"I thought that wasn't going to work out because she listened to Green Day."

"I was kidding. Kind of. So I'm going to give it another chance. She's cute; you'd like her if she were into boys."

"That's helpful."

"You really do need to meet someone new. Lisa was months ago. But anyway, man, I can call to cancel or you can come with us if you want."

"That's really nice of you, but, no, of course not. I'll be ok. You should go out and have fun. I need to charge my phone, stay with it in case there's any news."

"If you say so."

"Actually," he said, checking the batteries, "I'm going to do that now. But thanks for listening, and thanks for the beer."

"Any time, dude. Any time."

No calls came in that night. Lee got out his sketchbook and doodled for a while, but nothing inspired him, he was too distracted. He stared at the canvas he'd been working on for the past week where it was laid on a spread of newspapers to keep the paint off his teal carpet. The canvas was covered with muddled abstract swirls and eddies, gray and purple the prevailing colors, with the graceful arch of the St. John's bridge, chosen because it was the coolest looking one in Portland, seeming to coalesce out of the murk.

Lee remembered biking over that bridge with his brother earlier in the summer on their way to Sauvie Island, where they'd picked blackberries in the tranquil sunshine, pedaled down flat roads through endless fields, dove into the chilly waters of the Columbia and laid back on the beach drinking beers, eating sandwiches and talking about the tough breakups they'd both gone through a few months before. They'd vowed to each have new, better, less crazy girlfriends by fall to cuddle up with when the rains came, clicked their bottles together and drained them. And now, with September only a little more than a week away, all Lee had was a crush on his dentist. And Paul was fucking missing.

The painting wasn't quite right. It needed something more but he didn't know what. He stared at it, fiddling with tubes of paint but not wanting to squirt any out and waste it if he wasn't actually going to do any work. Paint wasn't cheap.

Lee picked up his phone, the power cord still dangling from it to the wall. Still nothing. Should he be calling people? Someone might know something more. But probably they wouldn't, probably he'd just make everyone worry, panic like he was starting to.

SEVEN

Lee stocked the rainbow of Stoli flavors, pulling the old ones out to push the new bottles to the back of the shelf. It was Tuesday afternoon, a little more than 43 hours after Paul was supposed to have shown up at their parents' house, and there was still no word from him. And Lee was back where he'd been forced to be instead of camping with his brother, keeping him safe. Though it was usually Paul who kept an eye on Lee, not the other way around.

The door dinged. Joseph walked into the store and smiled at him. Lee grinned back, walking with his box behind the counter. Joseph was an older guy in his fifties or sixties, though it was hard to tell, who was always, no matter the weather, bundled in a long ragged tan trench coat. He had wild gray hair and seemingly permanent stubble on his gaunt but friendly face. Lee wasn't sure Joseph was homeless, as he'd never seen him huddled on a corner asking for change, but he likely wasn't very far from it. And some of his customers definitely were. It made him feel like shit, taking their change and wadded bills for a plastic bottle of gin, but what was he going to do? It was his job, it was a free country and it wasn't his place to judge. He still often felt like an asshole, but with Joseph it was different.

He was taking his time as he always did, pulling different bottles from the top shelves and reading their labels then carefully returning them to their place. Things weren't busy and Lee looked forward to a long, friendly, rambling talk with Joseph when he finally made it up to the counter. Usually they discussed sports, often from decades ago, the Blazers or Los Angeles teams. Lee just pretended he knew what Joseph was talking about, nodded, smiled and pitched in with whatever halfway relevant observations he could come up with.

The door opened again and a tall officer in a lighter blue uniform than the Portland Police's came in, large black sunglasses hiding his eyes. Joseph quickly returned the sixty dollar bottle of whiskey he was looking at to the shelf and hurried out of the store. Lee hoped he'd come back, wondering if he'd done anything to make him afraid of the law. He really didn't seem like the type

But the cop was coming up to the counter and now Lee was the one getting nervous, though he couldn't think of anything he'd done recently that he could get busted for. They wouldn't take fingerprints off a dumpster. Maybe the officer just wanted cigarettes or a bottle of bourbon for after his shift. That happened sometimes.

"Are you Lee Garrett?" He had a slightly southern twang to his voice, like Lee's grandparents on his Mom's side.

"Yes, sir." He didn't just want cigarettes.

"I'm here to ask some questions about Paul Gar-rett, your brother."

Of course. "Have you found anything yet?"

"Not yet. We're just doing preliminary question-ing now, trying to figure out where to look, what to look for or if we even need to be looking at all. We wouldn't be, yet, if there weren't the chance that he's lost in the wilderness, which could be dangerous. I'm Sergeant Dennis Sorrel of the Oregon State Police." He held out his hand, which Lee took and tried to shake firmly. "Do you mind us doing this now? If you can't, I can meet you after work."

"Now's fine if you don't mind interruptions when someone wants to buy something."

"That'll work. So, when was the last time you saw your brother? The last time you heard from him?" Sergeant Sorrel pulled out a little black note-book and a pen.

Lee said, "We went out for drinks last Friday, when he was done with work, at a place kinda near my house, the Crow Bar. And I last talked to him on Thursday evening when I called to tell him that I couldn't come on the trip because the person who was going to cover my shift here on Saturday said she couldn't after all."

"What did you talk about on those occasions?"

"When I called, we didn't talk long. He said he really wished I could go and I said I knew, that it sucked. I told him to have fun for me, too. At the bar, I don't know what we talked about. Lots of things. I've tried to remember, gone over the conversation in my head a bunch of times by now. How much he loves his job, how much I hate mine. He told me for the millionth time that I should come work with him. We talked about beer, about the songs on the juke box, the war and Bush, about Michael Jackson. Friends we have in common and how they were doing. Probably a lot of other things, too. I can't remember exactly. We were drinking."

At that point the door dinged and Joseph poked his head in again. He was turning to leave so Lee said, "Don't worry, Joseph, come on in. It's fine."

Joseph quickly grabbed the bottle of the second cheapest rum that Lee'd known he'd pick eventually and came up to the counter.

"Is everything ok, Lee?" he asked.

"Yeah. Or, no, not really. My brother's missing. Sergeant Sorrel here is trying to find him."

"I'm sorry," Joseph said. "If there's anything I can do, let me know. You know I'd like to help."

"Thanks. I'll let you know if I think of anything."

Joseph paid with crumpled one dollar bills, and, as he always did, dropped his few cents of change into the penny tray. He'd joked that it was Lee's tip once.

"Good luck finding your brother," Joseph said. "It's no good when someone is lost." He waved, then ducked quickly out the door.

"Seems like a nice guy," Sgt. Sorrel said. "Anyway, do you or anyone you know have a spare key to your brother's house?"

Lee, a little nervous, said he didn't, then told him about going through the back window yesterday. The officer said it was fine as long as he hadn't disturbed anything.

They talked for another fifteen minutes. Sgt. Sorrel wrote down the contact information of anyone who might know where Paul was and asked questions about his mental state, life, work and camping habits. Finally he said, "Well, that's all I can think to ask for now. I'll call some of those numbers you gave me. Hopefully he told someone more precisely where he was going so we can narrow our search and make it easier to find his car. Anyway, here's my card. Call me if you can think of anything else I should know."

"You have people looking for his car? You think it's that serious?"

"We don't know. If he was in a wilderness area, it's certainly possible he got lost or injured, so we'd want to find him as soon as possible. But there are, as I'm sure you know, many other possibilities."

"Right."

"Thank you for your help, Lee."

"Thank you. Thanks you so much for looking."

"It's my job. And now I'll let you get back to yours. But we'll let you know the moment we find anything."

Sgt. Sorrel left with a wave. Lee went back to stocking the brightly colored bottles of Stoli. Paul hated vodka, would only drink whiskey, usually Maker's Mark. That last time at the bar he'd bought Lee a Maker's on the rocks instead of letting him buy himself a well whiskey and coke, telling him that he was doing his tastebuds a favor. Lee hadn't mentioned that to the officer. It wasn't important. But, of course, it was.

EIGHT

Lee, up front, surrounded by friends, bobbed his head and started swaying. Dragon Pig, a band he'd played in for a while before realizing he was a painter, not a musician, was starting in on what they always used as their last song, an epic ode to lost love that was a little more classic rock then their usual punky pop sound. It was impossible to judge objectively since he was still friends with all of them, but he thought they were great. He'd been dancing and playfully moshing, stomping his feet on the wooden floor through their whole set, though the place wasn't very full and most of the crowd in the wide room just stood around with arms crossed, bobbing their head to the beat. That was what people in Portland did at concerts, especially for the openers. Still, this was the most high-profile venue they'd ever played, a big step up from the crowded basements where most of their shows happened, and Lee was proud of them.

Conrad, the drummer, smashed on the snare, his long sweat-matted hair plastered over his face. He used to be Lee's housemate. Renee, his girlfriend, was the band's other founding member. She was the lead guitarist, but, though she had a good voice, absolutely refused to sing on stage.

For a little while Lee had played rhythm guitar and been the lead vocalist, singing the songs Conrad wrote about World War III, bicycles and break-ups. However, before they'd gotten any gigs, he'd decided that his voice was too atonal and yelpy and that his guitar playing was too clumsy and amateurish to front a rock band. Now he did the artwork for their albums, shirts and posters, having sold his guitar for paints and brushes.

Lee'd been replaced by Tom, a much smoother guitar player who was almost yodeling in melodic agony now. Brian, who Lee thought was probably the least talented of the group, played his bright yellow bass with a deadly serious expression.

With a last sustained wail from Renee's guitar matched to a lingering moan from Tom and a crashing of cymbals, they ended their set. Lee yelled, clapped and stomped his feet, but he knew the opener wouldn't get an encore. Looking back he saw that the rest of the audience was applauding, but they didn't seem as enthusiastic as they should.

"Those guys were pretty kick-ass as always," Elly said. "Hey, you want a beer?"

"Sure."

After a while the next opener came on. They were local too, and more popular than his friends' band. Everyone else got up to go to the stage but Lee and Elly stayed at their table in the back corner. He'd seen this band play a few times and he thought they were pretty generic. Elly said they sounded too much like the Foo Fighters.

About halfway through the set Lee saw Dragon Pig emerge as a clump from somewhere in the back. He got up, Elly following behind him. "Great job, guys," he yelled over the guitars, clapping Conrad on the back, shaking everyone's hands. "Pretty awesome playing this place, huh?"

"I'm glad you could come," Conrad yelled back, leaning down close. "How're you doing?"

"I'm ok," Lee said.

"No he's not," Elly shouted. "His brother was camping on the coast and has been missing since Sunday."

"Shit, man."

"Yeah, shit," Lee agreed.

"What do they think happened?"

"I don't really want to talk about it," he yelled. "Let's fucking celebrate your playing Berbati's, Dragon Pig's rise in the world. You guys sell any shirts?"

"With your art, how could we not?" Renee yelled back. She was tiny, with black hair, drastically cut bangs and sharp but pretty features. She acted tough but she could be hilarious and was very generous with her friends. He liked her and thought she and Conrad made a great couple other than their slightly disturbing size difference.

They went to the table where Teresa, Brian's girlfriend, pedaled the merchandise, a job Lee sometimes took when she wasn't available. She'd sold a few screenprinted shirts and burned CDs in cardboard sleeves, both featuring Lee's R. Crumb-like frenzied charcoal drawing of a dragon pig, smoke billowing from its snout. It wasn't anything like what he painted now. He thought it was ok, but looked forward to them coming out with a new CD for him to better showcase his talents on.

Conrad got him a beer, then Renee, though he protested, saying it was he who should be buying them drinks in congratulations for their show. Missing brother trumped performing at a big venue, he guessed.

Lee was drunk. He was dancing to the headliners, some indie band from Austin that was pretty rocking, pretty musically solid, in the midst of a mass of Dragon Pig and their friends. There was a girl next to him who he kind of knew, a friend of Tom's he thought, with whom he'd exchanged a few yelled words and smiles. She was cute, though a little taller than Lee usually liked, and she dressed maybe too mall-y for his taste. But, right now, he didn't care. He turned to say something else to her and then saw, past her in the crowd, Valerie. Whatever he was going to say was instantly forgotten.

She was stunning; this girl next to him, whose name he couldn't even remember, paled in comparison. He only saw Valerie in brief glimpses through partings in the swaying crowd and had to keep looking to convince himself it really was the girl who'd been poking around in his cavity-ridden mouth and causing him endless pain just yesterday, though it felt like a week ago. She was wearing a dress the color of a hazy sky with the sun trying to break through. It left her perfectly formed arms bare from the shoulders, her calves showing below mid-shin. Who wore something like that to a show at Berbati's on a Tuesday? And who was she with?

Lee drifted through the packed undulating audience towards Valerie, drawn almost against his will, because what could he say to her, how could he want her to see him drunk in his sweaty Dragon Pig tee-shirt with the hole in the armpit? It was hard to tell with the fluid crowd, but she seemed to be in a knot of about five or six people, mostly guys. Shit. Mostly guys wearing expensive looking characterless clothes, the only other girl in a red dress that revealed a chunk of bulging cleavage. They looked like the idiot suburbanites who ruined Portland on the weekends, coming to get in fights and clog the clubs, to stagger in heels through the downtown streets and then drive drunk back to Beaverton. What was she doing with people like that? One of the guys with the crewcuts was probably her boyfriend and Lee was about to retreat when she turned. Her eyes met his past the few people now between them and her face lit up in a smile. She said, "Hi, Lee!" and he felt his heart thump.

"Hi, Valerie," he said, retreat no longer possible. The band's singer was rambling on about how their tour was going and how much they loved Portland even though it stole its "Keep Portland Weird" thing from Austin, so they could hear each other without screaming. Not that he would have anything to say to his dentist.

"How are you doing?" she asked. "God, I'm so sorry how much that sucked yesterday." She didn't slur her words or anything, but he was instantly certain that she was drunk, too.

"No more pain, so far. You did a great job."

"I'm glad. How're you liking the show? Pretty great, huh?"

"These guys are pretty good. I came here to see Dragon Pig, one of the openers. They're friends of mine. Did you catch them?"

"No, we just got here for this band; they're one of Mary's favorites. It's her birthday. Mary, guys, this is Lee. He's one of my patients. We just met yesterday and here he is. Weird, huh?" Mary flashed him a smile, the guys waved or ignored him. At that moment, with a crash of guitars, the band started another song, drowning out Lee's call of happy birthday.

Valerie came up close to him and yelled into his ear, "It's cool that you're friends with a band that played here."

"I was in the band for a few weeks, actually, but with me as the lead singer they weren't nearly good enough to play anywhere."

"You sing? That's neat." He could feel her breath on his cheek when she talked and when he replied he was intensely aware of the small distance between his lips and her ear.

"If you count tone-deaf yelping as singing. Mostly I paint."

"I don't really do anything artistic, though I love all kinds of art. I'm a really good cook, though. That's my creative outlet."

Lee had noticed several glances coming from Mary and the guys. He decided it didn't matter. This girl was beautiful, it seemed like she was maybe into him, he was drunk and he'd lost his brother so who the fuck cared if she was his dentist. So he said, "Hey, Valerie, do you want to meet my friends who were in the opening band?"

"Sure." She smiled.

He headed away from her group towards the merch table where he'd seen them last and she miraculously followed him through the crowd. "I did the artwork for their shirts and CDs," he said, gesturing at the little pile in the corner, looking unprofessional next to the other two bands' layouts. The musicians weren't around.

"Cool! That's a pretty good drawing. It's funny. Is the band any good?"

"I like them a lot, but of course I'm biased."

"I'll get the CD, then." She pulled a billfold, something he wasn't sure he'd ever seen anyone use, from her small gray purse and peeled off a twenty.

"I'd feel bad if you didn't like it," Lee said.

"I'm sure it'll be good. And if not, it's not like it costs a fortune," she said, accepting her change.

At that point the band ended a song and left the stage. The crowd cheered and soon started stomping their feet for an encore. Lee scanned the mass of dimly lit people but wasn't sure where his friends were. Probably up in the very front, which wouldn't be easy to get to now that the place had filled up. He explained the situation to Valerie and said, "You want to just wait and meet up with them afterwards?"

"No, I think I'll head back to my friends," she said. He tagged after her, though he wasn't entirely sure that's what she wanted.

They made their way back around the edge of the crowd, which was stomping and clapping for the band to come back on stage, to where her friends were clumped. Lee cursed himself for losing the opportunity to keep her off alone. Once there, Valerie stayed slightly separated from them, closer to Lee than to Mary. "So, Lee," she asked, "What do you do with yourself when you're not painting, going to rock shows or getting your teeth drilled into?"

He spent all his time worrying about his missing brother. But he didn't want to talk about that now, wanted to forget, to lose himself with this beautiful girl. So he said, "I don't know. Work, hanging out with friends, hiking and camping, drinking at bars, watching movies. I ride my bike a lot. You?"

The crowd roared as the band rushed back onto the stage, launching immediately into their next song. Valerie didn't answer his question, turning forward and clapping. Lee faced the stage as well, though he was much more aware of the inches separating his side from hers than what the band was doing. She started dancing to the thumping drums and repetitive hum of the bass, moving her body naturally, unself-consciously. He wanted to dance with her, to ask her if he could. He needed more alcohol.

"I'm going to get a drink," he yelled into her ear. "You want one?"

"Sure," she said with a smile.

"What do you want?"

"A Bombay Martini. Please."

He smiled back at her. He wasn't sure how much that was going to cost, but he knew the booze wasn't cheap here. It was going to be more than the PBRs he'd been thinking of when he offered, certainly.

Everyone was watching the encore so the bar, a long curved slab of wood, huge shelves gleaming with bottles behind it, was empty. He yelled his order then spent most of the only twenty in his wallet on the martini, a well whiskey and coke and a two-dollar tip.

Keeping the drinks close to his chest, Lee worked his way through the crowd towards where he'd left Valerie. He didn't see her, then felt a hand on his shoulder. He turned and Valerie let it linger there a few seconds before pulling back. He held out her drink, which she took and raised up. The band's noise increased, rising to a crescendo. He thought he saw her lips say cheers so he clinked his glass to hers then drank, savoring the sweet of the coke and then the slap of the whiskey on his throat and its warmth in his stomach, wondering what she'd cheersed to, what he had.

That song finished, another one began, and Valerie started dancing again. She was utterly hypnotizing. To keep from staring he danced too, doing his best, swaying, moving his hips, taking little steps. It was hard with the glass in his hand and because he didn't completely feel the music, so he downed the rest of the drink in a gulp. That made dancing easier.

He wanted to turn to her, dance face to face, but he wasn't sure that was what she wanted. He kept turning his head to watch her. Twice he saw that she was looking at him, too, and they both smiled. Her smile was amazing.

Too soon the last song, more rowdy and punk than the rest, came to a crashing end, before Lee'd had the courage to do or say anything. And his friends would filter back here and find them or her friends would steal her away and that would be that; they'd smile, shake hands and go home, then he'd go to their dentist appointment in a few days. "Valerie, do you want to get another drink with me somewhere?" he asked.

She laughed and said, "I really shouldn't have even had that last one, shouldn't be out this late at all. I have class tomorrow morning." She giggled, possibly at the disappointed expression he was sure was on his face. But then her smile faded and he saw her think. She said, "Besides, I'm going to finish that root canal up for you in a few days. We can't really be going out for drinks together. But," she said, placing her hand on his shoulder, "this was fun, it was good running into you. I'll see you back at the dental school." She smiled at him then turned away to her friends, said something to Mary.

Lee, knowing his cue though hating it, slipped away into the crowd, looking for Elly, for any of his friends. He felt like he'd missed an opportunity, but what possibility was there? Like she said, she was his dentist.

NINE

"Is that his car?" Lee's dad asked, a hint of desperate excitement in his voice. A lean hand shielded his blue eyes from the sun.

"No, I think that's a Cherokee," Lee's mom replied quietly. She sat straight, her red lips set in a solid frown, her long auburn hair pulled tightly back into a bun.

"Yeah, his was a Wagoneer," Lee said.

They were driving northwest on Highway 30, on their way to Astoria and the coast. His parents had picked him up in their pickup with which they'd replaced the station wagon they'd had when he and Paul were kids. Lee was wedged into the uncomfortable middle seat. They were looking for any sign of his brother.

They'd driven up through industrial northwest Portland, past the turnoff for Sauvie Island and the derelict nuclear power plant rising eerily from the surrounding forest, then worked their way parallel to the slow wide Columbia River, often losing sight of it behind rolling hills, several times topping large rises to find breathtaking views of the water and the plains and mountains of Washington spread beyond. They passed lovely towns nestled among high green trees and drab industrial ones filled with concrete and dotted with brightly colored chain stores.

His parents had called yesterday after work. He didn't think there was much chance of finding Paul in the vastness of western Oregon, but he'd agreed instantly to the plan anyway. It was better than the worry and uncertainty that tortured him when he was doing nothing.

His mom, who was driving, had her mouth in a permanent frown. Other than that, he couldn't see any visible sign that this affected her much. His dad, on the other hand, was pale, and there were more lines on his already timeworn face. Black semicircles emphasized his red eyes.

They reached Astoria, a beautiful town at the wide mouth of the Columbia with a massive bridge arcing overhead. They drove up its hills, down the historic downtown streets.

Next they headed to Fort Stevens State Park, cruised through the parking lots under tall trees and down miles of winding roads. He and Paul had driven here on one of the first sunny days of spring with Lisa and Jenny. Lee remembered the girls laughing as a cold wind whipped at the edges of their picnic blanket on the sand, looking so pretty as their long hair, Lisa's dark, Jenny's blond, flew behind them. There was no sign of Paul here now, so they headed south on 101.

Past Seaside they came to Ecola State Park. It was the next major wild place down the coast with hiking trails and campsites. They scoured the parking lots again and didn't find his car.

"Do you think he could be here?" Lee's dad asked him as they were turning around and slowly heading down the long twisting road towards the freeway.

"It's possible."

"But then we'd see his car," Lee's mom said.

"He could have parked somewhere else and hiked in," Lee said.

"We should look."

"We don't have time to hike every trail on the coast," Lee's mom replied.

"I think we should look here. I just have a feeling, ok?" Lee's dad said. He tapped his hands on the dashboard repeatedly, nervewrackingly.

"Maybe we should, Mom."

"Fine."

They pulled a U-turn, parked and paid the fee. The day was sunny but wind whipped over them, bringing the smell of ocean with it. Lee stretched, feeling release from hours cramped in the car. Then, his dad in the lead, they started down a trail that led from the lot into a grove of thin sun-dappled trees. However, within a few feet they came to a fork and stopped cold.

They stood staring at the signs: a short path to the beach, longer trails heading north and south. "Well," Lee said eventually, "he was headed south, right?" knowing it was meaningless.

"Yeah, but most of the park, most of the trails, are to the north of us," Lee's dad said.

"Fine," Lee said. "We'll go north."

"We don't have to, I was just saying..."

"No, it's fine. Let's go."

The narrow dirt path wound its way now through dense trees, which rose gracefully, converging overhead to provide a green ceiling permeated by and glowing with the unseen sun. Just minutes from the parking lot, all sign and sound of human activity ceased except the thuds of their feet on the dirt. Birds called high and shrill and, faintly, they could hear the rumbling crash of the surf. Their trail didn't intercept any others, but little paths, probably created by deer, shot off through the undergrowth here and there. And what if Paul had gone down one of those, was just behind that tangle of vines, had broken his leg or been attacked by a cougar...

"Keep your eyes open," Lee's dad said.

"For what?" his mom asked. "What do you think we're going to find? Do you think he's just going to come walking down this particular trail three days after he's supposed to have shown up?"

"I don't know what, but just look, ok? We might see something that no one else would."

"Ok, Dad. We'll look."

The trail came into a field with a view of the ocean down below the cliffs on which they were hiking. There was a tan stretch of sand, people lounging and playing down there, and the brilliant profound blue of the water, speckled by the white of waves. The sky was cloudless, which almost never happened on the coast. A little steep trail plunged to the beach. What if his brother had tried to take that trail, or one like it in a more remote place, and tumbled down one of the cliffs that lined the Pacific, crashed to the rocks below or into the icy waters? Lee hated this idea, but that was, he thought, because it was perhaps the most plausible.

His dad and mom both stood, hands shielding their eyes from the sun, to look out over the long stretch of coast. He thought he saw tears shimmer in both their eyes. Maybe they were thinking the same thing he was, but Lee didn't dare ask.

"Maybe we should head back," Lee's mom said, finally. "We've got a lot of ground to cover today." There were no complaints.

Back in the car they continued southward. The Oregon coast was a gorgeous place, full of the white crash of surf, jutting rocks, hidden inlets with wide beaches, vast forests dense with evergreens and the smooth roll of hills, their grasses brownish now towards the end of summer, awaiting the ceaseless rain that was soon to come. Staring out the windows, Lee kept getting lost in the scenery, forgetting the specifics of looking for his brother and instead just feeling the empty depression that his brother's disappearance caused, just watching the gentle sway of waves before they broke far below, or the sun bouncing off the needles on the infinite green trees.

They stared at the cars on the roads, pulled off onto scenic drives and viewpoints, went to trailheads and parking lots, state parks and rest stops. Slowly they crawled their way down the coast looking for a black 1983 Jeep Wagoneer with a stripe of fake wood paneling on the side and a smashed-in back bumper that Paul had never repaired. They scanned every face for Paul: curly, wiry black hair above a tanned wide-featured, big-eared smiling face, his lean muscled body and his bulky orange backpack. They didn't go on any more hikes, just drove through Oswald West, Nehalem Bay, Cape Lookout, Carl G. Washorne Memorial State Park, plus a lot of smaller parks and reserves, and all the towns little and big on the way. There were a thousand turns they didn't take, a million roads down which they could have looked but didn't.

They said almost nothing. His parents didn't ask Lee how he was doing, how his job was working out or if he was looking for anything new yet, if he was dating anyone, how his painting was going or any of the other stuff they usually worried him about. They just talked about the task at hand; where had Lee gone with Paul when they went to the coast, had he mentioned any specific places, could they figure out where he might have gone hiking? Lee kept all except the essential details about their trips to the coast silent, but everything kept running through his head: the times he and Paul had struggled up a peak for overwhelming views of the rough coastline and curving ball of the planet covered with undulating ocean, or of whiskey shots followed by swigs of beer around a campfire on the dunes and drunken singalongs to the tinny sound of Paul's boombox. Or as children, running on the hardpacked sand near the water's edge, building castles and then bombarding each other's with stones while their parents reclined on bright plastic folding chairs, arms shielding eyes from the blinding sun that shone on their pale bodies. Talking about that would be way too dangerous.

Finally they reached Florence, which was the obvious point for Paul to have turned back on 126 towards his parents' town. Just south of them was the Oregon Dunes National Recreation Area; Paul could be there, but it was huge, stretching for miles south, and it was getting late. The sun was low on the horizon behind them as they reluctantly turned from the ocean. They had a long way to go, back to I-5 and then the two hours to Portland, then, for his parents, the further drive home. And yet they still turned into rest stops and scoured the main streets of the few little logging towns on the way.

Lee drove the last leg, piloting the truck through the darkness on the wide, straight highway. His dad was in the shotgun seat, leaning his head on the shoulder of his wife who was between them. His eyes were closed but Lee couldn't tell if he was asleep. It was going to be hours past their usual bedtime when they finally got home; the store opened very early each day to serve the farming community around it. Lee's mom was looking out the window on Lee's side but he felt that she was also looking at him.

"Do you think he could have run away?" she asked.

Lee started; the silence had been so complete for so long.

"What do you mean, Mom?"

"Disappeared on purpose. Gotten tired of life here, driven to Mexico, taken a plane to India. Maybe he was in trouble, owed money or something? Was he in any trouble that he wasn't telling us about, Lee?"

"No, no. He was happy. Mostly happy. He really liked his job, and I can't imagine who he would owe money to; business seemed good. He was as busy as he wanted to be all spring and summer and he hadn't bought anything big he could have owed money on."

"What about girls?"

"He wasn't seeing anyone, but that wasn't the end of the world for him."

"Could he have gotten a girl pregnant, could he be running away from that?"

"That's not how he would have responded if that had happened. I don't think he ran away, Mom." She didn't respond and Lee drove on in silence, thinking what an appealing idea it was. His brother, who loved the outdoors and adventure more than anything, picking up and disappearing, walking now through the jungles of Laos, rock climbing in the Australian outback or just hiking into the Cascades to live off the wild, a hermit in the wilderness he loved. He had talked sometimes, wistfully, about doing months-long backpacking trips or going to explore South America for a year, if only he had the money and the time. It was tempting. But his brother would have told him first if he had gone anywhere. He would have told him.

The freeway swept into downtown near the river then arced up over a high bridge with a sweeping view of city lights glimmering on the water. Lee almost never went this way, as it wasn't bikeable, so, as safely as possible he admired the scene in his rear view mirror and in quick glimpses back over his shoulder.

Soon they were pulling up in front of Lee's house. The silence they'd been driving in suddenly seemed like it had been loud when the rumble of the engine cut off. Lee's father sat up and looked around, surprised, somehow looking much younger. Then Lee watched as his dad remembered where he was and what was going on, and the haggardness and wrinkles rematerialized on his face.

"Do you want to come in?" Lee asked, though he knew his parents didn't like his messy, loud, run-down house.

"No. Thank you, though," his mom said. "It's late, and it's a long drive home."

"Thanks for coming with us, son," Lee's dad said.

"Thank you for taking me."

"I wish..." his dad trailed off.

"Me too," Lee said. They all got out of the truck and he embraced them both for a long time, wordlessly, clinging. When they left Lee stood on the front steps, watching the tail lights diminish down his street, turn, and vanish.

TEN

Lee walked towards Alberta Street with a backpack overloaded with small canvases pressing down on his shoulders, three larger paintings clutched awkwardly in his arms. He'd left work early so he could go up to Last Thursday, a monthly art event where anyone could set up on the sidewalk to sell their arts and crafts. Of course he might make less money in his attempts to sell his work than he would have staying the extra few hours at the liquor store, but he had to try. Painting was what he did, and someday he hoped he'd be able to quit his job and just make money from that. That someday seemed a long way off most of the time.

It wasn't a long walk from Lee's house. The street here consisted mostly of rundown apartments and industrial buildings with no windows. The whole street used to be like this, he'd heard, but now, further up where the art walk happened, it was dotted with galleries, coffee shops, restaurants and bars, though a few taquerias, tiendas, old time dives and corner stores remained from the neighborhood it used to be.

He found a spot in the heart of the busiest area, up against the blank white wall of some kind of car repair place. Usually he set up where it was quieter, closer to his house, but he wanted to make sure everyone saw him today, not to sell art but to run into friends of his brother to ask them what they knew. If he stayed in one place and let the crowd pass by, he figured he'd see more people than if he ran around looking. Pretty much everyone came to Last Thursday, especially on beautiful summer days like this. The sky was an unbroken cobalt.

As he scanned the few people wandering the street this early and the other artists and craftspeople setting up their wares, Lee thought back to his first Last Thursday. Paul had brought him when Lee had just moved to the city, saying he might want to try to sell some of his drawings here. At the time Lee had thought he was going to be a musician, but he'd appreciated his brother's interest. And he'd had a wonderful time walking up and down the crowded street with Paul, laughing, making jokes, watching the hippies, hipsters, punks and the cool parents with children perched on their shoulders. As night fell things grew crazy, carnivalesque. They saw jugglers, DIY clowns on freakishly modified bikes and a woman breathing plumes of flame into the air. Teenagers played rock music from front porches, a circle of African men banged drums on the sidewalk and DJs blared their music from storefronts.

They'd stopped frequently to chat with friends Paul ran into and he'd introduce them to his little brother who'd just moved to the city. That was well before Lisa and Jenny and Lee remembered Paul flirting for both of them with a table full of pretty girls in bright summer dresses next to theirs at La Si- renita where they'd stopped for giant delicious burri- tos. Lee had been embarrassed and thrilled at the same time by his brother's charm and brazenness, and had felt so glad he'd come to Portland.

Lee watched legs pass by. Shadowed folds in bag- gy jeans over black sneakers, pale well-muscled legs covered in wavy black hair with blue Tevas below, tiny legs lost in a swirling pink dress, tight khakis ending midway down wide rounded calves, small weary-looking feet in yellow high heels. His neck had grown tired looking up for people he recognized, but he figured anyone who knew him would stop.

"Hey, it's Lee, right?" Abby, a freakishly tall girl who Paul would often go kayaking and drinking with towered over him, her short flame red hair making her stand out even more.

"Hi, Abby," he said.

They'd only met a few times, at bars, both wast- ed or on the way to getting there, so he was surprised that she'd remembered his name and that he'd re- membered hers. "Is this your art?" she asked. He nod- ded and she moved in to take a closer look. "It's really good."

"Have you heard anything from Paul? Or about him?" he asked, though it was obvious she hadn't.

"No. I called him a few days ago, but he hasn't gotten back to me. I was going to ask you if he were here tonight, actually. Why?"

Lee told her about Paul's disappearance, how he was supposed to be back on Sunday. She put a hand to her mouth and said, "Oh my god! I can't believe that, Lee!"

She didn't know anything, hadn't talked to him for more than a week. They'd had tentative plans to go kayaking the weekend after next, that's what she'd called him about. There were tears in her eyes when she left.

A little later a middle aged guy with a large paunch pushing at a tight black tee-shirt, after ten minutes of peering closely at all the art but thankfully not asking Lee questions about where he got his inspiration and what it all meant, actually bought one of the little ones. It was a disembodied nose floating in the upper right of what looked like an oil spill in candy colors. He seemed pleasantly surprised when Lee told him the price.

When the air had cooled a little and the crowds were thick, Lee spotted Jenny, Paul's ex. She met his eyes, hers opened wide, and she strode towards him. "Jesus, Lee, I got a call from the police. I tried to call Paul but he doesn't answer. What's going on?"

Jenny's wavy blond-brown hair and blue eyes made her look like Sarah Michelle Geller, or at least that's what Paul used to say. She and Paul had broken up about a month before Lee and Lisa had.

"He went to the coast over the weekend and no one's heard from him since," Lee said in a flat voice.

"Jesus. Do you have any idea what happened?"

"No. The police are looking and we searched up and down the coast, but no one's seen or heard anything."

"That's so scary."

"I know. I gave the officer your number even though I told him you wouldn't have seen Paul in months. Sorry. I gave him everyone's number."

"Actually, that's not entirely true."

"What do you mean?"

"We, well, we saw each other a few times since the breakup."

"Paul never mentioned that."

"I guess not."

Lee looked at her. Paul had been so angry, so depressed and then so glad, so free, after they'd broken up. Had he really gone back and slept with her afterwards when he was trying to meet someone else? Maybe she meant they'd just hung out but he didn't think so. And if Paul hadn't told Lee about this, what else could he have not mentioned?

But that was stupid. Lee would have slept with Lisa on some of the lonely nights since their breakup if he'd had the chance. And he wouldn't have told Paul about it, leaving the impression that the break was clean, that he had moved on. Still, he'd thought his brother was stronger than that. Not that Jenny was so bad.

"Is there anything I can do to help?" she asked.

"When was the last time you heard from him?"

"About two weeks ago. I already told the police."

"What did you talk about?"

"He asked if I wanted to come over."

"And?"

"I told him no, that I was busy. It was because I was starting to date a new guy, but I didn't mention that to him."

"You rejected him?"

"It was two weeks ago. I rejected him months and months ago, when we broke up. We rejected each other and he didn't disappear then. Don't try to blame this on me, Lee."

"I wasn't."

"I don't think I could handle it if this were my fault," she said.

"Me neither. I was supposed to be there with him this weekend."

"Shit. Well, it wasn't your fault, Lee, just like it wasn't mine. And it won't matter because he'll show up soon, apologizing, saying the woods were so beautiful he just had to keep hiking, or he was on a cell-phone-free retreat with his tree-hugging buddies or something like that."

Lee was distracted by a glimpse of black hair that looked like Paul's. He saw the face. It wasn't him. "Yeah. I hope so," he said.

"Anyway, I should be going. Call me if you hear anything, ok, Lee?"

"I will."

She gave him a brief hug and then walked to a guy that Lee noticed for the first time who seemed to have been waiting just down the street. He was dressed like Paul often dressed and had a similar haircut but was blond, paler, less muscular and taller. Jenny took the guy's hand and they headed down the street together. He wondered if she'd cheated on him with Paul, if she'd cheated on Paul with him. Paul had never mentioned anything like that, though, and he and Lee had talked the subject of their breakups to death over endless beers and whiskey.

By the time darkness fell Lee had run into two more friends of and a guy who sometimes worked with Paul and none of them had known anything. All he'd done was spread worry and fear.

Lee was leaning over, stuffing the canvases into his backpack, when he felt a hand clap down on his back. "Lee, man, how are you? How's your tooth? Any word on your brother?" It was Patrick. Cindy, apparently back, was with him, as was Elly. That was strange, since they usually didn't hang out together when he wasn't around.

"The tooth hasn't really bothered me since they worked on it. Though I've been popping Advil steadily, just in case. And I have to go back soon to pay them tons of money to do more work. My brother's still missing."

"Shit."

Elly approached and gave him a wordless hug. When she pulled back Cindy gave him a quick hug, too. She was a short, pretty girl with curly black hair, dressed conservatively in a skirt and white blouse, probably having just come from work. Lee liked her and thought she was good for his friend, though of course he didn't get to hang out with Patrick as much as he had when he was single or when they could go on double dates. "Welcome back," Lee said.

"Thanks. I'm so sorry about everything you've been going through. But don't worry, it'll all work out, you'll see."

"We ran into Elly," Patrick said, "and we decided that the best plan would be to try to take your mind off everything. So come on, drinks are on us tonight."

"What about all this shit?" Lee asked, waving an arm at the big canvases still spread on the ground.

"You can put everything in my car," Cindy said.

"Thanks. But I don't know if that's really what I need. I should probably just go home."

"Why?" Patrick asked.

"I don't know. How can I have fun now?"

"How can anyone have fun ever?" Elly replied. "With the wars in Iraq and Afghanistan and millions of people going hungry and women being oppressed, there's always some reason to feel guilty and never have any fun. But fuck it, right? We can't mope about how awful the world is all the time, can we?"

"Um."

"Ok," Elly said, "I don't know if that was the most inspirational speech in the world. But screw it, you're getting drunk with us tonight and you have no choice. Let's go." She grabbed his hand and dragged. He let himself be pulled along.

All the bars on Alberta were always packed on Last Thursday so they piled into Cindy's Volvo and headed for a dive on MLK that Lee liked. They crowded into a booth and Patrick came soon with a pitcher of Pabst in each hand, came back a second time with a stack of frosted pint glasses he thunked down in front of them. They splashed the pale piss colored liquid into their cups. Lee raised his and took a long sip, lowering the level of beer appreciably. They were probably right. He did need to forget. Drinking had worked to take his mind off things at the Dragon Pig show. Well, drinking and running in-to Valerie.

"So, tell me more about your experience at the dentist." Patrick said. "I only got your message, but it sounded intense."

"It was shitty. At one point a professor told me, 'this is really going to hurt, so just hold on to your chair.' Can you believe that? This is 2005, not the Middle Ages. What kind of torture chamber do you work at, Cindy?"

"You don't even want to know what terrible things they do to the children in pediatrics," Elly said, laughing.

"It's not that bad," Cindy replied. "Everything is very high tech and professional there, they have tons of money. Though I guess I don't really know anything about the dentistry department. It seems to me that if you wanted to study dentistry or teach it, you must be somewhat of a sadist to start with, right?"

"Right," Lee said. "But at least they finally stopped the pain. God damn that hurt."

"Yeah. I've never heard Lee swear like that and I've heard Lee swear an awful lot," Patrick said.

"My dentist is really cute, so that's a plus at least," Lee said. "I ran into her at the Dragon Pig show, which you totally should have gone to, Patrick, and we kind of danced next to each other."

Cindy, laughing, said, "Now Lee, no hitting on your dentist. That's not appropriate."

"I didn't say I was hitting on her, just that she was cute. Forget appropriate, I don't think that's even possible. She said so, pretty much."

"Yeah," Patrick said. "That's like hitting on your teacher. It can't be done."

"Sure it can, you wimps," Elly said. "Teacher,

dentist, you can hit on anyone if you have the balls for it."

"No one's hitting on anyone," Lee said. "That's over. I missed my chance, if there even was one, at the show. Anyway, enough about me. We're supposed to be forgetting my problems, right? So, how was your trip, Cindy?"

Cindy told them about LA, then Elly about her last date and her date's inexcusable taste in music, Patrick about the leopard print wallpaper and all the hundreds of statues of Buddha in the house whose wiring he'd been updating. Lee mostly listened and laughed, occasionally making a comment. And he drank. After finishing his glass, he reached over to the pitcher to fill it, the froth hissing to the top. Did so again. Again.

They talked about politics and mutual friends and told stories from their past, though never ones that involved Paul. Elly got the next two pitchers. After one beer Cindy had started drinking Cokes, since she was driving. When he poured the last of the beer into his glass, Lee calculated groggily that he, Elly and Patrick had averaged more than a pitcher each and he might have had more than his fair share. He felt it sloshing in his stomach. His head was cheerful and foggy, his actions a little unsteady.

"Do we need any more?" Patrick asked.

"I don't know, I need to work in the morning," Elly said.

"Us too," Cindy said.

"One more pitcher," Lee insisted. "I'm buying."

"We said we were going to get you drunk, so we will. I'll get it," Patrick replied.

"Thanks. Thanks, guys."

Patrick filled Lee's glass to the top, then added a splash to his and Elly's, which both still had a little left. But it was right that he was drinking more, Lee thought. He was the one whose brother was missing.

With that thought, which had been mostly taken out of his head until then by the beer, friendship and laughter, Lee went silent and began draining his PBR one steady sip at a time though his stomach roiled. He poured himself another pint, then emptied the rest of the pitcher among his friends' glasses, spilling a little on the table. He raised his beer. "To my brother. To finding my brother!"

His friends raised their glasses and clinked them hard. A little sloshed onto Lee's hand. He drank deeply, trying to remember, trying to forget.

On the short car ride home, in the back seat with Elly, Lee kept sniffling, trying not to cry. "Patrick," he asked, "you knew him really well, how could he be gone? He knew what he was doing, he went backpacking all the time, he had a first aid kit and a compass. How could he possibly be gone?"

"I don't know man, I don't know. He could definitely take care of himself. Remember that time we were out with him and it started hailing practically golf balls out of the blue and he found us a freaking cave to take shelter in, then built a fire? When we were just out for a day hike, totally unprepared for that weather? That was like magic."

"I remember. I remember so many hikes, trips, nights camping with him. He must be fine, he must have just run away."

"Run away?" Cindy asked.

"Got tired of everything. Headed to Mexico or Laos or somewhere."

"Do you really think he would do that?" Elly asked.

"No. Yes. No, of course not. He would have told me first." Tears were streaming down Lee's cheeks. He wiped them away with the back of his hand, hoping no one would notice. Everyone fell silent.

"Well, we're here," Cindy said, too cheerfully. "Let me give you a hand with the artwork so you drunk fools don't ruin it."

When the paintings were put away they all went back out to the street. Patrick and Cindy gave him strong hugs and told him that everything would be fine. Then their car pulled away into the night.

"Are you going to be ok?" Elly asked.

"I don't know."

"Do you want to sleep with me tonight? Not like that, of course. But if you need to be with someone..."

"No. Thank you. You're wonderful, Elly." He hugged her, held on and found himself crying again. "Thank you." He didn't know if he could keep himself together without her and Patrick.

"No problem. Anything for a buddy, right? Anything you need."

"I think I need to pass out."

"Good call. You can start by letting go of me."

He was still clasping her tight, he realized, so opened his arms. Lee staggered up the stairs, fell onto his bed still dressed and kicked off his shoes. The room seemed vastly dark and empty. He wished he'd taken Elly up on her offer, wished even more he had someone to really sleep with, someone he loved to hold him now, to distract him, to care for him. He wished Lisa weren't gone, wished he had someone new. He wished his brother were back home. Maybe he'd hear from Paul tomorrow and everything would be explained, everything would be ok.

ELEVEN

Lee watched sunlight gleam off the Pacific, shielding his eyes and staring out at that endless cold ocean. It was Sunday. The last two days at work he'd been distracted, making stupid mistakes, thinking only of his brother, or he'd sat in his room listening to loud angry music and trying to paint, trying to bury all his anguish and worry in broad sweeping brush strokes. It was crap, the worst work he'd produced in years, he decided after he was done. A waste of paint and canvas.

His parents had picked him up very early that morning. They told him that Paul's bank account hadn't been accessed at all, that he hadn't booked any flights and that no calls had been made from or answered on his phone since the Friday of the weekend he'd disappeared.

They'd driven again down the coast, arguing over whether they'd turned down that road before, searched that particular parking lot. This time they put up bright yellow "Have You Seen This Man" fliers featuring a picture of Paul that Lee had taken on a hike on Powell Butte a few months before, wind blowing his hair back from his eyes, focused on something far past the camera.

Lee and his parents were hiking now in Oswald West State Park. It was spectacular: arrow-straight trees, sunlight glistening on the water, white clouds stalled in the sky. There were any number of places the path skirted a cliff and his brother could have fallen away to disappear from this world.

His mom and dad rounded a turn and vanished into towering trees. Lee stood still, his eyes tracing up and down the steep hillside, brown earth and green shrubs clinging to it, that fell away down to sharp rocks and white foaming water. It could have been here. Maybe there was a place where the earth was a little disturbed, a little raw, from Paul's hands grasping as he tumbled down, end over end, orange backpack entangling him, to crack his head on a rock below, a little red in the white spume and then sinking underneath the water, pulled by undertow deep, deep into the ocean and gone.

"Lee? Are you ok?" It was his mom. She and his dad had come back for him. She put a hand on his shoulder.

"What if he's gone? What if he tripped, fell and then drowned in the ocean?"

"Don't think that way, Lee," his mom said with a frown on her face.

"Then why are we out here?" he asked, his frustration, confusion and fear suddenly coming to a boil. "What are we looking for if that's not what we think happened? Do we think we'll find him here hiking down a trail a week from when he was supposed to come back?"

"Lee's right," his dad said, tears suddenly pouring down his lined face. "What if he's gone?"

"But it's not the only explanation," his mom said. "He could have simply left, run away somewhere without telling us. Or he could have been kidnapped, or any number of other terrible things. Things we couldn't do anything about. But why we're here now is that he could have slipped and fallen, yes, but he could have fallen into some ravine, broken his leg and be unable to get help, but he could still be alive. He had food and water with him. That's what we're here looking for. Not for the place he died, but for the place he could possibly still be alive and needing our help."

Lee stood there looking at his mother, who had her hands clenched, a cap advertising their store shielding her hard face from the sun. "You're right, Mom," he said, admiring her strength and willpower. "So we shouldn't waste time talking, we should be looking."

But they didn't find anything.

Lee stuffed a flaky crumbling forkful of his mom's chicken pot pie into his mouth. It was one of his favorite meals ever but he didn't really taste it now, staring over the old dining room table at the empty chair where Paul should be sitting. Lee came home quite a few times a year, for Thanksgiving and Christmas plus many random visits, and he always came with his brother. As far back as he could remember his brother had sat in that chair across the table from him while his mom sat next to Lee, his dad next to Paul.

"It's good having you home, son," his dad said.

"It's good being here." But that was a lie. It was painful, there were too many memories. Paul kicking him under the table or throwing peas at his head when his parents weren't looking, Paul sneaking the foods Lee didn't like, broccoli or overly salted cream of mushroom casserole, off Lee's plate to scarf it down himself. And a thousand more memories, just at this table.

"I hope the pot pie is ok," his mom said. "I had to make it yesterday and keep it in the refrigerator instead of making it fresh since we were out all day."

Lee hadn't known he was spending the night when they set out that morning, but obviously his mom had, though she'd just offered it as a casual suggestion, saying it would be nice not to have to go all those extra miles to Portland and back when they'd been driving all day.

"It's great, Mom." It was. He concentrated on the buttery crust, tender meat and vegetables in the creamy sauce inside. He'd tried several varieties of frozen chicken pot pies, even ordered them at a couple restaurants in Portland when they'd been on the menu since he loved these so much, but none of them had come anywhere close.

"Do you have enough money to pay for all your dental work?" his mom asked. All day they'd been talking like that, in fits and starts about anything other than Paul.

"I don't know. I still don't know what they need to do or how much it's going to cost."

"Well if you do need help, just let us know. We'll be glad to."

"You're closing the business every day to look for Paul and I know things have been slow anyway. Hopefully it won't be too expensive."

"You and Paul are the most important things in our lives," his dad said. "We can afford to pay for your dental work, anything like that if you need it. You don't need to question that, Lee."

"We could definitely afford it if you'd let my parents help us out," Lee's mom said.

"You know how I feel about that."

"I certainly do," she said with a little exasperation. "I knew how stubborn you were when I married you, so it's not like I wasn't warned." She smiled, wanly.

Lee felt the same way his dad did about taking money from his grandparents, tiny silver-haired people with casual conversational racism who'd never really forgiven Lee's dad for stealing their daughter away to Oregon. It was the same with Lee taking money from his parents. He'd helped out in the store, knew how little it made and that they didn't really save anything. It was one of the reasons neither he nor his brother had gone to college. He wasn't going to take any money from them, especially now.

For dessert they had brownies and milk that Paul had always complained came from California when dairies surrounded the town. Lee helped with the dishes, scrubbing them clean then passing them to his dad, who dried. Lee had never lived in a house with a dishwasher.

Without a word between them they watched an hour of TV, the end of a show on the Civil War and then one about lions, both on PBS. Afterwards Lee's dad yawned, stretched and got up, saying it was time for him to go to bed. Lee's mom rose too, they both kissed him on the cheek and hugged him tightly, said goodnight and went down the hall to their bedroom.

Lee got up and turned off the television, watching the picture contract into a bright point, buzz and then go dark and silent. In the room that had been his since he was six and moved out of the one he'd shared until then with Paul, he flicked on the light. His narrow bed was in one corner, the red dresser next to it. Some of his best high school paintings and drawings covered the walls along with posters of Miró, Picasso and Tanguy. His parents hadn't changed a thing, though his mom sometimes said that maybe they'd use the space for extra storage since he didn't come home very often.

He lay down on the bed. The alarm that used to be on the little table at its head was now beside his mattress in Portland. After setting his phone to wake him he undressed to his boxers and got under the blankets.

Lee expected to be up for hours, thinking about Paul, worrying through every scenario and conversation then starting over again. Instead he turned towards the wall like he had so many nights before and fell asleep in minutes.

"Are you sure you don't want us to stay with you?" Lee's dad asked the next morning. They were standing by the car in the parking lot of the dental school.

"It'll probably take forever. It did last time. Anyway, you guys need to go reopen the store. Even half a day's better than nothing, right? People depend on you. You don't want them to have to drive all the way to Eugene to get groceries."

"Everyone knows. They understand," his mom said.

"Right." He hadn't really thought of that for some reason, that of course the whole little town knew that Paul was gone, knew every detail.

"Anyway, we're not going to reopen the store. We're going out to the coast again," Lee's dad said. "That's why we're both up here."

"I feel so bad that I can't go with you. But it's so hard out there, with no idea where to look, what to look for."

"Your father insists that we keep going. But, really, what else can we do?"

"I wish I knew," Lee said.

TWELVE

"That went a lot better than last time, right? I'm so glad," Valerie said. She'd seemed a little embarrassed earlier, when she'd ushered him to the back and started working on his teeth without any smalltalk. Lee hadn't said much either, trying to figure out what, if anything, was going on between them.

Mouth full of dental dam and numbness, Lee just nodded. She'd spent the last what seemed like hours scraping away inside his tooth and then filling the hole she'd made with liquidized rubber she squeezed out of a sort of caulking gun, zapping it occasionally with some strange orange contraption that looked like a Fifties science fiction laser weapon. There had been no pain other than the initial prick of the Novocain needle. Thank God.

When all the dental equipment was removed from his mouth and he'd rinsed and spat, Lee said, "Thanks. That was the best root canal I've ever had."

"And also the worst, right? But why are you thanking me? I caused you ridiculous amounts of pain. You're supposed to hate me; I'd hate me if I'd caused that kind agony."

"The professor did the worst of it, so I'll just decide to transfer all my hate onto him, if you don't mind. We're going to be spending a lot of time together since there's so much wrong with my teeth, right? So hating each other wouldn't do at all."

"No, no it wouldn't, and that's nice of you."

Now that they were done with the emergency treatment they headed to Valerie's regular chair to do more tests. She led them down a hallway between two giant open rooms filled with row after row of dental chairs. There must have been a hundred of them and many were occupied. Dental students and professors in blue, pink or purple leaned down over their victims. The whir of drills was a low background noise. Valerie turned down one of the aisles and led him to a chair that had her name taped up on a white notecard. The one next to it said "Ellen Thomasson," and was decorated with little flowers in colored pencil. He was glad Valerie's was plain.

"I like your friends' band, by the way. Their CD's fun," she said.

He had been wondering if they were going to pretend like that night had never happened. "I'm glad. That was funny, running into you like that right after meeting you here."

"Yeah, it was. I had a good time, but I was pretty drunk and I think you were, too. Now, though, we need to get back to work."

Reluctantly Lee nodded. If he'd ever had a chance with this girl, and that was a big if, dancing next to her had been it and now it was gone.

Valerie took a bunch of X-rays then performed a long series of tests, poking and prodding. Throughout, she didn't talk about anything other than teeth. And he wasn't going to start a conversation while she was sticking things in his mouth.

When she was done she went to get a professor. She came back a few minutes later with a middle-aged woman with severe features and thick black hair pulled tightly into a large bun. Lee wondered why she didn't have to wear a hairnet when everyone else did. "I'm doctor Jazekova," she said with a slight accent, holding out her hand, which Lee shook. "Now let's see your teeth."

She stuck the mirror and pick into his mouth, less gently than Valerie had, then made disapproving clucking sounds. She and Valerie consulted the X-rays and engaged in a rapid fire conversation about tooth number 22 and other stuff he couldn't follow.

"Well, Mr. Garrett," Dr. Jazekova said, finally turning to him. "We've got a lot of work to do on you." Lee felt his shoulders droop. She continued, "You have eight definite cavities, two of which are distressingly large and close to the root so they could possibly end up being root canals, though hopefully we can get to them quickly and that won't be necessary. Plus we need to do a cleaning and scaling to get rid of the debris under your gums to keep them from causing more problems. There are a few other worrisome areas that could turn into cavities, or not. And we need to put that crown in when it arrives from the laboratory."

"Shit." He wished he hadn't sworn, but thought keeping it that tame was quite an accomplishment. "How much is all this going to cost?" He couldn't believe his teeth were that bad. He brushed twice a day, flossed fairly often. What the hell had happened? He was glad it was the professor who was breaking the news: one more person to hate instead of Valerie.

"I'm sorry it's so much," Valerie said quietly, her eyes lowered, handing him a piece of paper.

He looked over the bill. It came to $1,423 dollars, though it was clear that was just an estimate. That was five and a half month's rent that he was going to have to pay to be tortured in a dentist chair by a beautiful girl.

Valerie reached around his neck to unfasten his bib and her hand lightly brushed his face, accidentally, he thought. Lee decided there might be a slight blush on her cheeks when he glanced at her. He pulled off his goggles and stood. "Thanks," he said, though he wasn't exactly sure what he was thanking her for.

"There's no charge for the tests today, but you do need to pay for the root canal with the cashier on your way out."

"You're not making it any easier to like you, you know. Now I'll have to hate the cashier, too." She smiled then looked down. He said goodbye and left, only glancing over his shoulder at her once. She was peering into what he thought was probably his chart. He wondered what she was looking at, wondered if she was curious about him. Probably she was just wondering how his teeth got so badly fucked up.

An old lady with a dry wrinkled smiling face took his debit card and subtracted most of the money on it with one swipe. He signed, folded up the copy of his full-page receipt and left, his tongue feeling the new temporary crown, still slightly off despite all the adjustments, which fit in the gap where his tooth used to be.

On the way out to the bus stop he glanced at the bright yellow Oregonian box. The headline, huge and bold, said, "Katrina Slams New Orleans." From what he could see above the fold it looked like it might be a big deal, but no one had mentioned anything so maybe it wasn't. He didn't have any change on him to buy a paper, and after the root canal he probably couldn't afford it even if he did.

THIRTEEN

The next day at work Lee stared blankly ahead at the shelves, all the endless variations in shape and color of the bottles blurring before his eyes, replaced by a memory of his brother laughing on a foggy morning on the coast. And this was an improvement over thoughts of all the people who'd drowned in New Orleans, the unimaginable devastation there that customers had been telling him about all day. The world was shit.

Lee's phone vibrated against his thigh and his vision refocused. It was Patrick. No one was in the store, no one usually was on Tuesday mornings, so, despite the fact that it was against the rules, he answered.

"Hey man, it's me. I just saw the thing about your brother on the news. God, it's so fucked up. It seemed so much more real on TV."

"The news?"

"Yeah, the local TV news, channel 8, in between endless coverage of the hurricane. Which is incredibly fucked up, too, of course. They had your mom there, out on the coast, then showed a picture of Paul, his car and license plate number. They said he'd been missing since last Sunday and to call the police if anyone had seen him. It was creepy."

"Jesus. Thanks for telling me. I didn't know anything about it."

"I guess it's the logical next step, get the story out there to as many people as possible, see if anyone's seen anything or knows anything."

"Yeah, I guess."

"Anyway, I just wanted to let you know, let you know that people are taking this seriously."

"Thanks."

Lee hung up. He could call his mom and ask why she hadn't told him about this, but he already knew the answer. His presence wouldn't have helped, it had been hard and she wanted to spare him that pain. So he went back to staring out at the shelves loaded down with their bottles, gleaming in the sun that somehow found its way between the tall buildings to illuminate the liquor within. He wondered how much he'd have to drink to stop thinking about his brother and New Orleans, how many of those bottles he'd have to empty.

A tradition, started by someone who'd moved out long before Lee had moved in then passed down through roommates as they cycled in and out, dictated that there was a house meeting the last Wednesday of every month. Why Wednesday, why once a month, no one knew. It wasn't the most convenient day for them because Elly worked half the time, but no one had bothered to change it.

Tonight all four of them were here, for the first time Lee could remember with this particular set of housemates. Elly sat next to him on the couch. Doug, a barista and poet, was on a wooden chair he'd pulled in from the kitchen. He was a tall, skinny guy dressed in tight jeans, Converse sneakers and a black shirt for a band Lee'd never heard of. Perched on his sharp nose was a pair of thick-rimmed glasses Lee wasn't convinced he needed to see with. Kayt, the fourth housemate, who was never around much, lived, as far as Lee knew, off her parents, though she occasionally had temp jobs. She had dyed red hair with a few purple and one white lock scattered throughout in a kind of choppy semi-mullet, wore tight clothes that looked like they might have come from Hot Topic and talked about drugs a lot. She was settling into the orange armchair, crossing her skinny fishnet-stockinged legs in front of her.

"So," Doug said, starting the meeting, "Anyone got anything to say?"

"I do," Elly said. "I'm sure you guys all know what Lee here's going through, but I just want to make sure that we're all supportive. His brother's been gone for a week and a half now and this is hell for Lee. He obviously hasn't been around much and has tons on his mind, so I just want us all to be here for him, to cover his chores if he doesn't get to them, shit like that. Sound good?"

"You don't have to do anything special for me," Lee said. "I can handle it."

"Maybe," Doug said, "but we're happy to help out, too. If you need anything, just ask."

"Yeah. Totally," Kayt added.

"Well, thanks." Instantly there were tears in Lee's eyes. He needed to hold himself the fuck together. He turned away towards the wall and wiped at them with the back of his hand.

After a pause Doug said, "The basement smells pretty bad." It did, had for the past day or two.

"That was a batch of homebrew that didn't turn out so well. Sorry. I've been trying to air it out," Elly said. "And I keep meaning to get a bunch of incense to burn in there, but I haven't had time yet. I'll do it tomorrow. Besides, won't it be worth it once that works out and we have all the beer we can drink? Because of course you'll all get a bunch for having to put up with all that crap in our basement."

"Just do the incense thing tomorrow, ok?" Kayt asked.

"Sure."

"Anything else?" Elly looked around the room.

No one said anything. "Are we done, then?" Doug asked.

Everyone agreed. And so their house hopefully would continue to function for another month without any major drama or shakeups and ideally with a less stinky basement. Kayt headed out but Lee, Doug and Elly stayed in the living room drinking beers and continuing the ongoing discussion about how fucked up and awful things were in New Orleans and whether Bush was an incompetent idiot or actually evil. The enormity of the misery there, Lee thought, should help put his in scale, make it better somehow, more manageable. There were thousands of missing people there, lost brothers, husbands, daughters, everyone. It just made things worse.

FOURTEEN

Lee came slowly to consciousness, aware that some-where his phone had just made the little ding that meant he had messages. The noise reverberated pain-fully in his head and he had to piss. He was hung over.

He extricated himself from his tangled sheets, scooped up his pants from the floor, slipped his phone out of them and headed towards the bath-room. Last night came back to him dimly now, an evening of endless beers and then cheap tequila, through their meeting and then Elly's plan of zombie movies afterwards to distract them from all the real shit in the world. He let out a steady, utterly relieving stream while holding the phone to his ear between his shoulder and his head. "You have one new mes-sage," it said with chipper emphasis on "one," and then he heard his father's hurried voice say, "Lee, we just got a call, they found your brother's car! It's near Cape Lookout State Park, a little south and west of Tillamook. We're on our way there now! We'll give you a call when we know more, maybe you can meet us out on the coast or maybe they'll find him first; they've already started a huge search. I really hope you can come. I love you. We're going now, bye."

That meant Paul hadn't driven to Mexico. Fuck. But he could still be alive, he would have had food and water in his pack, he could, possibly, be near there and be ok. And Lee didn't think that park was too big, so they would find him soon if he were. He had to get there, now. He quickly called his parents, but the phone just rang through to the answering machine. They didn't have a cellphone.

It was 6:53 in the morning. Elly would still be sleeping, hung over, so he called Patrick. After three rings he heard his friend say, "You do know that it's not even seven in the morning, right, Lee?"

"They found my brother's car near Tillamook, outside of Cape Lookout."

"Oh. Shit."

He heard Cindy murmur something in the background and Patrick reply, "They found Paul's car." Then, to Lee, "Do you know anything else?"

"No. I just got a message from my parents, they're on their way there."

"They'll find him now that they know where to look, I'm sure they will."

"Are you working today?"

"I have one job this morning, another in the afternoon."

"Never mind then, I'll find someone else to take me there."

"What are you talking about? I'll call and reschedule. Be ready in half an hour, I'll pick you up."

Lee sat down in a patch of sunshine on his porch to wait. And then he realized he was supposed to work in a few hours. He got his boss's answering machine. "Hi, Amy, this is Lee. Remember how I told you my brother was missing? They found his car out on the coast and I'm going out there today to help look for him. I hope you can find someone to cover my shift. Thanks." And if she didn't like it she could go fuck herself. He was going to find his brother.

He checked his phone again. Still nothing. He got up to pace and found himself running his tongue over and over against the rough, alien presence of the fake tooth residing in the back of his mouth.

Patrick arrived fifteen minutes later. Lee got in next to him, saying, "Thank you so much, man."

"Of course. This is much more important than work. And Paul's my friend, too." Lee was glad Patrick had used the present tense, because he knew he'd slipped at least once himself.

Lee told Patrick what he knew, which wasn't much. "I should have looked up the number for the rangers or something," Lee said. "Do you think I should call 911?"

"Let's just go there and see what we see. There's probably someone to talk to who will know what's going on."

"Yeah, ok. I can't think clearly, this is too crazy. God, they found his fucking car!"

After that they became silent, neither knowing what to say, suspended in hope and fear. Patrick maneuvered his way onto the highway. When they were climbing west over the green hills Patrick flipped on the radio. Classic rock and meaningless DJ chatter filled the quiet air. They passed through suburbs and then wide flat fields.

Farmland was replaced eventually with forest, mist-filled valleys and hills that rose into sunlight. Lee checked his phone again and found that he wasn't getting a signal, so he stared out at the woods, paths quickly flashing by, leading off amongst the endless trees, never-ending trails that his brother could be wandering on forever. But now they knew where he'd left his car. They could find him now. Or what was left of him.

FIFTEEN

Finally they reached the town of Tillamook, set a little off the coast in a valley filled with lush green grass and armies of cows that passively watched their car rush by.

Lee and his brother had stopped at the cheese factory here last summer on the way back to Portland for samples and giant dripping ice cream cones that had tasted like heaven after a day of hiking on the coast. He remembered Paul, as they stood side by side looking down at a conveyor belt on which block after block of iridescent orange cheddar emerged from a tangle of machinery, saying that he was thinking of proposing to Jenny. He never had; things had gone downhill fast.

At Cape Lookout they stopped at the campsite to find out what was going on. While Patrick parked Lee walked up to the little hut where you paid, humming with nervous energy. A ranger stood there, a guy with an acne spotted face a few years younger than Lee, looking he was playing dress-up in the green uniform.

"Hi," Lee said. "I'm Lee Garrett, Paul Garrett's brother. I heard they found his car around here. Do you know anything about it?"

"Of course. I'm sorry, man, this has got to be tough. They found the car on a Forest Service road just outside the park, but there's no sign of your brother yet. Your parents are with Margaret Keller, who's in charge of the operation. Let me find out where they are, hold on."

He talked into a staticky radio, heard some short garbled replies and said, "They're hiking the trail out to the point. I wish we had someone to take you, but everyone available's out looking for your brother. I'll tell you how to get there, though." He gave them directions, then Lee shook his hand fiercely.

The road led along a bay of placid gleaming water over which they saw a strip of sand. Hills rose off to the side and they suddenly came to one that was barren, devastated, with stumps and fallen branches littering the ground. Paul had always hated the sight of clearcuts, though they were very common driving to and from the natural, protected areas in Oregon. The trees returned and the road rose into the woods. They found two State Trooper patrol cars and two Forest Ranger Jeeps in the parking lot for the trailhead that led out to the Cape but no one seemed to be around. He was sure he and his parents had been in this parking lot before, on one of their drives down the coast, but he couldn't remember any details.

"I can't believe all these cars are here for him, that things are finally happening," Lee said as they got out of Patrick's car and stretched in the sunlight that pooled down around them through gaps in the jigsaw puzzle of flat grayish-black clouds that hung low overhead.

The trail took them immediately into a dense forest, gnarled trees rising up all around, ferns flourishing on the side of the path. The light from the sky was cut off and everything was dim. Deer trails ran through the underbrush here and there and Lee had an urge to follow them off into the trees but stayed on the main path. They plodded down the trail side by side wordlessly, peering into the woods.

After maybe a half mile the forest opened up to their left and they saw that they were on the edge of a headlands, a cliff leading down to water and rocks far below, a beach on the mainland behind them. Seagulls swirled and cawed down there in the expanse of air. It was the kind of place that Lee had envisioned Paul slipping, crashing down and drowning. Lee was yanked from his reverie by a loud whackwhackwhack noise and then a helicopter lifted over the trees behind them, turned right and headed away, low, hugging the coastline.

"Do you think..." Lee trailed off.

"Yeah. They're looking for your brother. They're serious and we're going to find him. Today."

Things were finally happening. The mystery was going to be solved. There was a fucking helicopter out here looking for his brother. He hoped his parents didn't have to pay for it. Of course they wouldn't. This was a missing person, this was what the authorities were supposed to do. To find people in need. To find his goddamned brother.

They wound back into the trees and kept hiking. When the view opened again, miles later, to show the meadowed tip of the point they saw, walking towards them, a woman in a Park Ranger's uniform and with her Lee's parents.

Lee ran forward, stumbling over the uneven ground but not falling, then wrapped first his father, then his mother in a hug. The lady they were with was maybe in her forties, tanned and weatherworn, and she looked tough. "What's going on?" he asked her, asked all of them.

Lee's dad started to say something but stopped when the ranger spoke at the same time. "Good to meet you, Lee," she said, holding out her hand, which Lee took. It was cold. "I'm Margaret. They found your brother's car south of here, on a gravel Forest Service road just outside the park. We're searching down there, up here too, all the wilderness in the area, which is quite a lot. We'd have more resources but of course some people are still down in Louisiana, helping there. But we got a helicopter and a lot of rangers on the ground, plus dogs, so if he's still around we'll find him soon, don't worry."

Patrick caught up then and introduced himself. Lee's parents each hugged him, thanking him profusely for driving Lee out here. "Of course I wanted to help," he said.

"We saw Paul's car," Lee's dad said, "But they won't let us look around there."

"We're treating that like a crime scene," Margaret replied. "Not that we have any evidence that it is. But we don't want any clues disrupted, anything that could tell us where he went or what happened to him tampered with. Anyway, there was no sign of him there so it's just as likely he'd be out here. This is where most people go when they come to our park, here and down on the spit."

Lee's mom said, "We've been tramping around in these woods all morning and we haven't seen a thing. Not a footprint, a piece of litter or place where he built a fire. Nothing. No one has."

"We should go back to the car," Lee's dad said. "Lee needs to see it, to see if he has any ideas, any new insights."

"That's a good idea," Margaret replied. "They should be done with most of their work around there by now anyway." Lee couldn't tell if she were being condescending and didn't care. He did need to see Paul's car, the only thing they'd found, the only trace.

They took two Jeeps, turning off the main road onto a tiny gravel and dirt one that bumped through towering, dense trees. After about ten minutes they stopped. "Here we are," Margaret said, pulling off on-to a wash of dirt at the side of the road behind a parked and empty State Trooper car.

"Where?" Patrick asked. It seemed like they were amongst trees that were the same as the trees every-where along the coast.

"Lee's brother's car." And then Lee saw it, a glint of metal off to the right, off the road in a little clear-ing or gully or something, mostly screened from view by a thin layer of bushes and trees. It was his brother's Wagoneer, the wood paneling blending in with the woods. He pointed it out.

"Is that where you found it?" Patrick asked.

"Yes," Margaret said. "Or, rather, where some hunters found it."

"What the hell is it doing there, out of the park, off the road like it's hidden?" Patrick asked.

"That's what we need to find out. Lee, do you have any ideas?"

Lee didn't answer. He had let himself out of the Jeep and was walking towards his brother's car. Instead of cutting straight through the bushes towards it he headed down the road a ways until he found the little wash his brother must have driven up, a cleared area scattered with pebbles and fairly smooth dirt that water probably cascaded down in the winter. It went straight away from the road about ten feet, then turned back to the left, heading downhill. From here the car was barely visible.

He walked towards it, noticing faint tire tracks in some low, muddy areas, wondering why his brother would have gone this way. Though it was pretty smooth, not too much chance of damage or getting stuck.

Reaching the car, Lee looked but didn't touch it so he wouldn't tamper with whatever evidence might still be here. Peering in the windows it looked like everything was pretty clean, no litter or cans of soda, which was usual for Paul's car, for Paul's life. There was a West Coast map neatly folded shut on the passenger seat along with a well-used Oregon Hikes book and in the back was a big pair of bolt cutters with red plastic handles. No orange backpack.

Margaret, Patrick and Lee's parents walked up beside him. "Do you have any idea why he'd drive off the road like this?" Margaret asked.

"I don't know."

"Did he usually camp illegally?"

"Did you find a place he'd camped?" Lee asked

"No."

"No, we stayed at campgrounds. When one was available, anyway. I guess when we were backpacking and couldn't find a registered campsite we'd just find someplace, but not like this when a campsite's a few miles away. Unless it was full?"

"It wasn't that entire weekend, though it was crowded. We checked."

"Then I don't know. Maybe he wanted to get away from people, maybe it was too noisy there or something?"

"Maybe. How about the bolt cutters?" Margaret asked. "Did he usually have those in his car?"

"No. He probably had them in there from work, though. He's a landscaper."

"There aren't any other work tools in there."

"Maybe he just didn't have time to put them away with the rest of the stuff. I don't know."

After a stretch of silence Patrick said, "Your brother likes camping with people, doesn't he? That's what I remember. He likes talking to his neighbors, hanging out, meeting people."

"Yeah, he does," Lee replied softly. "He does."

"Do you know what I think?" Lee's father said in almost a whisper. "I think it doesn't make sense. He wouldn't come here on his own and hide his car like this. I think maybe someone stole his car, or maybe made him come here, someone who had something to hide. A hitchhiker he picked up, maybe."

"Don't be ridiculous," Lee's mom said. "He was probably lost, or it got late and he couldn't make it to the campsite before dark, so he decided to stay here."

"Then why didn't we find the place he camped?" Lee's father said.

"Well, the police dusted for fingerprints," Margaret replied. "So we might know soon if anyone else was in the car with him. Though of course it's hard in a car that lots of people have ridden in. And once we know that those turned out, we'll do a thorough search of the vehicle."

"You mean that actually could have happened?" Lee asked. His brother kidnapped, murdered, buried in a ditch by the side of the road somewhere or out in these dense woods? Or alive, tied up in a basement? That stuff didn't happen in real life, that was movies, bad crime shows on TV. Wasn't it? Of course he'd thought of all those possibilities before, run them and a thousand more through his head, but it was different to hear it from someone in a uniform, to hear that they were dusting for fucking fingerprints.

"We're not ruling anything out," Margaret said.

"Jesus," Lee replied.

At Margaret's insistence and over everyone's objections they drove back out to the point and searched again in the woods there, zigzagging back and forth, going off the trail, covering every foot of ground in the small bit of the park they focused on. Others were doing the same all over the area, the rangers told them, and they would have the park and surrounding wilderness covered within a few days, a week at most.

There were no paths where they walked so they stepped cautiously over projecting roots and around thickets, Margaret telling them several times to be careful not to damage the flora if it could be avoided. Lee stared into the woods looking for a footprint, a charred pile of logs, a hint of bright orange from a backpack hidden in a gully under a pile of branches and leaves. He saw nothing but an endless variety of plants and trees that he couldn't identify, a few tiny white flowers peeking up here and there and red berries hanging from bushes, heard no sounds but the rustle of birds and squirrels in the canopy overhead, and once the crashing of a deer or elk fleeing their intrusion. Margaret occasionally responded to the crackling of the radio at her hip in short, curt sentences that made no sense to Lee.

As they walked Margaret explained the steps that the authorities were taking. The Tillamook Police had run the fingerprints, would search for clues in the car and immediately around it and were conducting interviews in all the nearest towns. The rangers were leading the search of the woods with the help of State Troopers, who also supplied the helicopter and some police dogs. A boat from the Coast Guard was coming later to comb the water's edge around the point. The rangers were also calling everyone who'd registered at the campsite over the weekend, asking if they'd seen anyone who matched Paul's description.

Lee wished he knew more, could help more, but he couldn't think of anything else for them to do, any information they didn't already have. All he could do was serve as another pair of eyes.

"Shit!"

Lee whipped around to see his dad's feet flip up as he tumbled. His mom reached out a hand too late into the air where he'd been a second ago, but he was gone.

They'd been walking alongside a small stream, roughly following a meandering deer trail. Margaret, who'd been in the lead, rushed back past Lee who was still staring frozen and scrambled down the hillside after his dad.

Jerking into life, Lee ran back to the spot where his father had disappeared and looked down. He lay in a heap maybe five feet below them, a few feet from the trickling stream's edge. A small path of destruction led through the undergrowth, chronicling his fall. Margaret was beside him, asking if he was ok, if anything hurt.

"I don't know. Sorry."

"Don't apologize. We've been hiking all day and you must be exhausted. I just hope everything's ok. Let's see if you can stand." She offered her hand.

Lee watched. He was useless. His father could have plunged off the edge of a cliff and it would have taken him a minute to even move. He couldn't save anyone.

His dad rose with the ranger's help and brushed some of the twigs and dirt from his sweater and jeans. Then he took a step forward and winced, stopped. "My ankle," he said. "Sorry. It's not too bad." He took another step.

Margaret stopped him, bent to feel his ankle. She decided it was sprained, not too badly, and definitely not broken. "But it's more than past time for us to call it a day," she said. "The sun will set soon, anyway."

Lee checked his phone. No signal, but it was a little after 6:30. They'd been searching all day except for a short break back at the Ranger Station in the campground for sandwiches.

Putting one arm around Lee's shoulder, the other around his wife's, Lee's dad made his way back to the Jeeps. It turned out they weren't far at all, though they'd been walking for hours.

"Could you drop me off at my car?" Patrick asked. "Sorry, I really wish I could keep looking with you but I have a lot of work scheduled for tomorrow so I have to head back to Portland."

"Thank you so much for helping, for taking me out here," Lee said. His parents echoed the thanks.

"It's the least I could do. Do you need a ride back, Lee?"

He shouldn't miss more work, he needed the money, but he wasn't about to go back now, not when his brother was so close. "No, I'm going to stay out here until we find something," he said.

"Of course. Well, call me as soon as you have any news."

After Patrick drove away, Lee looked back into the forest of the Cape. In its depths, somewhere, maybe, was Paul, his older brother, fallen, injured, dying or dead. He desperately wanted to rush back in there, to run randomly from place to place until he found something. But his father was hurt and the sun was going to set soon. Others would look as long as they could and then there was tomorrow. But what if his brother died tonight and Lee could have found him, could have saved him?

When they reached the car he got in. He didn't think he had any other choice.

SIXTEEN

Friday was spent in a long and fruitless search with his Mom and Margaret, his dad staying behind at the ranger station with an ice pack on his ankle. Afterwards there were agonizing silences in their motel room, the TV droning away, Lee and his parents lost in thoughts that hurt too much to share.

The next morning Lee was waiting quietly with his parents, sipping bad coffee from Styrofoam cups, as the search team gathered in the parking lot. Then, chugging down the road, he saw Dragon Pig's dusty rusting touring van (not that they'd toured any farther than Seattle, and that was just once) with the stencils Lee'd cut of their name and a simplified version of their bestial logo in bright orange on the sides.

Patrick, Cindy, Elly and three of the four band members emerged from the van but before he could go to them a caravan of four more cars came into the lot. Piling out of them came various friends and coworkers of Paul's and Lee's, maybe fifteen in total, from Portland and from their hometown. "We're here to help look," Patrick said to Lee, putting an arm around his shoulders.

"Jesus, man, thanks. This is amazing." Lee felt his heart soar up, felt, maybe, a little hope again.

When Lee had talked to Patrick on the phone last night he'd said he might bring a few friends when he came back. Lee hadn't expected anything like this. Or this early: he'd never seen any of his friends out of bed before ten if they didn't have to work. The group looked sleepy and coffees steamed from paper cups and steel travel mugs in the hands of most. It was a gaggle of scruffy twenty-somethings, men and women, with hiking boots, fleeces against the morning chill and backpacks with Nalgenes sprouting from webbed pockets. Individually and in groups they came up to where Lee was standing with his parents and said how sure they were they'd find Paul, how glad they were to be able to help.

As Lee greeted everyone more cars pulled in with friends of his parents and others from their town: two teachers he and his brother had both had, farmers, the town's one police officer and a retired couple who didn't know Paul well but kept saying how happy they were to help.

Margaret, who was in charge of the search operation, said that all their extra eyes would be a huge benefit. She took control like a general, assigning people to different squads, each headed by a ranger, sheriff or police officer. With a sharpie and a large map of the area, she assigned different terrains to each group then sent them off.

Lee's father's ankle was still bothering him so he was going to stay behind again with the ranger who was coordinating the different groups via radio from the station. Lee said his goodbyes then went to join his mom and Margaret, though he wanted to be with his friends who he yelled thanks to yet again. They headed off into the woods once more.

That evening Margaret sat the Garretts down in her office, which had wooden walls covered in photos of her over the decades in seemingly every National Park in the country, smiling widely in front of all that wild beauty. Lee's dad was slumped in a comfortable looking swivel chair behind her desk, Lee and his mom were on hard wooden chairs facing it. Margaret leaned in the door frame. "I want to update you on the situation," she said. No one responded. Lee heard doom in her weary voice.

"The helicopter has covered the entire area several times and today was its last day. We don't think it's going to find anything. If there is anything to find it's going to be under the trees. The dogs couldn't pick up his scent leading from the car, though, and we didn't find any footprints. This would have been easier if it weren't summer; the heat dissipates scents and the ground's too hard to leave good prints. Plus it's likely he walked along the road for a while which makes him even harder to trace."

Why would he walk along the road? Because it was quicker to get wherever he was going than just diving off into the woods. But where was he going?

Margaret continued, "We've covered almost the entire park and most of the woods to the south where the car was found. But those woods stretch south and east for miles and miles, cut up by farms and logging operations, trails or towns here and there. If he kept going for some reason he could have ended up very far from here. Of if he hitchhiked or was abducted. Though of course the police didn't come up with anything when they dusted for fingerprints and searched the car."

"He wouldn't have hitchhiked away," Lee's dad insisted.

"Maybe not. But we need to consider all the possibilities and some of them aren't pretty. He could have gone out to sea, for example, slipped off a cliff, or perhaps gone swimming and been sucked out by the undertow."

Swimming. Somehow Lee hadn't considered that possibility. The water was icy on the Oregon coast but Paul went in sometimes. Skinny dipping at midnight, jumping in fully clothed when he reached the shore after a long day's hike. Paul was a very strong swimmer but something could have happened. A shark, or he could have been drunk or a wave could have taken him by surprise and knocked him under. And the tide could have come in and dragged out what he'd left on the shore.

Margaret had continued talking. "We could have missed him when we walked by, if he was down a steep ravine or under a lot of brush, though it's unlikely with the dogs. But, I hate to say this and I'm sorry, but if he did fall and injure himself it's most likely that he's dead. It's been two weeks. Not necessarily. If he had a lot of water and food with him and if he were unconscious when we passed by it is possible he's still alive. But I don't think it's a very strong possibility."

"He always carried extra," Lee said, then realized he'd used the past tense again. But really, what were the chances that Paul was alive? Unless he'd been kidnapped. Or hitchhiked or hiked his way out of his current life, escaping. Both of which would explain the hidden car. Neither of which seemed real or made any sense.

"We're going to continue the search tomorrow. With the extra manpower we should be able to cover all the area he could have gone within two days' hike by then, most of where he could have gone in three. Hopefully we'll find something. If not we're going to cut back the operation. Not give it up entirely, but cut it back. I'm sorry."

"What do you mean, cut it back?" Lee's father asked. "How can you cut it back if you don't know where he is, if you haven't found anything yet?"

"This search is very expensive. And with the disaster in New Orleans resources are being spread thin everywhere. When it becomes likely that we're not going to find anything we need to devote our time, money and manpower to other priorities."

"Jesus. Other priorities! What's more important than finding a lost kid? How can you say that?" Lee's dad demanded.

"I'm sorry. Hopefully, like I said, we'll find something tomorrow. With all Paul's friends looking, I have high hopes."

Lee was glad she did. He didn't.

Lee's parents went back to the motel they'd slept in the night before but Lee decided to stay with his friends. Elly had said he could sleep in her tent or set up his; she'd brought all his gear. The searchers got to camp for free. The campsite wasn't full, though there were a fair number of people enjoying the summer as it stretched into the first days of September.

They all sat around a boisterously crackling bonfire on the beach, burning driftwood and pallets that some of Paul's camping friends had brought with them from Portland. All of them were in a large circle which shifted constantly as people got up to get more beers from their coolers, to avoid the changes in direction of the swirling smoke or to talk to someone else. Lee had Elly on one side, Patrick on the other. Over the course of the hour or so he'd been there, sipping microbrews brought by the case, again by Paul's friends, and staring into the flames, everyone from the circle had come up to him, patted him on the shoulder. They'd all said brief words about Paul, how they loved him and missed him, how they were sure they'd find him. Lee thanked each of them sincerely for their help and held an image of that person with Paul in his mind for a moment.

Was this a wake, he wondered? Pretty much all of Paul's friends were here and they were drinking around a fire on the beach. Lee wasn't sure anything else would be more appropriate as a wake for his brother, not that he had ever been to a wake. But, no. This wasn't. They were still looking, they would all be looking together tomorrow. There was still hope, still too many possibilities, too many questions and mysteries. This wasn't a wake. If it were a wake he would be drinking whiskey.

"Does anyone have any whiskey?" Lee called out, suddenly feeling an intense urge for it.

No one did, at least no one in hearing. His brother would have had whiskey, Maker's. Lee opened another Black Butte Porter instead, and raised it towards the moon, which he suddenly noticed out over the choppy ocean waves, peeking between fragmented clouds that glowed with its light.

The ocean glowed too, whitecaps hovering like ghosts then crashing into dissolvement and chaos on the sand with a grumbling roar. Lee imagined stripping and running plunging screaming out into those waves, letting the water crash over him, purify him, carry him sailing back into shore. But it was too cold out there, much too cold and too dark. He'd need whiskey for that, too.

The moon was a glowing white circle through the red fabric of Elly's tent. She was a dim lump of darkness next to him, encased in her sleeping bag cocoon. Lee was in his. He didn't know what time it was or how many beers he'd had. They'd stumbled back here by the light of her wavering flashlight and quickly slid into the warmth of their bags.

Lee was thinking of all his friends and of Paul's, how good they'd been to come here and search when there were no clues except the car and the stupid bolt cutters. Suddenly Lee jerked upright. "Shit!" he yelled.

"What?" Elly moaned, not moving.

"The bolt cutters! When I ran into Jenny at Last Thursday she said something about Paul going on a trip in the woods with crazy nature-loving friends or some shit like that. Paul's friends were pretty much all here and none of them are crazy environmentalists, right?"

"What the fuck are you talking about, Lee?"

"What if he was hanging out with crazy nature types, but maybe they weren't hippies, maybe they were eco-terrorists or some shit like that. And he had the bolt cutters in the car because he was doing some kind of sabotage, breaking in somewhere! That's why his car was hidden off the road! That's why he's missing, why he disappeared! He's running from the law, or something happened, something went wrong! We need to go tell the rangers!"

Elly sat up too. "Lee, dude, it's the middle of the night and we're drunk. They're not going to listen to any crazy theories we come running in with now. But," and she slowed, mulling the idea, "what if you're right, what if that is what happened? Would you want to go to the rangers then, to the authorities? Wouldn't that be like turning him in?"

"Oh, fuck. I hadn't thought about that. Do you really think that could be what happened?"

"I have no idea. What we should do is get some sleep, think it over and talk about it again in the morning. Or, hopefully, find him in the morning so we don't have to worry about this crazy shit."

"Right. Ok."

They were quiet then but sleep didn't come. Lee tried to think whether Paul could be an eco-terrorist. He was definitely an environmentalist, giving money to Greenpeace, drinking tapwater out of Nalgenes, riding a bike when he could, buying organic produce or growing it in his garden. And he loved nature more than anything, clearly wanted it protected. But he'd never been a violent person. The most radical thing Lee could remember him doing was voting for

Nader in 2000, and that was only after he'd decided that Oregon was going to Gore anyway. He'd never really talked about doing anything extreme. Except, Lee suddenly remembered, once.

They'd been fishing for salmon on the Rogue River this May, right after Paul and Jenny had their breakup. They'd planned it as a long weekend for Paul to clear his head, camping, kayaking and fishing. Lazily they cast their lines into the gorgeous blue fast flowing river, not caring if they caught anything, talking about everything except Jenny and drinking a lot of beer and whiskey.

And they hadn't caught anything until the last day, when the clouds that had been threatening all weekend finally broke into a light drizzle. Lee had wanted to pack up and go home but Paul insisted on giving it one more try. So, shivering in their rain shells, watching drops pucker in the still places on the edge of the river and drip from the tall trees, they cast their lines one more time, drinking coffee spiked with Maker's to fight the chill and cure their hangovers. And, almost immediately, Paul got a hit.

Just a few minutes later he expertly hauled into the shallows a beautiful salmon the length of his arm, which thrashed back and forth through the water with a violent grace, shimmering silver.

"Do you want me to net it?" Lee asked.

"No," Paul had said. "No, she's too beautiful, too rare. I know we're allowed to catch her, so the government must think there's enough, but we don't need her. Her life's hard enough with the fucking dams everywhere blocking her path, with the big farmers stealing her water to grow their pesticide tainted foods in dry valleys and with everyone dumping their toxic shit into the rivers. And who the hell are we to drive her and everything else extinct when they were here so long before us and our stupid civilization. They're so goddamned beautiful and powerful, and it's so amazing that they can find their way to the same place generation after generation. It would be better if we blew up all the dams, the logging trucks, the tractors and the irrigation canals, all of it, everything. But we can start by letting this beauty go, letting her swim, letting her live freely." And with tenderness he'd reached down, grasped the fish where it swam and with a quick jerk freed the hook from its lip. Instantly, with a flash of silver, it was gone.

"Sorry about being so dark," Paul had said then with a weak laugh.

"You're going through a lot," Lee'd said. "And besides, that was beautiful. But now, if we're not going to be catching fish, shouldn't we get out of the rain and back to the car where it's warm?"

"Sure thing, bro."

Paul hadn't said anything like that before and he never did again. Lee'd discounted it then as his brother being depressed and angry about Jenny, about everything, and hadn't really thought of it until now. But what if that was the start of something, if Paul had driven home thinking about it, about how to put those thoughts into action? Lee wouldn't know how to find a group like that but his brother knew more people than he did so maybe he had a contact and started going to meetings, making plans, plotting the action that would cause him to hide his car in the woods and vanish from his life? Maybe, maybe... It was so, so much better than thinking he'd fallen off a cliff and drowned.

Lee thought of Paul tossing a Molotov cocktail at a logging truck, breaking the links in a fence to let caged animals free, planting explosives at a dam. Then of Paul drowning, Paul tied up in a basement somewhere, Paul swimming strongly into the ocean towards the setting sun, and he didn't know when these thoughts turned into dreams.

The sun smeared down into the clouds that hovered on the edge of the ocean, lighting them a dirty golden color. Lee stood with his parents, his dad leaning his weight against his wife. Scattered along the beach's length were couples watching the sunset on blankets spread out in the sand.

"I'm going to go back with my friends tonight," Lee said. "I really want to stay and keep looking, but I have to get back to work." He'd agonized about that decision all day as they combed fruitlessly through the woods yet again, woods that looked exactly the same as the ones they'd been in the day before and the day before that. What won out was the thought that, if there was anything to the eco-terrorism idea, it was something he could best look into back in Portland. If Paul had been an eco-terrorist he would be nowhere near here by now, he would have escaped.

"If that's what you need to do, I understand," his mom said.

"Maybe I should stay," Lee said, changing his mind again.

"No," his mother said. "You need to go and get back to your life, at least for a while. But we're glad you could help us this weekend. And thank all your friends for us again, they were amazing. Thank them so much for their help."

"And thank you," his father said, reaching out to sling his arm around Lee's shoulder. "Thank you so much, son. I don't know if I could have handled this without you. Without both of you," he said to his wife. Tears ran down his cheeks. Lee was surprised that he wasn't crying and that his mother's eyes were dry, too. Lee had a theory now, a hope, but what did it mean for his mom? Was she accepting this? Numb? Giving up? He didn't know. He didn't even know what he felt, what he believed, now.

SEVENTEEN

Lee slouched in a beat-up armchair in the large but cluttered cafe where his housemate Doug and other tatooed hipsters worked, looking out the plate glass window onto the dark street. He was waiting for Jenny. On the drive back from Cape Lookout a light, chilly rain had begun to fall, the first of autumn. And if it were falling in Portland it would be falling back on the coast, washing away all signs of Paul. Lee sipped a delicious Stumptown coffee though it was almost seven-thirty in the evening. The caffeine was probably fine; with all the thoughts racing through his head it wasn't likely he'd be able to sleep tonight anyway.

The place was closing soon and Jenny was late. Finally he saw her walk in, shutting a bright yellow umbrella. She scanned the room until she found him, then strolled over. "What did you need to talk to me about, Lee?" she asked. "Is it about Paul? Is there any news?"

"You said something when I ran into you at Last Thursday about Paul going on a retreat with crazy nature friends, or something like that. What did you mean?"

"I didn't really mean anything by it. I guess I just thought he'd been hanging out with some environmentalist recently," she said, sinking into a chair next to his.

"What environmentalists?"

"Well, I don't know any of this for a fact, but it just seemed like maybe his ideas about the environment had been getting a bit more extreme. And that it had to do with some new people he'd been spending time with."

"More extreme how? Like eco-terrorism? Where are you getting this from?"

"Just stuff he'd say sometimes when he'd come over. About how none of us were doing anywhere near enough to stop the destruction of the planet, how just driving a Prius and buying organic bananas was a joke compared to all the shit that was going on, stuff like that. He was darker. And once when I asked him to come over he said he had couldn't because he had a meeting to go to, but when I asked what kind of meeting he said it wasn't important and changed the subject. Somehow in my mind those two things became connected, that's all."

"Why the hell didn't you tell me any of this? Or the police?"

"Like I said, because I didn't really know anything. And because I figured if there was anything important, you, his family or friends, people who were still actually involved in his life, would know about it. How could he have not told you if he was doing something like that?"

"Fuck," Lee said. "I don't know. I think he would have told me, but if he was serious maybe he would have kept everything secret. Maybe he only hinted at it to you because you weren't really a part of his life anymore, didn't talk to anyone. Christ. Do you know anything else? Names, where he met these people, what the group was called?"

"No. He never talked about any of this directly and I could just be making the whole thing up. But, God, Lee, do you really think this could be why he disappeared? You said eco-terrorism. Do you know anything? Do you think he could have done that?" She reached out and put her hand on his, then quickly pulled it back.

"I don't know. There were bolt-cutters in his car, which was what made me think of it in the first place. I don't know anything, but this could be real!"

"Maybe. God, that would be so great to have a reason, to have him alive, a fugitive, an eco-terrorist." Then she sighed. "But, no. Think about it, Lee. Paul wouldn't do anything that extreme. This is just our minds playing tricks on us, wanting to come up with explanations. I can't really believe he'd do anything more than go to meetings and talk about this stuff over beers, if that. Would he have actually done something so radical that it required disappearing afterwards, leaving his life behind? I don't really think that seems like Paul. Do you?"

Lee tried to think. It was so tempting to believe all this as an alternative to the thought that Paul was gone. But could he really be an eco-terrorist, or the run? It was hard to believe. But not impossible. "I really don't know," he said.

The guy behind the counter came to collect Lee's empty coffee cup and told them that they'd be closing in a few minutes.

"I guess I should be going," Jenny said, rising. "I'm really sorry to have gotten you all worked up if this turns out to be nothing. But if you do figure anything out, please give me a call right away."

"I will," Lee said. She put her hand on his shoulder for a moment then walked out the door into the rainy night without a backward glance. Lee sat there, lost in thoughts, until they kicked him out.

As he was walking home, rain seeping into his sweatshirt, Lee's phone rang. It was his father, and Lee could tell he'd been crying. "Since we didn't find anything today they're cutting it back, cutting everything back. There's only going to be one ranger keeping up the search with us full time and it's not even Margaret. They just called to tell us."

"I'm so sorry," Lee said.

"We're going to keep looking, your mother and I," he said. "My ankle's almost healed."

"I'll come out again soon. I shouldn't have come back tonight."

"You have things to do. We understand."

And he did have things to do. He had to find out what kind of eco-terrorism Paul could have been involved in, how that could explain that he was still alive somewhere so it didn't matter if they were searching the coast or not. But he still didn't know anything, so wouldn't say anything, wouldn't get his father worked up about this until he had some sort of proof.

When Lee got home he borrowed Doug's laptop. Buzzing from anxiety, excitement and caffeine, his fingers tapping incessantly on the keyboard, he followed link after link about Northwest eco-terrorism. There was the Environmental Liberation Front putting metal spikes in trees to shatter sawblades and burning down housing developments, and Tre Arrow, one of their local heroes, currently fighting extradition back to the US from Canada on charges of setting fire to cement and logging trucks here in Oregon. He'd been arrested in Victoria for shoplifting bolt cutters. Bolt cutters! Lee remembered Paul saying Tre Arrow was an idiot when that story broke, committing petty theft when he was a wanted felon. But maybe he'd just meant that he could do it better. It was so tempting to think of Paul that way, disappearing as an environmental hero. But groups like that didn't just post contact information on the internet, obviously. Indymedia, which was Lee's first idea for finding those kind of people, had posts about environmental activists being shot at by loggers and Oregon's forests being wrongfully clearcut, but no recent actions or protests. However, later in the week there was a talk on tree-sitters in Northern California. Maybe someone who knew something would be there. It would be way better than doing nothing.

After two days spent obsessing over eco-terrorism to no avail at work and at home, Lee went back to the coast. With no ranger accompanying them, he and his parents drove to a place well outside the park, down a bumpy dirt road through dripping,

122

mossy forest. The trees here were younger, smaller; they must have been logged within the past 50 years. When they parked, pulling off the road into a ditch amongst trees that looked just like those they'd passed and those up the road, Lee asked, "Why here?"

His mom unfolded a map of the area. Large swathes had been crossed through in black sharpie. She put her finger on a little road just on the outer edge of the marked-off terrain. "We're searching this area today."

Lee's mom held the map while his dad pulled out a compass. They consulted it briefly, then his mom pointed into the woods. She counted off her footsteps under her breath as they tramped into the muddy forest. They went slowly to accommodate Lee's dad's slight limp. After two hundred paces, or what would have been that many if they hadn't had to reroute to avoid gullies, fallen logs and impenetrable thickets, they turned, walked fifty paces, then turned back with military precision. They didn't talk, the only noise the crunch of fallen leaves under their boots, the metronomic repetition of the count of their footsteps by Lee's mom and the occasional caw of a disturbed bird.

Lee kept his eyes darting here and there into the woods around him. But, he knew, it had been two and a half weeks since his brother disappeared. If they found anything here now it would probably be a corpse. He couldn't think that way, though, that couldn't be right, something else must have happened. Paul was a fugitive, he was an eco-terrorist. But yesterday Lee had spent hours at the Central Library, reading every paper for weeks before and after Paul's disappearance, turning his fingers black from the ink, and had found no mention of any act of eco-terrorism. He longed to tell his parents about the theory but really he knew nothing. It wouldn't be fair to get them excited over something that could be a phantom, a fantasy. Which is what it felt like now, back on the coast, the trees swaying above in a wind that occasionally whipped down around them, cutting through Lee's thin layers. There was no rain but water was everywhere: drops dripping down from the trees, dark puddles reflecting green and gray and beads on the bladelike leaves of ferns.

They didn't find anything. After their day's search, his mom precisely, with a sharpie and a ruler, X'ed off their lack of discovery on a previously green sliver of the map.

EIGHTEEN

Lee pushed open the door and entered the cafe, its walls decorated with photographs of revolutionaries in Central America, quotes from Marx and block printed artwork featuring fists and stars. A slide of a giant redwood was projected on a screen that looked like it belonged in an elementary school classroom. A tall guy with a shaved and stubbled head, torn jeans and a woven Mexican sweater stood beside it. About half the audience, mostly white kids with an assortment of dreadlocks, patched hoodies and large piercings, turned to look as Lee ducked in and sat in an empty wooden chair towards the back. The guy up front pressed a button and the slide clicked to show, from way down below, a woman up in the giant tree on some kind of platform, waving.

"This is Mary from a few years back when we first started setting up our platforms on Sundance, a redwood which is over one thousand years old..."

With more slides the guy described their tree sit in Humboldt County, Northern California. Activists lived in platforms that they'd constructed high in a grove of endangered old-growth redwoods to keep people from clearcutting the trees and making them into jacuzzis and decks. Some of them had been up in the redwoods for over a year continuously. Lee imagined his brother dropping out of his life to live in a tree. It didn't fit, Paul needed to move and explore. And sitting in a tree didn't jive with the bolt cutters they'd found in his car, either. Those implied something more active, more destructive. Like Tre Arrow burning trucks on Ross Island, like PETA or ALF or whoever it was breaking into labs and factory farms to free oppressed animals. Like sabotaging dams to help the salmon return home.

Lee spent the rest of the talk looking around at the maybe fifteen people in the audience. Who of them might know his brother? How would he find out? He went up and got a beer for courage. When the talk ended the floor was opened to questions. There were a few about how to help and one asking if the presenter knew anything about a tree sit going on in Australia, which became a lecture from the questioner about the tree sit in Australia. Lee downed the last of his beer in a gulp then raised his hand.

"Hi," he said when he was called upon. "My name's Lee. My brother, Paul Garrett, disappeared on the coast near Cape Lookout two and a half weeks ago. He was a tall guy, late twenties, looked a little like me but an inch taller with shaggy black hair, bright blue eyes and kind of big ears that stuck out a little. I was just wondering if anyone here knew him, knew anything about him. Sorry to disturb your talk, but if any of you do know anything, I'll stick around so please come find me afterwards. Thank you."

Everyone had turned to look at him and Lee tried to figure out if any of them knew anything. He couldn't tell, couldn't read their faces. Then someone else asked another question and all their attention turned away.

When the questions were over the guy up front thanked everyone and people scraped their chairs back and left or went up to the counter to order. Lee stayed in his seat, watching the audience as they passed. A few said they were sorry about his brother but no one stopped. Then the guy who'd given the talk broke away from the group who'd surrounded him and headed towards Lee, who stood. "I'm Jonah," he said, offering his hand. "I'm really sorry to hear about your brother."

"Thanks," Lee said. "Did you know him?"

"No, I'm sorry to say I didn't. I'm based down in California, don't know too many people up here in Portland. Why did you come here to ask, though?"

"His ex-girlfriend said he'd maybe been hanging out with some extreme environmentalists, though she didn't know who. I thought there was a chance that someone in the audience for this talk would know him through that."

"How extreme are you talking?"

"I don't really know. There were bolt cutters in his car when it was found abandoned at the coast. She, the ex, said he wouldn't really talk about it."

"This is going to sound harsh, but if anyone's doing illegal stuff, more illegal than our tree sits, they're not going to admit that they know him. ELF and all those people are very secretive, especially with all the arrests over the past few years, with the FBI targeting them as eco-terrorists using the bullshit Patriot Act. If I did know him through something like that, and I don't, I wouldn't admit it to you. Sorry, but I don't think you're going to have any luck here, or anywhere else, really. They're not going to leave any traces behind if they did something like that. And if they do leave traces, the Feds will find them before you do. Good luck, though. That's really tough."

"Thanks." Lee looked around one last time at the crowd but no one was looking at him, no one knew anything. It was hopeless.

Lee had another beer at the cafe then switched to whiskey at a dive just up the street, thinking it should be Maker's but not willing to pay the extra unless there was a reason to celebrate. And this was the opposite of a celebration. Even if his brother had been an eco-terrorist there was no way to find out the details, no way to know anything. Lee was stuck in the same hell of uncertainty he'd been in before, only it was worse now because he'd been so excited, so sure he was on to something.

Lee sat at the bar alone, downing shot after shot of harshly burning liquor, handing over wrinkled bills, not caring that he needed the money for the dentist, not caring about anything. He just wanted to drown the hope and despair and the endless cycle of thoughts that led in circles. And then, as he smacked another empty shotglass to the wooden bar, his stomach roiling, he knew where he had to go.

Lee pedaled through the night, the rain having thankfully stopped. He probably shouldn't be biking this drunk, he thought, but screw it, the only person he'd be likely to kill would be himself. He made it to his brother's place safely and wheeled the bike around back, leaning it against the utterly dark, silent house. It fell with a clattering crash and Lee cursed then held still. There was no movement, no noise, no one coming to investigate.

Kneeling on the cold, wet ground, Lee pulled at the stuck window. It didn't budge. Leaning back, putting all his weight into it, he pulled harder but there was still no give. He needed light. His phone, that would work. He pulled it out and flipped it open, casting a faint blue glow, and pushed it up against the window, straining his eyes. It was locked, the latch was shut from the inside. Why had he fucking told the cop about this way in, how could he have been so stupid?

Lee went back out into the garden, looking for something with which he could smash the window, a shovel maybe. He needed to get in. If there was any evidence that Paul had been an eco-terrorist it would be in there. As he searched between the planter beds, dimly illuminated by the neighboring houses and streetlights, he smelled something faintly acrid. It was the tomatoes, a row of towering plants, their beautiful bulbous heirloom fruits having ripened and fallen to the ground where they were rotting.

How could Lee have not thought about the garden, the plants unwatered except by the rain, probably dying, the food wasting on the vine? And how could Paul? Paul had lovingly cared for this garden as a showcase for potential clients, as a source of local food, as a favorite hobby. How could he let it die? How could he leave it, Lee, his parents, his job, everything behind? He hadn't loved the garden more than the wilderness, that was true, but it was so hard to believe that he would just let everything rot. And even if he had, what the fuck was Lee doing here thinking about smashing in a window? He'd been in there, the cops had too, and there was nothing to find. What, was his brother going to have left a note taped to the fridge saying "I'm going to go blow up a dam, please water my garden?" God fucking damn it.

Lee grasped a tomato plant by its thick stem and yanked, uprooting it. The fruits thumped invisibly to the ground, water sprayed up from the leaves and the appetizing smell of tomato foliage filled his nostrils, drowning out the stench of the rot. Tossing the innocent plant aside, Lee threw himself to the cold wet ground, face first, and sobbed. He'd had so much hope. The eco-terrorism thing had seemed like it might finally solve this disappearance, give meaning and reason to it. And now he was exactly where he'd started, knowing nothing, mired in endless mystery and misery. A few more days of his brother being gone had passed and with them the likelihood of ever finding out what happened to Paul was diminished even further.

As Lee lay there, damp seeping up from below, rain started to fall, steady and drumming, splattering on the plants, landing on him, soaking him through. He let it.

NINETEEN

The next morning at work Lee moved slowly, as if he were drugged, occasionally hugging himself and shivering. He had no idea how long he'd lain in the garden or how he'd found the willpower to get up and ride home. Or how the hell he'd made it in to the store this morning, how he moved, lived, at all. He'd probably catch pneumonia and die, but for now his body felt healthy. Lee wished he were sick; his health seemed a perverse irony, a cruel contrast to the state of his mind.

A yuppie guy and Joseph were the only customers and Lee looked forward to Joseph coming up to the counter and, with his conversation, if only for a few minutes, breaking the endless churning cyclone of thoughts that wrenched through his brain.

In the curved mirror overhead Lee saw the smeared image of the yuppie, a pasty man with wispy brown hair, pick up a bottle of top shelf tequila, read the label then slip it into the bulky Patagonia jacket he was wearing. Lee's hands clenched on the edge of the counter and he felt his mind fill with white rage.

What fucking right did this rich fuck with his expensive shoes and khakis and two hundred dollar new jacket have stealing his fucking tequila?

The guy spent a few more minutes looking around then walked past the counter to the door, giving Lee a wan smile of perfectly straight white teeth. Lee gave him a tight grin back.

By the time the door dinged at the apex of its opening Lee was on the man, not aware of having moved past or over the counter, realizing just now that his hand was reaching out and clasping the collar of that coat, feeling nylon and Velcro bunch up in his fist as he yanked with all his strength. The thief stumbled backwards and suddenly there was an explosion, glass and liquid hitting his feet and legs, tequila glugging out of the shattered bottom of the bottle on the tile floor. Human weight hit Lee and he turned it, shoving the man into the wall beside the door, the wire rack holding the Portland Mercury clattering away from his madly scrambling legs. Lee smashed the yuppie's upper body, still held by the scruff of the neck, into the wall with a thud, pulled back on the collar and pushed forward again. The man crumpled to the floor, arms going over his head.

Lee felt a hand on his back, a voice saying, "Isn't that enough?" His left leg was flexed for a kick though he hadn't made a conscious decision to do that, to do any of this. He wasn't sure what he would have done or when he would have stopped.

He turned. Joseph was there, a worried look on his face. "Shouldn't you call the police?" he asked. "Maybe the nice one who was asking about your brother will come."

Lee stood there shaking, the world refocusing. Where the hell had that come from? He hadn't been in a fight since sixth grade, wasn't a violent person, and he'd followed store policy and called the police, letting the suspects go, when he'd seen shoplifters before and was on his own. But of course he knew where it had come from: Paul. It was driving him crazy and he had to get a hold of himself. God he hoped the guy wasn't too badly hurt, wasn't going to sue. The shoplifter was getting up now, untangling his legs from the newspaper rack. There was fear in his eyes and his hands were shaking.

"I, I forgot I had that in there," he said. "You're not going to call the cops are you?" His clothes were rumpled but Lee didn't see any blood on his face. He must have gotten his arms up in front of him when he hit the wall. Both times.

Lee glanced back at Joseph then up at the video camera that was sure to have caught the whole thing. What the fuck should he do? What were his options? Call the cops, keep the guy here until they arrived. Let him go. No one would look at the tape if nothing was reported. Probably.

"I'll give you a hundred dollars if you don't call the police," the guy said suddenly.

"What you broke is worth almost that much," Joseph said calmly.

The guy pulled out a wallet and rifled through it. "I've got one hundred and fifty dollars, one hundred and fifty four," he said.

"One hundred and fifty's about right," Lee said, his heart racing. The guy pulled it out, two bills, and handed them towards Lee. He'd been right to kick his ass, this guy carrying around that much cash, stealing for fun. Fucking asshole. Lee took the money. "I don't ever want to see you in here again."

The man scurried away and Lee said, "Thank you, Joseph."

"I was just trying to help out," he said. "Did you ever find your brother?"

"No." He said it flatly.

"Oh, no. Well, we'll find him, don't worry."

"Thank you," Lee said wearily. No one was going to find Paul. It was going to be a mystery forever, agony forever. He went over to the cash register, rang in the bottle of destroyed tequila and got the change from the hundred dollar bill. He walked back around the counter and over to where Joseph had returned to examining bottles like nothing had happened. Lee reached out, touched him on the shoulder, then offered out his palm, the coins resting on top of the small stack of crisp green ones and the worn fifty. He needed it more, deserved it more than Lee did. Lee didn't deserve anything.

"You don't have to do that, I was just helping out," Joseph said. "I couldn't take all that. You were the one that caught the man."

"You stopped me. I don't know what would have happened, but you stopped me. Take it, please."

Joseph looked at him, down at the bills then back up into Lee's eyes. Lee tried to convey with his gaze how much he needed Joseph to take the money, to make himself feel right about the situation, to make up for the fact that he'd almost kicked a man on the ground and didn't know if he would have ever stopped kicking. Joseph's hand darted out, took the money and secreted it away in his coat. "Thank you," he said.

"Thank you." Lee reached out his hand and Joseph shook it firmly. "Just don't spend it all in here, ok, Joseph?"

"Of course not. Thank you again." Joseph turned and walked towards the door.

"Don't you want your usual bottle?" Lee asked.

"Not tonight. I've got to go find your brother tonight," Joseph said.

"Thanks for trying," Lee replied, "but you shouldn't bother. No one can find anything, there's nothing to find. He just fucking disappeared."

"I'm still going to look," Joseph said over his shoulder. And then the door dinged and Joseph was gone. Lee was alone in the store. He went into the back to get the mop, the broom and the chemical cleaners that would hopefully overpower the smell of tequila. While he was sweeping up the broken glass then mopping the white tiles until they gleamed he kept looking up at the boxy little camera pointing at the door, pointing at the scene of the crime. He knew no one usually looked at the tape. And if someone did? Then he was fucked. But he was fucked anyway. Everything was.

TWENTY

The waiting room smelled of wet humanity. Lee scanned the line of dentists for Valerie. When his eyes found hers she smiled and he felt some of the darkness in him lighten and lift for a moment. He walked towards her purposefully. Yesterday he'd almost killed someone for shoplifting and his brother had blown up a logging truck or fallen off a cliff and there was no way to know which and nothing to lose.

"Hi, Lee, how're you doing today? Teeth still feeling ok?"

"Valerie, will you go out on a date with me?"

Valerie's smile lingered for a second then faded. There was conflict in her eyes then steel as she made up her mind. "That's nice of you to ask, Lee, but that could never work. You're my patient, we have a professional relationship. It would be against the rules, to say the least. So I'm sorry but I'm going to have to say no. Now, if you'll follow me to the back, we have a lot of work to do today."

And now everything was shit, everything. He couldn't argue with that, couldn't believe he'd even asked in the first place. He followed after her, dragging his feet.

She put goggles on his eyes and a bib around his neck, carefully not touching his flesh, very professional. "Mr. Garrett, open wide, please," she said. In her gloved hand there was a long needle.

Could she really stab him with a needle then drill into his teeth calmly after he'd made a fool of himself, after she'd rejected him like that? But he deserved it. He opened.

"This might sting a little," she said. She was going to kill him. But there was just the mildest of pricks, then another. And then, in his mouth at least, he didn't feel a thing. She went away while the Novocain did its work, leaving Lee alone with the endless cycle of his miserable thoughts.

Valerie returned. She fumbled around on her tray with her instruments, came up with a metal rod with sharply pointed hooks on both ends. His eyes shifted to her firmly set mouth then back to the metal tool, the tiny pinkish reflection of her face, or what he thought was her face, trapped in its curve. And then the hook shook a little. It moved towards his mouth then pulled abruptly back and Valerie tossed it with a clatter onto the tray with her other instruments. Amazingly, she laughed.

Lee looked up and saw a shy, glowing smile on her face. "You know what, Lee?" she said, "I will go on a date with you. What the hell, right? There are tons of other patients here, hundreds of other dental students. I can say there's a scheduling conflict or something and they can find another student to work on your teeth."

"Thass gwate. Thang oo," he got out between his ballooned, numb lips. Valerie laughed again, at him this time, but kindly. He wished she'd made this decision before she'd pumped him full of Novocain.

"But it would be hard to explain if we sent you home without doing anything at all today," she said thoughtfully. "Lee, is it ok if I do a cleaning and fill a cavity this morning and then we go out sometime this weekend? I know it's a little weird, but this whole thing has been, right?"

"I gueth tho," he said and smiled. He'd have a date this weekend. If they didn't need him out on the coast to look for his brother.

"I'll try my hardest not to cause you any pain. Though I can't believe you want to go out with me after what I put you through that first time. But that's not my fault, right, you hate the professor for that? That'll work?"

Lee just nodded, smiling. And Valerie started scraping away at his rotting teeth. Tenderly, if such a thing were possible.

TWENTY-ONE

Valerie's plan was to go see the swifts. Lee'd heard of it, thousands of birds flying into the chimney of an elementary school in Northwest Portland every night in September, but he'd never been.

The sun, which he'd thought might be gone for good behind the unending gray drizzle, had come out again, shining on the glistening sidewalks, raising small clouds of steam that glowed in the evening light.

Lee'd taken the streetcar from work to where it stopped being free then walked the rest of the way past the fancy houses of the neighborhood. Eventually he came to a grassy hill alongside the large elegant reddish buildings of the school, a tall brick chimney rising from one. The lawn was filled with Portlanders in fleeces, sweatshirts and rain shells, prepared for the chill of the coming night. They sat on blankets spread over the grass in groups and pairs, children running between them, laughing. A few small black forms darted through the air but nothing impressive was happening yet.

Lee scanned the crowd for Valerie but didn't see her. He pulled out his cellphone and saw that he was just on time. Hearing his name called he looked up and saw her walking towards him, a paper Trader Joe's bag swinging from her hand. She looked amazing in tight jeans and a simple maroon shirt that brought out the warm colors in her brown hair. Hell, she looked great in scrubs, so of course she did.

"Hey there," she said when she reached him. "How's it going?"

"I'm doing pretty good," he said, and it was true just then, with her pretty face smiling at him. "How about you?"

"Well, school was a bit of a bitch today, but other than that, good. How're your teeth doing, and the temporary crown?"

He liked that she'd sworn. "You're not my dentist anymore. Besides, it's the weekend, so you're not allowed to think about teeth for the next couple days."

"You're right, sorry. Force of habit."

"No need to apologize, I was kidding. My teeth are fine. Anyway, let's find someplace to sit."

They claimed a patch of open grass with a view of the chimney. From her bulky purse Valerie pulled a small thin blanket that looked like it had been woven somewhere in Central America. When they sat their thighs touched, which Lee told himself there was no way to avoid while staying on the little blanket and off the damp grass. He felt her warmth through their jeans. Also from Valerie's purse came two plastic wine glasses and a corkscrew, a few knives and plastic plates. He had no idea how all that stuff had fit in there.

In the shopping bag was hummus and pita, brie, blue cheese and crackers, carrots and celery with dip and a bottle of local Pinot Noir. "I hope everything looks good to you. I'm a vegetarian, did I mention that before? It's not a problem, is it?"

"Of course not, and thanks for bringing all this stuff. One of my best friends is vegan. And I cook vegetarian most of the time." Because it was cheaper.

"I have been since I was nine," she said.

"That's great. I think I would have starved if I tried going vegetarian when I was a kid. My dad's from a farming town and my mom's from the South. I don't think either of them could imagine dinner without meat."

"I've got my parents mostly trained, not that they'll ever really get it."

"I don't think my parents would even be trainable. Anyway, everything looks great," he said.

They splashed wine into the little glasses surreptitiously, not knowing if drinking were allowed. She raised hers slightly and said, "To utterly inappropriate and unprofessional first dates."

Lee laughed and, looking into her eyes, a lovely mix of coffee bean browns and lakewater greens, said, "Cheers." He took a sip. "Delicious," he said and it was, not that he knew anything about wine.

For the first few minutes they ate in a slightly awkward, nervous silence broken only by comments on how good something was, offers and acceptances of more and thanks when they handed each other cheese-laden crackers or hummused pitas. Then Valerie said, "I've been listening to the Dragon Pig CD more. It's not the kind of music I'm usually into but

I've decided it's great for cleaning the house. I was wondering how they came up with the name, though."

"You know, I'm not really sure. It's the name Conrad and Renee had when they first told me about the band. I always just assumed it sounded cool. I'll ask the next time I see them."

"I don't know how you could have drawn the Dragon Pig without knowing the deeper significance behind it, Lee," she said with a laugh. "But, really, it doesn't matter. I was just curious."

"Well now I am too. Anyway, what kind of music do you listen to, if it's not indie punk or whatever the hell it is my friends play?"

"All sorts of stuff, but usually mellower. Jazz and folk, a lot."

"Elly, my housemate, the vegan one I mentioned, used to be in a folk band, Lolita, or maybe they were more bluegrass. They were great, anyway, maybe even better than Dragon Pig. They never came out with a real album, but I could burn you a CD with some of their songs."

"Lolita?"

"Yeah, I guess my friends don't have the greatest taste in band names, do they? They all looked like hardcore lesbian punks but played this gorgeous, mellow traditional music. It was a little bit disconcerting, actually."

She smiled and her greenish eyes sparkled when they met his. "How many other bands are you friends with?" she asked.

"Just those two. Though I know some other musicians through them."

"That's two more bands than I know. All my friends in Portland are dental students, like those guys I was with when I met you. Some of them are great, but I hung out with a much more creative crowd when I was an undergrad."

"I was worried you were going out with one of those guys when I first saw you."

"God no, they aren't my type at all."

"And what is your type?"

"Like I'm going to tell you. I'd either stroke your ego or hurt your feelings. Let's just say it's not them and leave it at that. And you, Lee, what's your type? Do you usually hit on your dentists?"

"You're right, that question's a trap."

She grinned, then her eyes focused past him, widening, and she said, "Look!"

Around the chimney was an aerial ballet as thousands of black flecks swirled, inscribing a whirling circle, a pattern coalesced from the chaos of individual swifts acting as one. Lee'd been so captivated by Valerie that he hadn't noticed and she hadn't either. It was a good sign.

The swifts dove down in a shimmering mass, neared the entrance to the chimney where maybe a few birds arced down and into it, then the mass rose again and turned with a pulse against the deepening blue of the sky. They rushed outward in a wide curve then arced down again towards the chimney. Other specks twirled here and there in the periphery like bits of ash from burning paper, flicking at random, little clumps forming, tracing their own circles and disbanding, an incredibly complex series of movements forming patterns in the sky. Swifts were still coming from all corners of the air, some so high that a hundred of them appeared as a small puff of smoke.

Wordless, Lee and Valerie watched. Around them the crowd murmured appreciation while children shrieked in delight. The sky gradually darkened to an imperial bluish purple. Lee reached out and took Valerie's hand, she squeezed back and they stayed that way, their fingers intertwined. The dance of the swifts changed, the circle turning into a downward spiral funneling towards the chimney. More and more birds entered at each pass, those that didn't swooping up again for another round. It was hypnotizing.

Lee didn't know how much time passed but eventually the number of swifts in the air lessened as they settled for the night into the chimney. There were just little clumps darting here and there as the evening air grew chilly and dark.

"That was amazing," Lee said.

"Yeah. How could so many thousands of birds fit in that chimney?" she asked.

"I have no idea. And they were flying like they had one mind, instead of the anarchic mess you'd expect, that you'd get if you had that many people trying to go somewhere at once."

"I know. And how did they even find the place? It must have been after they stopped heating the school with it, one swift just said, hey, look, here's a chimney that seems nice! And then to somehow find their way back to just exactly here, year after year, generation after generation."

"I can't believe I'd never made it out to see that before. Thanks for suggesting it."

"Thanks for coming."

They looked into each other's eyes for a moment and some softness Lee saw there made him lean forward and touch his lips gently to hers. He pulled back for a second, saw confirmation, and leaned in again, wrapping his arms around her. As they kissed he closed his eyes and saw the afterimage of dancing swifts spiraling downward behind his eyelids.

After they'd made out for an endless few minutes, Valerie pulled slightly back and rubbed her arms, shivering. With a smile she said, "So what now, Lee? What were we talking about?"

Lee tried to think and realized that whatever they'd been talking about wasn't important. It had been nice and fun but if he wanted this relationship to go anywhere now, to be at all honest, if he wanted this magical evening with the swifts to mean anything, he needed to tell her about Paul, even though it seemed so hard to break her smile that way. He said, "Valerie, there's something I have to tell you. My brother Paul is missing. He disappeared on the coast, where he was camping, almost three weeks ago, right before I met you. They found his car out by Tillamook, but nothing else."

"What? Jesus, Lee, I'm so sorry!" She leaned over and put her hands on his, concern in her eyes. "Do they know anything?"

Lee hesitated, gathering his thoughts, then he launched into the whole story, trying to tell it calmly, of their endless searches by the coast, the excitement when the car had been found, the bolt cutters and the eco-terrorism and all the dead ends, all the worry and despair. Everything but beating up the shoplifter. "I'm sorry to lay this all on you on our first date," he said, "But I thought you needed to know."

Without a word she wrapped her arms around him. She was so soft and warm, felt so right. He wanted to cry but held himself back with a shudder. Being held, letting the story out and being heard made him feel emptied, lighter, free. She kissed him softly on the top of his head then pulled gently away. "Thank you," he said.

"Of course. God, that's all so hard. I can't believe it, can't believe you can even function with all that shit going on."

"I'm not doing that great. But when I'm around you, well, you make me happy, as happy as I've been since I found out. Tonight especially, but even flirting with you at the show, even you working on my teeth. I couldn't really forget everything, of course, but tonight at least I could put it aside and function a little better. Thanks to you."

She looked into his eyes, her gaze steady and deep. "Actually, I guess I did know there was some pain in you, somehow. That might have been why I was drawn to you at first; I like taking care of people, it's partly why I'm becoming a dentist. I didn't think it was something like this, though, something so big, dramatic and immediate. Such a fresh wound. But I can tell you're brave, that you're doing your best with this, though of course it's so, so hard."

"Thank you," he said again. "So, where do we go from here? I kind of ruined our lovely evening, didn't I? We can't really talk about anything else now, can we? So, how 'bout those Blazers, huh? It just doesn't work."

She smiled sadly. "You didn't ruin anything, Lee. You needed to tell me and I'm glad you did. If you need to keep on talking about it, please do."

"I think I'm ok for now. It did feel good to tell you, though. Thanks so much for listening. And I guess maybe we should just end our evening now so you can have time to think about all this."

"We don't have to. I'd be happy to stay with you if that's what you want."

"No, this has been a great night and I don't want it go downhill because neither of us can stop thinking about Paul. I'd like to see you again soon, though, if that's ok."

"Of course." She leaned in and kissed him, slowly, lingeringly, then pulled back.

"This has been way better than you drilling into my teeth," Lee said.

She laughed, reached out and gave his hand a squeeze. "You sure you're ok?"

"I'm not ok. But I'll have another date to look forward to, and that'll help."

"Alright then, Lee. Have a good night and stay strong. I'll talk to you soon."

Then she got up and walked away. He followed her with his eyes for a moment, then his gaze drifted up. Here and there, lone swifts still darted, almost invisible against the darkening sky.

TWENTY-TWO

Lee felt excited jitters in his stomach when he saw Valerie's name on his buzzing phone the next night. "Hi," she said. "It might be a little weird to call you so soon but there's a conversation I think we need to have and I have an insanely busy week coming up, so this might be the only chance we get."

"What?" Lee felt his chest constrict with the fear that she'd decided this was a terrible idea after all.

"Lee, I had a great time last night. But I need to ask you something. Do you think you're ok to be dating now? It's such a horrible thing that's happening to you, and maybe you need your time and energy to deal with that, to look for your brother and to be with your family."

"Doing that all the time is driving me crazy, Valerie, thinking about nothing but Paul. I need something different, something happy in my life and I feel like I had that last night with you. I need something to look forward to."

"Are you sure, Lee? I don't want to just be a distraction, either."

"You're not. You're wonderful, Valerie, I felt that from the first time I saw you. I need to give this a try. Of course it's going to be hard, but we can take it one date at a time, just like the start of any relationship, right? And I thought last night was a really good start."

"It was a great start. If you think you're up for it, I'll take your word, I guess. Because I really do like you, Lee, and I'd like to help if I can. So, sure, we'll take it one date at a time. But I probably won't be able to go out with you again until Friday."

She was worth waiting three weeks for. Lee said, "Friday's great."

"Anyway, Lee, how are you?"

"I'm ok. There's nothing new, no news. We're going back out to the coast to search this evening, not that we're going to find anything."

"That's got to be hard."

"It is. Anyway, how are you doing?"

"I'm a little overwhelmed. I've got a ton of stuff to do at school this week and some tests I have to study for."

"What kind of tests do dental students take? Do you have an hour to see how much agony you can cause some poor schmuck with a drill?"

"Very funny. There is so, so much stuff to study, so much you have to know in order to become a dentist. I should have kept you as a patient; I could have studied for every dental problem in the book just by looking into that mouth of yours."

"Very funny."

"I'm kidding, of course. But is this really what you want to talk about?"

"It is. I spend every minute, pretty much, thinking about my brother. It felt really good talking about him with you last night, and I'm sure I will again. But right now, let's try to forget about that. I don't know that much about you, and you don't really know me. So, yeah, tell me about dental school, about your life. Please. I really do want to know."

So she did, talking about arrogant professors and clownish fellow students he should hope didn't get assigned to him and then somehow about her home town and childhood then his, the conversation flowing easily, occasionally punctuated by laughter. Lee switched his cellphone from his right ear to his left when it started aching. He wandered around his room but wasn't aware of it, aware only of Valerie, envisioning her in his mind as their words tumbled together.

Eventually she told him she had to study for a while before going out with her friends. "You have to study on a Saturday night?" he asked.

"I should have been studying last night, too, but instead some boy distracted me."

Lee was smiling as they said goodbye and hung up. He felt warmth in his chest, replacing the cold dread that he was used to there by now.

A minute after finishing his conversation with Valerie, Lee heard a knock at his door. He opened it to find Elly grinning at him. "Was that your new girl-friend?"

"What, were you eavesdropping?"

"Noooo. I was going to drop by and heard you on the phone so I stopped by again a little later and you were still on the phone, and, since you never have calls that last for more than two minutes, I figured..."

"Well, yes, you creep, that was Valerie."

"How'd the date go last night? Though I did notice that you were here in the morning and that she wasn't."

"It went great. We're going out again on Friday."

"Taking it slow, huh?"

"Yeah. Her idea; she's busy."

"Well, congratulations, man!" She hit him on the arm, hard. "It's awesome that you met someone. And a soon-to-be dentist at that. You'll have it made."

"We've gone on one date."

"Plus she's looked inside your mouth at your rotten teeth and drilled at them for hours. That's got to count for something!"

"I guess so," he said, laughing.

"Anyway, it'll be great. We can go on double dates if I decide to keep going out with Steph. Or triple dates, with Patrick and Cindy, if triple dates exist. And if engaged fuddy-duddies like them still date."

Lee laughed again and was about to respond when he heard a honk outside. His parents. "Shit, I'm not ready. Go down and stall them, ok?"

"Sure thing. I like your parents, though I feel so bad for them. For you, too, of course, but especially for your dad. He seems so lost..."

Lee threw a change of clothes into his backpack, stuffed in warm waterproof layers for the lashing rains he expected on the coast and laced up his hiking boots. After bounding down the stairs he found his mother standing in the doorway talking to Elly. She gave him a hug and said that his father's ankle was bothering him on long car drives so he'd stayed back at the hotel. "Are you coming with us, Elly?" she asked.

"I wish I could, but I have to go to work in the morning."

"Well, thank you again so much for coming last weekend. All your support meant a lot to us."

"I wish I could do more."

"We all do," Lee's mom said.

They searched all Sunday in an unceasing cold, drizzling rain. They found nothing.

Most of the long, now too familiar route back to Portland Lee and his mom drove in silence, but when she was exiting the freeway she said, "You know, Lee, we're going to have to give this up sometime soon."

Lee didn't respond, staring out the breath-fogged window at the rainy streets, running his tongue again and again over the fake crown on his tooth, feeling its rough edge. He was doing that frequently now, mostly when he was out at the coast and, though he worried that he would knock it free, he couldn't make himself stop.

"We need to reopen the store, we're not making enough money and the shelves are starting to empty out since we haven't stayed on top of reordering. We can't afford to keep paying for a hotel. And we can't keep trudging through the woods getting our hopes up with every flash of color we see and then having them dashed again and again, slogging through mud and rain endlessly, seeing over and over again the places our son, your brother, could have been lost."

Not looking at her, not saying anything, Lee reached out a hand and put it on her shoulder. And, hoping she could see him, he nodded, not daring to speak, trying to keep the tears from spilling from his eyes. He knew she was right.

"Thank you, Lee. But convincing your father of this, that's," she sniffed back tears and snot, "that's going to be the hard part. I tried explaining it to him, that we're going to have to pin our hopes on unlikely scenarios: that Paul ran away, that he was kidnapped and might escape or the police could find him, that he somehow lost his memory and couldn't find his way home. We'll always have those hopes, and I don't know if that's better or worse than knowing for sure, but we'll always have them with us. But despite them we're going to have to accept that there's nothing we can do about it and that, to us, realistically, he's gone. If he was alive out on the coast, we would have found him. He's, we've got to accept that he's probably... Probably gone."

"Mom," was all Lee could say, putting his hand back on her shoulder, feeling it tensed, hard and solid. They pulled up in front of his house. Lights glowed from its windows into the darkness. She was right, though he hadn't put it to himself in that way. Or thought of his brother losing his memory. That could be, that might... "The hope is probably worse," he said, thinking of the dead ends of the eco-terrorism theory.

"Probably." She leaned over and gathered him into her arms. They held each other, tears running silently down their cheeks, for endless moments. Then Lee's mom sniffled and pulled back. "Well, I should get back to your father, try again to tell him this. Though he won't want to hear it."

"Thank you, Mom. Thank you for telling me."

"You already knew."

"You're right."

"Take care of yourself, Lee."

"You too."

He got out then and waved, still crying, as his mom's car pulled away and became ghostly red taillights trailing into the night and then gone. Then he sniffed and wiped away his tears. Like his mom, he would be strong.

TWENTY-THREE

Lee pulled his bike down off the hook and exited the MAX in Gresham, the suburb to the east of Portland. Looking for a street sign, he tried to get his bearings among the stripmalls and single story houses. He'd gotten a text at work from Elly telling him to meet her at an address out here that ended, "It'll be worth your while. And totally unethical, maybe." How could he say no to that?

Lee found the first street she'd mentioned in her directions and was pretty sure he knew which way south was so he hopped on his bike and started riding into the dusk. It took fifteen minutes that should have been five if he hadn't taken a couple wrong turns to find the place.

It was a small square house painted a peeling sky blue. The grass was neatly mowed behind its chain-link fence and rose bushes lined the short path to the door, bright green with yellow and orange flowers showing their first hints of brown and death. Elly's car was parked out front. Wondering what this was all about, he knocked.

Lee laughed when Elly answered the door, and said, "You look so... professional."

"Shut up." She was in slacks and a tucked-in blue shirt, her piercings were gone from everywhere except her ears. He'd only seen glimpses of her dressed like this when he caught her sneaking out to or back from work. "Anyway, come on in."

He followed her into a dim house, the curtains all drawn. She led him down a short hallway to a living room filled with plump couches and armchairs. On all the walls were paintings, framed and unframed, of people, horses, landscapes and sunsets, all in bright washes of color done in a loose, flowing style that reminded him somewhat of Georgia O'Keefe. He wanted to go look closer, but Elly said in a loud voice, "Lee, this is Mrs. Tanner," and gestured to an armchair that was turned mostly away from him towards a window. He'd dismissed it as being heaped with blankets. The blankets moved now and a small pale wrinkled face surrounded by a halo of white hair smiled at him from behind thick glasses. She extended a hand that looked like skin stretched tight on a latticework of bird bones. He took it gently and shook, once up, once down.

"Nice to meet you, Mrs. Tanner," he said.

"A little louder," she said, loudly.

"Nice to meet you."

"It's good to meet you, too."

"Mrs. Tanner, Lee is an artist, like you."

"Oh, isn't that nice? I painted all of these, did you know that?"

"No, I didn't. They seem really good. Do you mind if I take a closer look?"

"Not at all. It's good to have people see them. I can't really myself these days, even with these ridiculous glasses; my sight is mostly gone. But I can still see the colors. I do love the colors."

Lee went to the walls and started working his way around. Elly came to join him.

"These are mostly just the ones my husband loved best. He passed away twelve years ago, bless him. There are lots of others around, too. Has Elly told you about my husband?"

"Not yet," Elly said. "You should, Mrs. Tanner."

The paintings were very good, Lee thought, better than his, definitely, better than almost anything you saw around Portland, on the street or in galleries. The colors were clear and pure, joyous, and gave a warmth to each subject. The lines were sure and the slight abstractions of the forms revealed a deep emotional level to them somehow. His favorite was a face set in a blurry green and yellow background, a middle aged man depicted in tones of the earth soaked in sunlight. A smile was just breaking out on his lips, warmth and kindness in his eyes echoed the color of the greenery around him. "That's my husband," Mrs. Tanner said, but Lee had already known that.

"It's wonderful."

"Thank you."

Lee moved on to the next painting and Elly followed. "These are great," he whispered to her now that their backs were turned to Mrs. Tanner. "But what am I doing here? I know you're not allowed to have guests over while you're working."

"She has a whole room full of art supplies that she doesn't use anymore," Elly whispered back. "And I know you're running out of everything, don't have the money to buy more with your stupid dental crap."

"So, what, we're going to steal from this sweet old lady? Elly, I..."

"No, idiot! We're going to convince her to give them to you. Some of them. She can't use them anymore, she's practically blind, like she said. And you need them."

"Still, that's got to be against the rules."

"Well, yeah, I probably could get fired for it, if that's what you mean."

"You're a really great friend, have I ever told you that?"

"Not nearly enough."

At this point they'd come around to the last painting, a dog leaping into sunshine-filled air. Lee usually hated any kind of painting of pets but this one really made him feel the love the artist had for the animal. "These are great. You're really talented, Mrs. Tanner," he said, loudly.

"Thank you. Now take a seat, please. I don't get many visitors."

"When did you paint all of these?" Lee asked, settling onto a couch.

"Oh, when I was younger. These ones are mostly from twenty, thirty years ago, after my son moved out for college. That's when I really took up painting again and when I was best. I could keep it up until two years ago, though. Then I finally realized I couldn't see enough to make anything but a muddled mess."

That's what everything he did was, Lee thought: a muddled, abstract, meaningless mess. "I'm sorry."

"Psh, don't be sorry for me, I've had a beautiful life. I haven't told you about my husband yet, have I? Oh, he was such a good man. He was in the army in World War II, in France and Germany, if you can imagine. We met when he came back at a dance for returning soldiers. It was a little scandalous, my dating then marrying a man who was Hispanic, but I didn't care, I was in love. His family changed their name when they moved up here from Guatemala, if you're wondering. I didn't change my name back, I would never do that."

"Oh. He was quite handsome," Lee said, looking back up at the picture. Mr. Tanner was a little pudgy and balding, but he was still very good looking. It was the eyes, mostly.

"You should have seen him when I met him," Mrs. Tanner said. "Elly, dear, bring out the pictures."

Elly brought out a thick photo album. It was almost all pictures of her husband, Hernando, who really was handsome in his uniform. Flipping through they watched him grow older, fill out, lose his hair, but in all the pictures his eyes were smiling like in the painting on the wall.

"Mrs. Tanner has lots of pictures," Elly said when they were done. "And lots of paintings."

"What kind of painting do you do, Lee?" Mrs. Tanner asked.

"They're usually kind of abstract atmospheric swirls with objects floating in them. That's what I've been doing recently, anyway. I've tried all sorts of things, lots of styles. I really like your paintings, though, how clear the colors are, so maybe I'll try something like that."

"Now don't copy me, young man," she said, laughing.

"Not copy. Just be inspired by."

"Well that's ok. That's more than ok."

"What kinds of paints did you use, Mrs. Tanner?" Elly asked, though Lee could clearly see that they were mostly watercolors with a few oils here and there.

"All kinds. Mostly Aquarelle for my watercolors. They have such beautiful tones. But I've tried everything: oils, charcoal, pencil, pastels. I don't like that acrylic stuff. It's too plasticy. Watercolors are by far my favorite."

"I've never really tried watercolors," Lee said.

"Oh, you have to. They give such pure, clear, glowing color."

"Lee doesn't have much money for art supplies right now, Mrs. Tanner," Elly said. "He had a root canal and has to spend all his money at the dentist."

"Ooooh, I hated the dentist," Mrs. Tanner said. "All my teeth are gone now, though, so that's something to look forward to with age," she said with a gleeful chuckle. "No more dentists, just dentures." Lee laughed with her.

Elly said, "Lee's paintings are really good. He sells them sometimes."

"Mm. Well, he was nice to come out and visit with me today, to look at my pictures. I can see what you're up to, Elly. I'm blind, you know, not senile. I suppose I could give him some of my paints since I'm not using them any more. Remind me to find some for him to take home at the end of our visit."

"That's very kind of you, Mrs. Tanner," Lee said.

"I don't use them," she said again with a wave of her hand. "Now, tell me about yourself, Lee. Is Elly here your girlfriend?"

"She's not my girlfriend, but she is one of my best friends," Lee said.

"Well she is a very sweet girl. You'd be lucky if she were your girlfriend."

"That's true."

They chatted for an hour more, or mostly Mrs. Tanner chatted while Lee and Elly listened. About art and how the Portland area had changed and, mostly, about Hernando. Eventually Elly said that it was time for Mrs. Tanner's pills and for Lee to get going. So, Mrs. Tanner leading the way pushing a walker, they went to a back room filled with canvases leaned against each other on the ground, more hanging on the walls. The aggregated color was overwhelming.

Mrs. Tanner walked over to a cabinet that was partially obscured by paintings which she had Elly move out of the way and started opening and closing drawers, pulling out materials. "I've got a good bunch of beautiful watercolors here for you to start out on and a pad of great paper," she said. "And when you run out, you can come back and visit me again and show me what you've done. I can see the colors at least. We'll talk for a while and then you can get more. How does that sound, young man?"

"It sounds great, Mrs. Tanner. Thank you." He wasn't sure who was taking advantage of who, now. Which was perfect.

"What will you paint first?"

"My brother," he said, though he hadn't know it before he said it. Lee would paint Paul just like Mrs.

Tanner had painted Hernando. "My brother is missing, he has been for weeks."

"Oh my, that's terrible, Lee. What happened?"

"He was camping at the coast. They found his car but nothing else. And no one has any idea where he is or what happened to him."

"That's so tragic. I'm very sorry."

"Thank you."

"And I think painting your brother is a good idea, Lee. Painting Hernando helped me get over his loss, helped keep his memory alive."

"That's good to hear, Mrs. Tanner. That's what I'll try."

Lee tore up his first two attempts with watercolors that night. But the third, based on the picture they'd used for the Have You Seen This Man poster, seemed like it might have promise.

TWENTY-FOUR

Standing in his brother's garden Lee breathed deeply
to steady himself, to make sure he was ok. Then he
took hold of a fat, round orange tomato, felt its
weight in his palm and pulled it from the vine with a
sharp twist. He placed it gently into a plastic Fred
Meyer shopping bag. Going down the row he picked
the fruits that had ripened but not fallen. The tomatoes, whose leaves were withered and yellow, seemed
to have produced even more than usual, and soggy
red masses were piled on the ground. The plants'
deaths wouldn't be in vain; all those seeds on the
earth would ensure that another generation of tomatoes would grow here.

Next Lee went to the greens. Most of the lettuce
had bolted, with bright clusters of flowers perched on
high stocks, but a few were still good and he harvested those, then took some more leaves from the kale,
which had been growing strong all spring and summer and might last months more. He cut the few un-
withered and unbolted stalks of basil but left the ore-
gano, thyme and sage to live another year.

The summer squash were huge dying jungles, all their leaves browning and covered with a white mold, but there were yellow squash in there and zucchinis, some overgrown to the size of footballs and arms but a few newer ones still small and tender. Lee took them all, loading up his backpack. The biggest stuck out the top when he tried to close it.

Finally Lee dug, sticking a trowel he'd borrowed from Elly into the damp earth at the base of sickly-looking root vegetables. He unearthed dirty gems of topaz and rust colored potatoes, the fat bulbs of onions and branching, finger-like carrots, a shocking orange once the dirt was brushed away. Some had started to go bad but he took those, too. The damaged parts could be cut off.

After hanging a bag by its straps over each handle bar and cinching his backpack around his waist, Lee turned back for another look at the garden. This food was going to rot if he didn't take it. Paul would want Lee to harvest what was still good. Many plants had withered but others were alive, brought back and nourished by the recent rains. Weeds were everywhere: dandelions, grasses, clovers and other small, green, thriving things. He could come back in a week and there would be more food here, there would be food until the frosts came. And Lee would come back. He would water if it didn't rain, he would take care of this place. For Paul. Or for Paul's memory.

Lee and his parents were trudging through another carefully partitioned chunk of forest together, miles from where the car had been found, a light rain misting down. Lee's mom had picked him up the night before after a whispered phone call explaining how impossible his father was being and asking if Lee could please come out to support her, to talk to him.

After a deep breath, Lee said "Dad, Mom and I think that maybe, maybe it's time for you two to go back to the store, maybe just come out here once or twice a week..."

"You want me to give up, too?" his dad interrupted, stopping and standing tall. It was like he'd been waiting for Lee to say that, and probably he had. "I can't believe you want to give up looking for your brother too, Lee!"

"It's not giving up, it's just realizing that searching here is hopeless," Lee's mom said with a tone that suggested she'd made the same point over and over again. "We've covered every area he could walk to within three or four days and it's been too long for him to have survived here realistically. That doesn't mean he couldn't be somewhere else or that he still couldn't be safe or make it home someday. It's just going through these horrible woods over and over again, slogging through this mud and rain, getting crazier and crazier that's not doing anyone any good. And besides, we need to get back to the store."

"The store? This is about money? Who cares about money when our son could be out here needing our help?"

"It's not about money, Dad, did you even listen to her?" Lee said, his voice rising. "I know you just want to help get him back, that's all either of us want too. But I don't think, and Mom doesn't either, that we can help here anymore. Of course we're not giving up on Paul. We're just giving up on finding him out here. The Park Rangers said the same thing when they stopped looking."

"I can't believe you're both abandoning Paul!"

"We're not," Lee's mom said, and he could hear exasperation in her voice. He felt a little of that too, but mostly he felt queasiness in his stomach at the pain he was causing his father and at the accusations his father was making, because of course he felt that way too, of course he sometimes thought he was abandoning Paul by not being here every day, by fucking around back in Portland instead, by giving up. But his mother was right, they couldn't find Paul safe here and they had to get on with their lives.

Lee took two steps towards his father, who tensed slightly. Lee wrapped his arms around him, held him tightly. He was shocked at how small his dad felt, how frail, even though he knew they were the same height and basically the same build. Or had been. "I'll come out here to look on Sundays with you if you want, Dad. But you do need to get back to the store. It's not for the money. People count on that store, the whole town does."

Lee's father patted him on the back then pulled away. Without a word or a backwards glance he walked quickly into the woods.

"Should we follow him?" Lee asked.

"Maybe we should give him a few minutes to be alone, to calm down."

"I think we should follow. He seemed really up-set..."

"No, you're right, Lee. I couldn't handle it if he fell again. God, I just wish he could finally pull himself together."

"I'm sure he can. But this is so hard... It'll take time."

Lee's father had vanished behind a tangle of trees but he couldn't have gotten far. They started walking briskly in the direction he'd taken.

Before they caught up to him they heard a shout. A moment later they saw Lee's dad running back towards them, crashing through the ferns and bushes, something brown clenched in his hand. "Look!" he yelled. "Look!" he repeated as he pulled up before them. They saw that he held a dirty, well-used gray boot. "I found his boot!" he said. "He was here, he is! We just need to keep looking!"

"Where did you find that?" Lee's mom asked, her eyes wide.

"It's like I was being guided right to it. And I checked, it's his size!"

Lee reached out to take the boot from his father.

Lee's mom, excitement in her voice now, asked, "Where? Were there any other signs of Paul?"

"It was down in a narrow little gully, partially covered by leaves. I don't know how I saw it. Like I said, I felt like I was being guided. And I didn't see anything else but I didn't look, I rushed back here to show you so we can start the search again!"

"Jesus, his boot? I can't believe it, this changes everything!" Lee's mother said, a note of hysteria in her tone.

"No," Lee said, quietly, finally, the deadness of his voice matching that in his head. "No. It's not Paul's."

"How do you know?" Lee's father asked accusingly. "It's his size, it was near where his car was, it looks like the boots he wore!"

"It's not. Paul would never wear a boot made in China," Lee said, holding out the tag. "He'd never wear a crappy cheap boot like this."

"Are you sure? How do you know that?" Lee's father asked.

"I know. I know what he liked, I went to Next Adventure and REI with him all the time but he'd always special-order his boots online or go to the Danner store. They were really expensive but he'd always talk about how great they were, how they were worth every penny." He handed the boot back to his father.

Lee's mother's excitement turned instantly to anger. "How could you run away from us and then get our hopes up over someone else's goddamned boot! How could you?" she demanded.

"I'm sorry. I was so sure it was his, lying down there hidden…"

"It's good that it's not his," Lee said. "Good. Because if it were his, it would mean he was here, and if he was here he'd be dead. Remember?" He said this last part to his mom, hoping to cool her down to the lifeless cold he felt inside himself, to calm all of them down.

"Jesus, Lee," she said. "I can't handle this. Come on, we're going back to the car, I'm driving you back! We're not going to accomplish anything here."

"I'll drive him," Lee's father said. "You always do. I'm sorry. I'll drive."

"Fine," she said. "Fine. Lee, maybe you can talk some sense into him. No, wait, that's stupid. We're getting out of here, we're checking out of the hotel today. He's not here, that's not his boot and we're leaving together. We need to get out of here."

"But..." Lee's father trailed off. Then he looked down at the boot in his hand. He let it drop to the muddy earth. "Ok," he said.

TWENTY-FIVE

The door dinged and Lee looked up from the pad he was doodling on behind the counter. Joseph walked in dressed in a new trench coat, much cleaner but otherwise identical to his old one. He smiled and said, "You look good, Lee. What's the occasion?"

"I have a date. You look good too."

"Thanks." Joseph checked to see that the store was empty then said, "Thanks for the money. It helped out. I got a new coat, I got a lot of things. Thank you."

"You're welcome, man. And thank you."

"Any news on your brother?"

"No." He thought of all that had happened since he'd last talked to Joseph: the boot, his parents giving up the search, the acceptance, sort of, that Paul might be gone. "No, no news."

"Well, I'm still looking. I'll let you know when I find something."

"I appreciate it, Joseph, I really do. But I don't know that it'll do any good. A lot of people have looked."

"It's not a problem. And thank you again. It's good that you have a date. I hope things go good for you. They need to. Things balance out."

"Sure." But, as wonderful as Valerie was, of course a good date couldn't balance out the loss of his brother.

Joseph picked out his bottle quicker than usual and left after shaking Lee's hand. And then Lee went back to what he'd been doing all day at work, all yesterday too: doodling his brother in various settings, possibilities for paintings, none of which seemed quite right. Though the one at home of his brother's face squinting into the distance still seemed like it could end up being really good if he just kept on working at it.

The streetcar crawled through downtown towards the address Valerie had given him on NW 23rd, nicknamed trendy-third, a ritzy area Lee didn't know that well. He clenched a bottle of wine, a bit more expensive than the Charles Shaw he usually bought, by the neck in one hand, balanced a bowl filled with a salad that had spent the day hidden in the back of the Coke fridge at work in the other.

Lee arrived at an old, fancy looking brick apartment building. He found Valerie's name on the brass panel, pressed the button and, seconds later, the frosted glass door clicked open with a buzz. He walked through a marble lobby decorated with fake flowers to the elevator, which had a beautiful old wrought iron cage. It was a little terrifying as it rattled its way up four stories but he survived to walk down a thickly carpeted hallway to her apartment.

She opened the door with a gorgeous smile, wearing a heavily stained flowered apron. He wanted to kiss her but held back, feeling a little awkward. "Sorry about this," she said, gesturing down, "I'm a total mess when I cook and dinner's not quite done. The apartment's a bit of a mess, too. I meant to clean up more but I've been really busy."

"There's absolutely nothing to apologize for," he said. "You look wonderful. So does your place." Behind her were windows looking out to the dark west hills, nice furniture that definitely hadn't come from the side of the road and framed art on the walls. There were a few papers on tables and counters here and there, a blanket thrown over the edge of a couch, but it looked pretty clean to him. If she thought this was a mess he never wanted her to see his house.

"Well, come on in." He walked past her, placing the bottle of wine in her hands, showing her the salad. "They both look great," she said. She reached out and touched his arm. There was still that thrill that he'd felt when she'd tapped his back at the dental school that first day. "Anyway, I hope you like tomatoes. I went a little crazy at the farmer's market so there's going be a lot of them with the dinner tonight. You're not allergic, are you? I should have asked."

"I'm not allergic to anything. And I love tomatoes. There're some in the salad too, which, by the way, needs dressing; I didn't want to get it soggy on the way here. Olive oil and vinegar would be perfect."

"No problem! Just make yourself comfortable and I'll finish things up in the kitchen. We'll be eating in ten minutes."

"Anything I can do to help?"

"I've got it taken care of."

"You sure?"

"I'm sure. It might be a little early for me to start revealing my dark secrets, but what the hell, right? I'm a bit of a control freak when it comes to cooking. Nothing else really, just cooking. So you'd be better off staying out of the kitchen, at least at first. Sorry."

"Yes ma'am. And thank you for cooking. I really meant it when I offered to take you out for dinner."

"I wanted to cook for you. And you can cook for me next time."

When they sat down at the table over a plate of bruschetta, Valerie asked, "So Lee, how are you doing?" She gazed steadily into his eyes.

"It's been tough. Two days ago, out on the coast, my father found a boot." He paused.

"A boot? Was it your brother's?"

"That's what my dad thought. He came running back so excited, clutching this boot he was so sure was Paul's. But it wasn't, it was some cheap Chinese thing that Paul would never wear."

"I'm sorry." There was such kindness and pain for him in her eyes.

"I'm not." Lee paused, breathed, then rushed on, his words no longer calm, unable to stop. "If it was my brother's boot it would mean he was there and if he was there he'd be gone. And he probably was, and is, and that's what we need to accept. But we also need to accept that since we haven't found him there're these other possibilities, endless possibilities of what could have happened to him so that there's no closure and no end. So maybe I wish it was his boot so we would be able to know. But he's probably gone and my dad can't accept it, which is driving my mom crazy. But they're not going to stay out on the coast anymore. And do you know what's really been torturing me? That boot. It's not my brother's boot so who the hell's is it, the same fucking shoe size as Paul, and what's it doing out there? How can you lose one boot, leave it behind?" He came to an end and sniffed in through his nose, trying to hold himself together.

Valerie was looking at him, her eyes wrinkled around the edges with worry. He tried to meet her compassionate gaze, then, because tears were forming in his, looked down again. Not saying anything she got up, walked behind his chair, wrapped her arms around him and pulled him close. Lee relaxed into her embrace, soaking in her warmth and comfort, feeling some of the tension leave his shoulders. After a few minutes he said, "Thank you, Valerie. I think I'm ok. Now, let's eat this great food you've made us."

The bruschetta had thick slabs of flavorful tomato that dripped their juices when he bit into them, luckily onto his plate not his shirt. The salad was next: lettuce, carrots, onions and tomatoes. "All the ingredients are from Paul's garden," Lee explained. "I went back there a few days ago and harvested what hadn't gone bad and died. There was a lot, actually. He really loved his garden, took such good care of it. I wanted to share it with you."

"Thank you, Lee. That's really touching." She put a bite to her mouth, a reddish-purple leaf of lettuce and a little yellow tomato. "It's fabulous. Home grown vegetables are always the best."

The main course was a delicious roasted tomato, cheese, yellow squash and polenta casserole of which they both had seconds. When they'd pushed their plates away, Lee took a sip of wine and said, "So, Valerie, you've been so good at listening to my troubles. Is there anything you want to talk to me about?"

"All my problems kind of pale in comparison to yours, Lee. My Grandma has the flu back East, but she's tough, she'll be ok."

"Are you close to your grandparents?"

"She's actually the only one left, but I'm really close to her. She'd take care of me in the afternoons when my parents were away at work, she and my Grandpa. We still talk on the phone a couple times a month."

"I'm sorry she's not feeling well."

"I'm pretty sure she'll be fine, though it'll be good to see her again for Thanksgiving. And how about you, Lee? Are you close to your grandparents?"

"My dad's parents both passed away when I was in high school. They lived in our town so I got to see them all the time and had a really good relationship with them, especially my Grandpa. My mom's parents live in Georgia and we're not that close. I think they can't really stand the fact that my dad stole my mom away to Oregon back when they were hippies in the seventies. They made a big deal of welcoming us the few times we visited but it's never felt at all genuine or real."

"That's a shame. They haven't forgiven your dad for something that happened decades ago?"

Their talk continued through families to funny childhood stories as they cleaned up together in the kitchen, Lee feeding her dishwasher while she wiped down the counters and stove.

When the kitchen was cleaner than Lee's kitchen ever was they moved to the couch. During a slight lull in the conversation Valerie scooted in closer to him and he leaned in and kissed her. As they made out Lee wondered if it were weird for her tongue to be playing over teeth she'd been drilling into a few weeks before. He pushed the thought from his mind and just enjoyed the moment, pulling her closer, running his hands up and down her back.

After long minutes of this Lee leaned back a little and said, "We don't have to do anything tonight, you know. I'm happy just kissing you, just being with you." And he was, he realized with some surprise. Of course he wanted her, badly, but he really didn't want to push things too fast, to risk ruining this one good thing he had in his life.

"That's sweet," she said, leaning in for a quick kiss. "But we'll just see where things go."

Things went, not long after, to her bedroom. There was a blue blanket sloppily thrown over white sheets on the wide bed. A real bed with a wood headboard, unlike the mattress on a boxspring on the floor in his room. Some clothes were scattered on a dresser and in a corner. "Sorry it's a mess," she said.

"I really, really don't care," he replied, laughing. And then they were falling on top of the bed, lips and bodies pressed together. He reached around and found the zipper for the dress she'd had on under the apron and carefully pulled it down. She helped and together they lifted it up over her head. She was wearing a tan bra and black panties and she was the most gorgeous woman he'd ever seen, her legs strong and smooth, her stomach flat, little breasts perfect, lustrous hair exploding brown behind her smiling face. He kissed her lips, her neck, down the middle of her chest to her stomach, his hands cupping her breasts. Rearing up to lift off his own shirt he felt her hands on his belt buckle, fumbling then pulling it loose, yanking the belt free then playing again with the button on his jeans.

Their hands and mouths ran lightly over each other's bodies. He worked his hands behind her back, got her bra on the first try. In awkward jerks they removed the rest of their clothing.

"Wait," she said.

"Do you have a condom?" he asked. He thought there might be one in his wallet in his jeans wherever they'd ended up, but he didn't want her to think he was someone who carried a condom all the time. Besides, if it were there it probably would have gone bad from lack of use.

"In the bathroom, I hope," she said, getting up. "I'll be right back."

He watched Valerie's pale lovely form walk away, marveling at his luck, his fate, at how perfect this was, how beautiful she was.

Valerie came back with a strip of three condoms in shiny red wrapping. When one was on she scooted forward, straddling him. "Are you ready?" she asked.

"God yes," he said. She lowered herself down onto him. At first he was worried, wanting it to go well, scared he wouldn't be good enough or last long enough since it had been months, but soon he was lost in the movement of their bodies, of kissing her and the excruciating pleasure he felt as she moved over him and then later under him. Her moans were musical. They intensified, he felt her contract around him and he let go, a quick burst of light followed by a wave of peace. Maybe a bit sooner than he would have liked, but it didn't matter. He drowsily kissed her head, her cheek, her lips. She smiled and wrapped her arms around his sweaty back, holding him close for a second then pushing him gently away.

Afterwards, lying on top of the covers, tracing a finger idly around the curves of her body, he turned his head to find her turning hers and their eyes locked, smiles on their faces. Lee thought that maybe he was in love, but that was stupid, he barely knew her. And then he felt guilty for being so happy when his brother was missing, when his parents were so miserable. She snuggled against him and fit perfectly in his arms against his body. Soon, he was lost in deep sleep.

Lee awoke sometime later to find himself squinting into imperfect darkness in a strange bed, much too warm. He pushed the blankets back and heard a groan where he now saw Valerie on the other side of the bed. Her back was turned to him, her hair, what he could see peeking out from under the tightly tucked blankets that he'd just disturbed, was tangled chaos. He patted the blankets back down around her, sealing her in. He couldn't believe he was in her bed, how lucky he was, how wonderful she was.

Then, with a jolt of fear, he looked around until he located the glowing green numbers on a clock beside the bed. 3:27. He found his jeans and set an alarm on his phone. God he wished he didn't have to go to work in the morning, wished he could sleep in with

Valerie, wake to make love, drift off again. Wait in line to get brunch with all the hungover hipsters then spend a day doing whatever she wanted. Not that he knew yet all the kinds of things she spent her weekends doing. He was looking forward to finding out.

An insistent trilling and buzzing, which was somehow an earthquake in his dream, brought Lee to groggy consciousness. "Who's calling?" he heard Valerie mumble. He realized then it was his alarm and fumbled around on the floor by the bed until he'd found and silenced it.

"No one, it was just my alarm," he said. There was no response and Valerie's face, turned towards him now, was slack and peaceful. He leaned over and lightly kissed her parted lips but she didn't wake up, didn't even stir.

Lee splashed water onto his face, dressed then went to her bed again. He kissed her. No response. Called out her name. Nothing. So, feeling terrible, he reached down, placed a hand on her shoulder and shook.

"Mrmrm, what?" she asked, her eyes still closed.

"Valerie, it's me, Lee. I have to go to work."

She opened her eyes then squinted at him. "Really? It's Saturday." Her scrunched up face was incredibly cute.

"Really. I told you last night."

"And you're all dressed. Why didn't you wake me up, Lee?"

"You're not an easy girl to wake."

"That's true," she said through a yawn. "Do you have to leave right away?"

He glanced at his phone. "Yeah. I'm running a little late already, sorry. I had a great time last night, Valerie, and wish it didn't have to end so soon."

"Me too. You can't call in sick?"

"I shouldn't. I had to miss a lot of days already looking for my brother and your dental school isn't cheap." He watched her carefully to see how she reacted. She'd known he was poor, he thought, but maybe not. He wondered how big a problem that was going to be, the fact that her family had money and his didn't, that she was in graduate school and he'd never been to college.

"I guess that's true," she said seriously. "This isn't just an excuse to leave after we've had sex, though, right?"

"Of course not. Last night was wonderful, all of it, every minute I've spent with you has been. I'm going to call as soon as I get to work, wake you up again. I want to be with you again, Valerie, as soon as you have time."

"I can't at least make you a quick breakfast?"

How could he say no to that? Breakfast was delicious, as were their parting kisses. Lee left for work thirty minutes after he was supposed to have arrived.

TWENTY-SIX

Lee pulled out his phone and called work as he jogged towards downtown, knowing he could run faster than the streetcar. No one answered. His boss occasionally came in on Saturday mornings but didn't seem to be there now.

Breathing heavily, his armpits and back slick with sweat, Lee unlocked the door, slipped inside and locked it behind him. The clock showed that it was seven minutes before the store opened. No one was there. He could do all the pre-shift work during the day if it was slow and no one would know he'd been almost an hour late. A great hour, but it couldn't happen again.

After work Lee went to cash the paycheck that had been waiting for him. It was much smaller than usual, reflecting all the days he'd taken off work to look for his brother. He signed the back, stuffed it in the envelope and fed it into the greedily sucking ATM. When he checked his balance, he cursed.

"Ok, now we scale this fence," Elly said.

Dave Garlock

"Scale the fence? Seriously?" They were in a parking lot in industrial inner SE, their bikes pulled into the shadows and locked together. A tall chain link fence stood between them and the darkened recesses where, Elly claimed, there was a dumpster full of hummus.

"Seriously. Not just anyone's going to wander in there so you almost always find something good."

"We got a lot of pizza at the last place and that was out in the open. Even vegan pizza for you."

"We were lucky, that dumpster's usually completely picked over."

"And that Trader Joe's dumpster I told you about was easy, no climbing, and it was amazing. It's not too much further south."

"The one where your tooth started killing you? I'm not going south of Powell tonight, thank you. And this break in the rain's probably not going to last forever, so get your skinny butt up that fence. I'll keep watch."

Lee had never been much of a climber. He put his hands on the cold slick metal bar on top and yanked, scrambling with his feet on the bowing fence until he perched at the top, awkwardly straddling it. He paused, wondering how to get down.

"We don't have all night," Elly whispered.

He braced his hands, swung his other leg over, then tried to lower himself but one hand slipped on the rain-slicked bar. He felt himself tumbling, landing on his feet with his body crumpling down, bracing himself with his palms on the rough wet concrete. Cautiously, he rose.

"Are you ok?"

182

Lee felt himself over. "Yeah, I guess so." His ankles seemed untwisted, his knees unsprained. Which was lucky since he had miles to ride to get back home.

Elly scrambled over the fence gracefully and fluidly despite her stocky five-three form and the pack bulging with pizza slices on her back. "Follow me, you klutz," she whispered, touching him lightly on the arm.

They rounded a corner and found themselves in a small courtyard between this building and the next, a grove of bamboo shimmering in the breeze, a tile floor under their feet. Overhead, a flickering orange-ish light eerily illuminated the scene. A bench ran against one wall under an awning. It seemed like it would be a nice place to take a lunch break in the summer. He wondered if the hummus place were hiring and if it paid more than the liquor store.

Elly made a beeline for a dumpster Lee hadn't noticed in the back corner. She lifted up the lid and whispered, "Hey, we're in luck."

Lee walked over and peered in. Elly's flashlight played over a pile of plastic cartons in one corner of the almost full dumpster. She reached in and pulled a few out. "What do you prefer? Original, garlic, green onion? Ooh, and we've got some dip in here, too." She pulled out a different shaped package. "And the sell-by date is yesterday, so this hasn't been sitting here long at all."

They loaded Lee's backpack with several different flavors of hummus and dip, taking extra roasted garlic since Elly said it was the best. They could have fit more but only took what they and their housemates and friends would eat before it went bad.

After Elly scrambled back over the fence Lee stood before it uncertainly. He took off his backpack and tossed it over to Elly, who caught it easily. He put his hands on the metal, pulled them back. After a deep breath he threw himself forward and up, not pausing at the top but heaving both his legs over, pushing himself off for a controlled landing this time, thumping to his feet on the pavement.

Elly mimed applause. "Much better," she said. "Now let's get out of here."

They rode their bikes side by side down dark empty Portland streets, puddles splashing up to spatter onto their legs, streetlights shining through the branches of trees casting strange huge shadows.

Lee said, "Thanks for taking me out tonight. I'll have pizza and hummus for days, a lovely balanced diet. Things are a little tight with all the dental crap and taking Valerie out isn't going to be cheap, either."

"Glad to help."

"If there's anything I can do for you, just let me know. Well, anything that doesn't require money."

"You could ask your new girlfriend if she has any single hot rich lesbian friends."

"What happened to Steph?"

"Nothing yet, but I don't think it's ever going to get serious. I think she knows it, too."

"That sucks. Anyway, what makes you think Valerie's friends are rich?"

"She's in graduate school to become a professional, you said her place is really nice and she comes from a wealthy suburb. Those kind of people only know people who have money, too."

Lee thought of the crowd she'd been with when he met her. "Maybe. I can ask when I see her next."

"Thanks, buddy. A rich girl's just what I need, so I don't have to keep doing this gross digging around in dumpsters stuff."

"Oh come on, you know you love it."

"It's true. You know me too well, my friend. So you'll have to find me a rich hot lesbian who loves dumpster diving."

"I'll do my best."

"It smells great in here," Patrick said of the pizza in the oven as he walked in, offering up a six-pack of Full Sail Amber. "You're going to turn me into a dumpster diving punk yet." Lee'd actually been a little surprised that his friend, who he hadn't seen in a while, had accepted his invitation to eat a dumpstered dinner after what had happened last time.

Lee shook Patrick's hand, pulled him in for a loose hug then led him into the living room where hummus had been scooped into bowls, surrounded by some pita and chopped up vegetables, some of which were from Paul's garden. Elly came in from the kitchen, smiling, and shook Patrick's hand. "The pizza should be heated up in a few minutes, good timing. And now we can start in on the appetizers. Thanks for bringing the beer."

"Don't mention it."

They settled onto the couches, cracked open their bottles. Lee raised his and said, "To helping the environment by eating all this food that would have just gone to waste and to helping my wallet, too, one dumpstered meal at a time."

"Sure," Elly replied, smiling. "To saving the planet by breaking into heavily guarded dumpsters instead of heavily guarded logging camps. Or, shit, Lee, I'm sorry, I shouldn't be joking about that."

"It's ok. It's fine," Lee said. From Elly it was, though it still hurt.

"Why are you sorry?" Patrick asked. Lee hadn't told him about that theory, hadn't told anyone besides Elly and Valerie.

"You know the bolt cutters in the car?" Elly said. "Well, Jenny, Paul's ex, said he was hanging out with some crazy environmentalists and Lee thought those might be connected, might be the reason the car was hidden."

"Yeah," Lee said, "But I talked to some tree-sitter guy who said no would tell me anything even if they did know something and I looked in all the papers and nothing like that happened. It's a dead end. Even if there were something to it there's no way to know, just like with every other damned thing about Paul's disappearance."

"Shit, man," Patrick said. "But if he was involved with something like that someone must know something, right, one of his friends must have been in on it, brought him in, right? Maybe they'd talk now, since it's been like a month, so Paul would have had plenty of time to get away."

"Has it really been a month?" Lee asked. He did a quick mental calculation and figured that the month anniversary was coming up in a few days. He wondered how he could have almost let it slip by unnoticed, when earlier he'd been counting the days and hours obsessively. "A whole fucking month. I really can't believe it. I can't believe he's been gone so long. It seems like forever and it seems like I just saw him last week."

"So here's what you do," Patrick said. "You have some kind of anniversary for Paul, for his disappearance. And you mention something about this eco-terrorism stuff when everyone's gathered together and watch their faces to see if anyone shows any recognition, see if anyone knows something."

"I don't know about that detective shit," Elly said, "but an anniversary, a celebration, seems like a good idea. Go back to the coast one last time, have a fire, drink some whiskey."

"Yeah," Patrick said. "If I got carried away with that detective shit, as Elly so eloquently put it, I'm sorry. I'm sure you've thought all that through. But, yeah, talk about how great a guy Paul was, try to move on, as much as you can not knowing what the hell happened to him."

"Maybe," Lee said. "Not like a funeral or a wake or anything, since we don't know where he is, since he might still be alive, but saying goodbye to that damned place and yeah, celebrating Paul, moving on from there into whatever it is we have to do now. That seems right. That seems good. Really good."

Lee was excited by the idea. He'd get the friends that had come out to look for Paul together, have another fire, sip whiskey, laugh and cry. At the coast, on Cape Lookout. And it was possible someone would know something they hadn't been telling about Paul's eco-terrorism, though he doubted it, didn't really believe that was real anymore. He wished he could do it on the month anniversary but he didn't even know when his brother had disappeared, just knew it was sometime over that horrible weekend. A month from any of those days would be in the middle of the week, not enough time to plan things. Lee worked Saturday, so Sunday.

"Could you guys come on Sunday?"

"Of course" Patrick and Elly said in unison.

"I need to call my parents, then," Lee said. "And everyone else."

"After our delicious pizza," Elly said.

"Right. After the pizza."

Lee's mom thought it was a great idea. She said that maybe it would help his father to give up his searches on the coast, to which he was still returning frequently despite the boot, despite everything. If she could convince him to come.

TWENTY-SEVEN

Valerie drove Lee towards the coast in her newish Honda Civic. This would have been their fourth date; he'd asked her to this gathering on their third, a lovely after-work hike in Forest Park. And now she was going to meet all his friends and family. It was too soon, it was weird. But she'd said of course she would come if he wanted her there, that she would be there for him. She was wonderful.

"You go camping often?" Lee asked, looking to the back seat of the car where their backpacks were bumping together. Hers didn't look like it had been used much.

"Nope. I got all this stuff when I moved out here to the great Northwest, thinking everyone went camping all the time, but I'm always so busy. An ex was involved, but that didn't last very long after the trip to REI."

They hadn't discussed exes yet and Lee wasn't sure he wanted to, so he let that slide. "Well, hopefully we can go camping again together sometime soon under better circumstances."

"I'd like that," she said, smiling. "Because I'm not so sure I'm going to be camping tonight. We both have to be back at OHSU really early in the morning. It probably makes more sense to sleep at home tonight."

"We'll see," Lee said, looking away out the window at the outlet stores they were passing. He had his heart set on one last night out at the coast to honor his brother fully.

"Anyway, how was your second appointment without me? How're you liking Bas?" Valerie asked. Bas was Baskar, Lee's new dental student. He was professional, bland, boring, nice enough. "He's fine," Lee said, "Actually the appointment Friday went pretty well. He did a filling that went very smoothly and the best part was that they'd fucked up the crown at the lab or something so it didn't fit right. They had to send it back and I get to put off paying for it for another few weeks. That's going to be helpful."

"It's good that you're making it through this without putting everything on credit cards. I'm going to have a ton of debt when I graduate. Dental school isn't cheap."

Lee hadn't even considered putting everything on credit cards. Probably because he didn't have a credit card, never had. It had never made sense. He always had enough money in his bank account to pay for what he needed. "I guess I'll try to struggle on without debt as best I can," he said.

"I do always seem to fall for starving artist types."

"What, I'm just another in a line of poor painters you've dated?" He said this lightly, but it did sting a little bit.

"That's not what I meant," she said with a grin. "Some of them were sculptors." She laughed and a second later he laughed with her. "But really," she added, "I think it's good to talk about our exes, it's a good way to get to know someone and to learn from past mistakes." She said she'd moved to Portland with her boyfriend of two years from college, a writer and reporter, when she got accepted to graduate school here, that he was the one who was excited about camping in Oregon. After a few months, though, he hadn't found a job, hadn't made many friends and decided he hated the constant drizzle so moved back to Philadelphia. Lee said he couldn't imagine anyone being dumb enough to leave her for any reason, let alone because of a little rain. She'd also dated someone from her school here for a month or so but that had ended three months ago. There hadn't been a real spark, a real connection, she said.

Lee told her about Lisa, who was also a painter, a more successful one than he was, about their rocky year and a half of making out in dive bars and small fights at art openings, and about the hours long shouting match that ended it. Neither went any further back, not that Lee had much further to go: two girlfriends in high school and another one, Sue, for a few months before Lisa in Portland plus a handful of dates that didn't go anywhere and a few one night stands.

The road to the coast was so familiar that Lee didn't even really see it now but Valerie pointed out how lovely the hills and forests they were traveling through were, exclaimed at the cuteness of the young cows standing in the green fields when they neared

Tillamook. It turned out she'd never been there, just gone to Astoria once, Seaside another time. Lee told her they'd have to go to the cheese factory but realized as he was saying it that this was a part of the coast he'd probably never want to return to.

They turned towards Netarts then again towards Cape Lookout. In the dusty parking lot they pulled in alongside the familiar caravan of cars from Portland, the cars that had been out here to search when there was still hope.

Lee took Valerie's hand and, nodding at everyone or saying hi but not stopping to talk, he made his way across the parking lot to his parents. They stood by their truck talking with Abby, Paul's tall kayaking friend. Or at least his mom was talking. His dad was off to the side looking down at his feet. Lee had told everyone to dress normally but his mom was in black. His dad's western shirt was one of his brightest, in contrast, his jeans some of his most worn. "Lee!" his mom said when she saw him, gesturing him in for a quick hug then pulling back and saying, "And this must be Valerie. So nice to meet you!" She offered her hand and Valerie shook it, smiling.

"Nice to meet you too, Mrs. Garrett."

"And I'm Simon," Lee's dad said, holding out his hand. "Thank you for being good to our son." Valerie shook his hand, too. This was going to be weird, definitely, her meeting his parents a few minutes before meeting all his friends just a few weeks after she'd first met him.

Abby had waved and walked off to leave them alone. "Lee," his mom said, "I think this was a wonderful idea, getting all of Paul's friends and the family again together to say goodbye, or at least to say good-bye to this place."

"Thanks," Lee said. Valerie squeezed his hand.

"I have a few things to say, your father might too when it's time. Anyway, Valerie, tell me about your-self. You go to dental school, is that right?"

As they chatted Lee watched them closely, hop-ing they'd like each other, worrying more, he real-ized, that Valerie would like them than the other way around. His dad was distant, didn't say much.

After a few minutes Lee's mom said, "Well, we should let you catch up with your friends, too. It was lovely meeting you, Valerie."

"You too, Mrs. Garrett, Mr. Garrett. Simon. And I'm so, so sorry about Paul; it's got to be incredibly hard not knowing what happened. I wish we could have met under happier circumstances."

"Me too," Lee's dad said.

Elly, Patrick and Cindy were standing together with Conrad and Renee by Dragon Pig's van so Lee led Valerie there next. It would be good for her to meet some of the most important people first, before they all became a blur of forgotten faces and names.

"Guys, this is Valerie," he said, wondering if he should have added "my girlfriend," if she would have thought that presumptuous, if she minded that he didn't say it, if she noticed at all. "Valerie, this is Pat-rick, a friend of mine for years and years and his fian-cée Cindy. Elly, my housemate and another great friend. And Conrad, an ex-housemate of mine and his girlfriend, Renee, both of whom are in Dragon Pig, whose great CD I forced you to buy." He wondered if

Valerie would look down on Elly's punk haircut, on Conrad's giant ear studs or Renee's homemade clothing. He needed to stop worrying, just relax. It was impossible.

Elly said, "Ah, the mysterious Valerie. We've heard a lot about you. All good, of course. It's wonderful of you to put up with our friend here. He's a great guy, as I'm sure you know, and it's good that he has someone to be with while he's dealing with all of this." She gestured at the dusty parking lot filled with cars and people milling around.

"I've heard great things about you guys, too," Valerie said.

"I was the one who brought him to OHSU, because she works there," Patrick said, nodding at Cindy, "So we brought you guys together, kind of."

"I thought you met her at our Berbati's show," Conrad said.

"Well, both, kind of," Lee answered.

"Oh?" asked Renee. "Do tell."

"Well," Valerie said, stepping in bravely, "I shouldn't admit this but he was my patient first, which is very unprofessional." Everyone laughed. "So you did bring him to me, Patrick. Thank you. And the day after I first looked at his teeth we met again at your show, though I'm sorry to say I got there late and missed your band, which I'll have to rectify the next time you're playing," she said to Conrad and Renee. "Then a little later we decided we'd rather try dating than dental work and so here we are."

"Well I'm glad you two did meet," Cindy said. "You seem like a great match."

"Thanks," Valerie and Lee said at the same time.

"Anyway, I have more people to introduce this lovely lady to," Lee said, "though I'm sure she's going to forget all the names. We'll see you guys later." They went off into the milling crowd. Lee looked back to see them leaning in amongst themselves, obviously to compare their opinions of Valerie. He hoped they approved. He hoped she approved of them. But then he had to smile and make another introduction.

Eventually Lee cleared his throat then called out, "Excuse me." A few people looked at him. Feeling like an idiot he yelled it again and again until he thought he had everyone's attention. In a loud voice he said, "Thank you all for coming here today. Now if you'll follow me we're going to hike out to the point and then anyone who wants to say anything, to tell a story about Paul or whatever, can do so." He turned and headed to the trail, Valerie at his side. The crowd, maybe thirty people, family, friends and coworkers of Paul and Lee, followed.

The path followed the edge of a tall cliff then cut inland, meandering through deep mossy forests. It was probably too long a hike but Lee couldn't imagine doing this anywhere else. Luckily it wasn't raining. "So, what do you think of everyone?" Lee asked.

"Yeah right, that's an easy question to answer after meeting all the people in your life within twenty minutes. They seem great. I like your parents, your friends. Patrick and Cindy seemed really nice. Everyone did."

Did that mean she didn't like Elly? But she'd just met tons of people. Of course she couldn't give him detailed judgments, it was impressive she even remembered two names. "I'm glad," he said.

"I just hope they like me. They all seemed really friendly but maybe they're jealous and suspicious of this stranger swooping down on their friend, their son, while he's grief stricken and stealing him away."

"Don't be ridiculous. You're a wonderful, beautiful girl and they can tell that, not someone who's taking advantage of my grief. I'm the one who seems like maybe I took advantage of my terrible situation to get you to go out with me."

"I didn't even know about your brother when we started dating."

"I know that. Anyway, I'm sure they liked you. What's not to like?" He wrapped an arm around her waist and pulled her to him as they led the way down the trail.

When they arrived at the point there was still a good distance between the reddish sun and the Pacific waters that awaited it. A few clouds hung above the horizon but it was a mostly clear, chilly evening.

At the tip of the cape was the clearing, with cliffs falling away to the water on each side, where he and Patrick had encountered his parents and Margaret on the day they found Paul's car. A little bench stood at the head facing out towards the ocean. Lee jumped up on it and turned away from the sea towards the gathering of people he'd brought here. Over the past few days he'd tried to write a speech, had crossed out sentence after sentence and finally given up, hoping he could improvise something, that he could just speak what he felt. He was acutely aware of all the eyes on him. Gulping, he wished he wasn't the center of attention, that he wasn't the first to speak, that he had the yellow legal pad with neatly written notes he saw clenched in his mom's hand. He cleared his throat and then spoke.

"Thank you all for coming here today," he said. "As you know, Paul Garrett, my brother, disappeared a little more than a month ago. His car was found near here, near this beautiful point that sticks out into the Pacific. You, the Park Rangers and especially my parents searched here tirelessly, but we didn't find anything. And if he were lost here we couldn't find him safe now. We don't know what happened to him, we may never know. He could still show up, he could still be ok. But not here. So, tonight, we're going to say goodbye to this place and, though we can't really say goodbye to Paul because we don't know what happened to him, we're going to celebrate and remember him.

"As you know, my brother loved the outdoors. Loved this ocean and this ragged, stunning coastline. Loved all of nature. So this State Park is the perfect place to remember all the wonderful times we had with him on this coast, in the hills and mountains we passed through on the way here, east in the Cascades and the desert, in all this state's rivers and forests and ski slopes. He loved those places and he worked to protect them, volunteering time, giving money, doing everything possible. It seemed like he'd give his life, do anything, to protect the wilderness. So if he is here he would be glad to be in a place so beautiful and unspoiled." He'd looked over the crowd at this last part but hadn't seen anything unusual. Patrick had said that he would keep an eye on everyone. Nothing was going to come of it, though, no mysteries were going to be solved.

Lee sniffed back tears and turned to look out at the sun that was giving the clouds an orangeish glow around their edges as it lowered past them, composing himself. Then he said, "Paul was the best brother I could have possibly asked for. As a kid he wasn't ashamed of playing with his little brother, didn't mind me tagging after him everywhere. Of course there were only maybe ten kids in town so limited options might have had something to do with it, but even as kids we were great friends. And then when he moved to Portland he didn't mind me following after him again to the big city. In fact he encouraged it and worked hard to make me feel at home there, introducing me to his friends, taking me on his trips, going out for drinks, opening his life to me. We were friends just as much as we were family and I can't believe I've lost, may have lost, one of my best friends and my only brother."

Lee sniffed back tears and continued. "I, I don't really know what else to say. I tried to come up with a story that encapsulated Paul, and our relationship, but I couldn't. There were too many and all of them meant too much. I loved him. I love him. I'm sure all of you do too. So if any of you have anything to say, stories to tell, please do. Thank you." He stepped down from the bench. Valerie was right there and he sunk into her arms, resting his head on her shoulder.

There was a slight pause then the dull thud of someone jumping up onto the wooden bench. Lee looked up over Valerie's shoulder and saw the Tony's squarish, crew-cut head. "Um, hi," he said, "I'm Tony, a friend of Paul's since we were little kids. I don't know a lot of you since I went away to Afghanistan with the Army and then, unlike seemingly everyone else from town, didn't move to Portland. But even though Paul had his life in the city he always kept in touch, giving me a call every time he came back, going out for a drink or to watch a game on TV, or just calling to ask how I was. That was one of the best things about Paul, how he always had time for his friends no matter where they were, no matter who they were, no matter how many people he knew, he always had time to make you feel like you were an important part of his life, if that makes any sense." It did make sense to Lee, it was part of what he'd been trying to say. There was always time for a beer or hike with him, for advice when he needed it. It was the same, he knew, with all these people here and with his parents. Tony had gone on, saying, "And because of that I know he wouldn't, couldn't abandon all of us, that something must have happened to him, some terrible accident. Like has happened to so many people. But I'll always remember our games as kids, some of the only kids around, with little Lee tagging along, playing catch in the fields or skipping rocks on the pond in the sun as if nothing could ever change. And we're all going to miss him so much."

Tony jumped down. After another pause Abby stepped up on the bench, towering over them. The clouds were red, orange and gold now, the sun dropping further down but still distinct from its bright reflection that was shimmering on the waters below. "Um, hi, I'm Abby," she said. "Paul and I were good friends, we went kayaking what seems like every month on all the rivers in this state and a few others, and we drank rivers worth of beer at all the bars in Southeast Portland. And he was always there for me. With consolation and advice about problems with boyfriends and with jobs, with a loan of gear or money. And on the river he was a rock, never panicking when things went wrong, never making a mistake. I remember one time we were out on the Deschutes on a class three with my sister from Kansas who'd never gone kayaking except on easy stuff the day before and she tipped and went under and the boat popped back out without her even though she was wearing a life vest and I was panicked and frozen but instantly he was diving out of his boat and then before I had time to do or think anything they emerged together, way upstream. Her foot had caught in a rock but he'd pulled her free in well under a minute from when it had happened, and apart from a scraped ankle she was fine. She had a huge crush on him after that, which I totally understood. Paul was such a wonderful guy and I, we all loved him. He was my best friend. I miss him so much and I can't believe he still hasn't come back." Crying, she stepped down.

Several more friends of Paul's told mostly tearful stories of how he'd been there for them, of trips they'd taken, places they'd hiked and camped, how much he'd meant to them. Sal, the employee who'd worked for his landscaping business the longest, spoke briefly and told how Paul always treated his employees as friends, was the best boss they could have had. Lee hadn't even thought about them, really, how they'd have to find new work. Hadn't thought about Paul's business, his house, his stuff or any of it in any coherent fashion, even when he'd been there taking care of the garden. All of that needed to be dealt with. Rent was going to be due on Paul's place soon. Rent, even though people had been telling him he was throwing his money away and should be paying a mortgage ever since he started renting a whole house for him and Jenny, for himself alone afterwards. He'd always said he wasn't ready to be that settled. And who was going to pay that rent? He wondered if his parents had dealt with this stuff without mentioning it to him. Wondered if his mom had. Someone must have paid it already for September, paid for that house to sit empty and abandoned. He'd have to ask because they were going to have to do something about it soon. Jesus. Could they let the house go? What if he came back? But the whole point of this was that he probably wouldn't. Fuck. He couldn't believe still, maybe ever, that Paul, who everyone was saying such great things about, was really gone.

Once it seemed that all the friends who were extroverted enough to get up there and talk, which was a lot of them, had gone, there was a long pause. Then Lee's mom stepped lightly up onto the bench. Her eyes, Lee saw, were dry. She glanced briefly at the yellow paper in her hand. Behind her the sun touched the waters and, as she spoke, started flattening, smearing into a band of gold on the horizon. The clouds took on shades of purple edged with magenta. "Thank you all so much for coming out here to honor the life of my son," she said. "It means a lot to me to hear your stories, to hear how much you all cared for him and he for you. It's wonderful to learn things I didn't know about him, things I missed because he moved to Portland, followed by our younger son Lee. It's good to hear that his life there, and all over the state in the nature he loved so much, was happy and rich and full of friendship. It's good that the little boy who so loved the camping trips we'd take as a family to Crater Lake, to Lassen, to the Sisters or the coast, that the little boy so awed at all the tall trees and the snow-covered mountains grew up into a man who turned all that into the most important part of his life. And there's a temptation to blame myself because that's how he vanished from our lives as well, but I think that's wrong, I think that denying him what he loved most would be worse than losing him to it. Still, it's hard, so hard not knowing what happened. But I have to thank my son Lee for coming up with the idea for this as a way to say goodbye to the searching, goodbye, at least for now, to Paul, our oldest son. It's so hard but we do need to realize that, probably, he's gone from us, that, probably, we need to move on. Until we know for sure it's fine to have hope in our hearts, knowing that there is still some small chance that he'll come back to us. But if he does it will have to be as a wonderful surprise. Because until then we need to move on with our lives, accept his loss and honor him, but to pull ourselves together for the future. I believe that's what he would have wanted." And she stepped down.

Lee looked over at his father to see if he was going to say anything but he was still looking down at his boots, which he scuffled in the dirt, tears running freely from his eyes down over his drawn cheeks. He showed no sign of moving forward. Lee looked back and saw that the sun was a bright neon sliver, just the top visible, painful to observe, over the lip of the water. The clouds looked bruised. Everyone was silent. And then the sun was gone.

After the unplanned moment of silence stretched into the awkward and the night began settling quickly around them, Lee said, "Thank you all again for coming, for everyone that spoke. We'll head back to the parking lot now. For everyone who can stay we'll have a bonfire on the beach. I'm sorry it's a Sunday, sorry that some of you have to go back to work in the morning and won't be able to stay. But thank you all so much for coming."

They found their way back with the wavering beams of the flashlights Lee had told people to bring illuminating the muddy path in front of them. He heard someone, he couldn't tell who, whisper, "Isn't it too early to do this kind of thing? It's only been a month," and he wanted to tell him that it wasn't like that. It wasn't a funeral, it wasn't a wake, it was different. But maybe it wasn't and maybe it was too early. At least for the kind of stuff his mom had said. He didn't know. It had seemed so good to hear those stories, to bring everyone together.

Lee found himself walking besides Patrick. He tapped him on the arm then whispered, "Did you see anything suspicious? When I mentioned Paul giving his life?"

"No dude, sorry. It was a dumb idea."

Lee saw his father walking alone in the front, his strides hurried as if he were trying to escape into the darkness. After thanking Patrick for trying Lee ran up and placed a hand on his father's shoulder. "Everyone's speeches were great, weren't they, Dad?" he asked.

His dad stopped and gave him a wild look, his eyes gleaming in someone's swinging flashlight beam. "How can you say that? Everyone was giving up, you and your mother too. I don't understand how you can give up on your brother when we don't know anything, when anything could have happened. I don't know how you and your mother can think that your brother is dead, have a service for him. I don't believe it. I know he's alive somewhere, somehow. I won't accept that he's dead."

Each time his father spoke the word "dead" had been like a punch to Lee's stomach. He realized that no one else had used that word the entire night. "I'm sorry, Dad," was all he could say.

"I don't know if that's good enough," his dad said. "I don't know if anything can make up for you all abandoning Paul." He strode away, Lee's hand falling from his shoulder. Lee, in more pain than he'd felt all day, though earlier he had thought he was being healed, watched him disappear into the darkness.

TWENTY-EIGHT

They roamed over the beach lit in black, white and blue by a fragment of moon that shone overhead, searching for driftwood to burn. When Lee judged that their pile was high enough he leaned into the center, where a pyramid of dry twigs surrounded a mound of newspaper, and struck a match against the side of the box. He cupped the sizzling flame in his hand to keep the breeze coming off the water from extinguishing it. Gently he touched it to the paper, heard a hiss then a whoosh of oxygen rushing into the now lively dancing ball of flames, which quickly subsumed the small sticks and twigs and began licking up at the logs above. Lee stood back and watched the fire grow.

Bottles traced circles through the crowd. Many people refrained after the initial cheers to Paul though, claiming they were driving back soon. Lee drank from each of the several fifths of Maker's Mark making the rounds each time they were placed in his hands, refusing the beer and other liquor. His parents had already left, coming to hug him goodbye, his mom hugging Valerie too. Lee's father didn't say anything about what he'd said before, didn't elaborate or apologize. Others had come to shake his hand or hug him and announce their departure, claiming early work the next morning or homework they had to get done. He didn't know if anyone would camp with him. He didn't know if Valerie would.

She was beside him now but was turned talking softly to a girl he didn't know, the girlfriend of one of Paul's camping buddies, maybe. Valerie wasn't drinking much. She'd said she wanted to keep open the option of driving home.

Lee felt a tap on his shoulder. Looking up he saw Paul's friend Tony, the one who'd been in the Army, leaning over him. "Do you want to take a walk with me?" Tony asked.

"What's up?"

"I just think we should go for a little walk. There's something I need to talk to you about."

"Ok." Lee took another swig of whiskey, feeling it glow in his sternum, and rose unsteadily. As they left the fire's warmth the chill of the night quickly cut through his clothes. They headed towards the water and the rumbling crash of waves drowned out all but the occasional faint bark of laughter from the group around the bonfire.

Tony lit a cigarette, the flare from the lighter revealing his serious face for a second. "Lee, there's something about Paul I think you don't know. But I want you to stay calm; it didn't have anything to do with your brother's disappearance or I would have told you already."

"What are you talking about, Tony?" Lee felt his heart start to beat faster.

"I really shouldn't say anything. But he was planning on telling you about all this the weekend he disappeared, if you'd been there. And you're his brother so you should know. Maybe you know a little already. I feel like you do and that's why you said some of what you did in your speech. Swear, though, that you won't say anything or talk about this with anyone."

"I swear. Just tell me what you're talking about!"

Tony breathed in deeply and his cigarette flared. Then he let out a plume of smoke, dimly visible in the ember's glow. "Ok Lee, here it is. Paul formed this group called the Coyotes. I was part of it with him and a few other guys. We discussed environmental issues, how to help the planet: taking down dams, sabotaging logging trucks, all that Monkey Wrench Gang and ELF shit and how we could do it smarter, better, safer and more effectively. But it was just talk over beers, just boasting. Paul wouldn't have done anything, no one would have done anything. We weren't anywhere close to that point yet. And if we ever got there I was going to be in charge of any actions because of my experience in the military. He wouldn't have done anything without me."

"Jesus. So Paul really was an eco-terrorist!"

"First of all, eco-terrorism is the government's term so they can lock up people who are committing minor "crimes" for years and years. But like I said, we weren't going to do anything, probably, and if we were he wouldn't have done it alone."

"He wouldn't have been alone. I was supposed to be there!"

"I know, but he was only going to tell you about this shit. You would have been new, green; he wouldn't have gotten you involved in anything yet. Maybe when you couldn't be there he decided to practice or scout something out and that's why he hid his car. But he wasn't doing anything illegal, he's not on the run from the law or any romantic bullshit like that. He just had some kind of terrible fucking accident and now he's gone."

"How can you believe that when this was real? Fuck, the Coyotes? Why coyotes?"

"There's this story from the Native Americans around here about how Coyote freed all the salmon from a trap some cruel sisters were keeping them in, gives them to all the tribes in the region."

"The fucking salmon!" Lee exclaimed, thinking of his brother's rambling speech on the river. "Who else was in this group? Maybe they know something more."

"They don't. And I'm not going to name any names. They were people Paul trusted and that's as far as I'm going to go."

"Jesus fuck," Lee said. "This whole thing is crazy. My brother was the head of a secret group plotting to blow up dams..."

"We never got to plotting, picked specific targets, anything like that. I told you, it was just talk and very possibly that's all it ever would have been. But now your brother's gone and nothing will ever happen. I'm sorry, Lee." He reached out and put a hand on Lee's shoulder.

Lee looked up into his eyes, which were lit by the glow of the cigarette and the moon's light reflecting off the rolling ocean. They looked sad, remorseful and honest. But what if he were saying all this to throw Lee off the track, telling him a little so he didn't find out everything? The tree-sit guy had said they wouldn't tell him anything. So if Paul had done something, if Tony had even been there with him, what then? They wouldn't tell him, they'd try to shut the possibility down just like Tony was doing now. But no, Paul was going to bring Lee into the group, make him a Coyote that weekend. Maybe they would have done something bold and crazy and powerful later, together, with Tony and the rest of the group, but instead fucking fate had Lee work that weekend and Paul fall from a cliff or whatever had happened to him and everything was ruined. Unless Paul was tricking Tony, too. God, the possibilities were endless, agonizing. And there was still no way of knowing anything for sure.

"Thank you for telling me this, Tony," Lee said, though he wasn't sure he was actually thankful for the knowledge.

"Paul was going to tell you that damned weekend. And you needed to know. It's hurt me keeping this from you and everyone these past weeks. The only reasons I did were that I didn't want to talk about any of this on the phone and that it really doesn't change anything. Just don't saying anything to anyone, especially not the cops but anyone, ok? We don't need people arrested for conspiracy, which is the kind of shit they do these days. You swore, Lee."

"I remember."

"I should go now. There's nothing more to talk about, I think, but if you have any questions you know where to find me. God, I really hope I did the right thing by telling you this, Lee." He dropped the cigarette to his feet, ground it into the sand with a quick turn of his boot, then knelt to pick up the butt. Without another word he turned and strode away past the fire and towards the parking lot. Lee was alone on the cold dark beach, not seeing anything because his mind was filled with images of Paul blowing up a logging truck or Paul practicing that and falling off a cliff instead.

When Lee finally headed back to the fire he saw Valerie coming out to greet him. "I was wondering where you'd gone off to," she said.

Could he tell her? He'd sworn to tell no one and there was nothing to tell, right? If he believed Tony then even though Paul had been a Coyote it wasn't the cause of his disappearance. Telling her would just get her as riled up as he was over nothing, right? And he'd given his word. So he said, "I was just talking to a friend. Anyway, thank you so much for coming with me to this. It's really great of you, being so kind when we've only gone out a few times."

"Of course. It was beautiful getting to know your brother, hearing all those stories about him. And it was nice meeting your parents, your friends. I feel like I know you much better now."

"And you still want to be with me?"

"Of course! Why wouldn't I?"

Because he'd just lied to her. "Because my dad hates me for giving up on Paul, because I always tagged after my big brother, because my friends are punks, because I don't have any money and have a shitty job. Because I'm giving up on my brother who could still be out here somewhere!"

"Jesus, Lee. Those things don't matter or they're not true. You didn't give up on your brother, you honored him. I really thought it was beautiful. And so great that you could get everyone together, organize such a wonderful memorial pretty much by yourself. And I liked your friends, as much as I got to meet them. Lee, don't worry. Everything's going to be ok." She wrapped him in a hug.

"Thank you. Though I wish you were drinking, too." He didn't deserve her no matter what she said.

"I told you, I should get back, get a decent night's sleep and a shower before going to dig around in someone's mouth in the morning. And you should too, before having someone digging around in yours. It wouldn't do to puke on Bas when he's drilling out one of those cavities. Though it would be funny."

Lee didn't laugh with her. He couldn't tell how drunk he was. He wanted to stay one more night here on the coast that his brother loved, the coast where he disappeared because he was a Coyote or for reasons that had nothing to do with that. Wanted to stay here wrapped in Valerie's arms all night, listening to the crashing waves. Going back would be abandoning his brother just like his father had said, and what he'd just found out could mean that his father was right. "Maybe I'll just sleep here by myself," he said, hoping she'd change her mind.

"Come on, Lee," she said, letting him go. "It doesn't make any sense."

"Fine," he said, turning from her towards the glow of the fire, which sent billowing smoke, lit red from below, up into the dark night. "Whatever. I need another drink." And he walked away, ignoring her when she called his name.

The crowd around the fire had dwindled even further when he returned. Elly, Patrick and Cindy were still there though, and a few others. Patrick had a bottle of Maker's Mark. Lee went over, wrapped one arm around his neck and took the bottle with his other hand. "To Paul," he said, taking a sip, then another. But it wasn't Patrick he wanted to be holding, even if his crazy plan had somehow worked. Lee was being a petulant asshole, he realized. "To Paul," he yelled again, echoed by others around the fire. He emptied the rest of the bottle onto the flames, which sputtered and steamed. Then he turned and headed in a run towards the parking lot. He hoped that it wasn't too late, that Valerie hadn't gotten into her car and driven back to Portland, that he hadn't thrown away something so good in his pain and confusion.

But she was here, coming out of the darkness of the beach towards the fire, and she wrapped her arms around him. He said, "I'm so sorry, I was an asshole, of course you don't have to camp with me for a few hours only to get up at five in the morning hungover to go to work. It was stupid, it doesn't matter."

"No, no, I'm sorry, I was being insensitive. You lost your brother and I was worried about a little sleep, of course we can camp here if that's what you need to do."

Then they looked at each other, their faces painted bluish from the light of the moon, and both laughed weakly. "Our first stupid fight," Valerie said. "So, what do we do now?"

"We'll go. We can come back here or go somewhere else and camp some other time when it makes more sense. We had the speeches and the sunset and the fire and the whiskey. That's enough, this was good."

"Are you sure? Because I'm serious, I will stay out with you here tonight if that's what you want, if that's what you need to make peace with your brother, and then I'll happily give you a ride back to OHSU in the morning."

"No, it's stupid, you're right. We'll go. Just promise we'll camp some other time together."

"I promise."

"Valerie, I, thank you. I love you."

He cursed himself for saying it as soon as it was out of his mouth. He wasn't even sure it was true, though it had been in the moment he said it. It was way too soon for that. She made a soothing noise and brought him to her, kissed him deeply then held him close. She didn't, though, say she loved him back. The kiss, the offer, the apology, were more, much more, than enough.

They went back to the fire and Lee gave his friends long hugs goodbye, thanking them again for coming out and making it such a wonderful night. If anyone was disappointed that he wasn't camping with them they didn't say anything. Maybe no one was camping. Patrick said he'd make sure the fire was put out safely. Then, his steps not entirely straight and steady, Lee made his way back to Valerie's car with his arm around her waist. He looked back at the camping stuff, unopened, unused. But it was ok. And maybe holding off sleeping here would somehow hold off the final giving up on Paul. Maybe it would be more in line with what his father wanted, more in line with the idea of Paul as a Coyote.

When Valerie started up the car the little blue readout showed that it was 10:21. "Huh, I thought it was much later," she said.

"We'll get a little sleep after all," Lee replied.

"We can go back out if you want, stay longer."

"No, it's time to go. Thank you so much, Valerie." He put his arm around the back of her neck, kissed her check.

She backed up the car and said, "Now, how do we get home?"

Home. Her place, where he was sure they'd stay. He was drunk but he still knew the route. So they began the long drive back through the darkness.

That night Lee held Valerie in his arms but they didn't, by unspoken mutual consent, make love. Still it felt calming and right just to hold her, her back to him his arm around her stomach. Soon she was breathing heavily, asleep and comfortable in his embrace, and he felt a little peace, though he couldn't sleep. His mind was consumed by thoughts of exploding dams, coyotes, salmon and Paul.

TWENTY-NINE

When the alarm's shriek tore him from vague, unsettled dreams, Lee found that Valerie was still in the same position in his arms. This was what was real, he tried to convince himself, not tales of Coyotes that led nowhere, that didn't solve anything. To try to shut down his mind he kissed her neck and she murmured then pulled away to swat at the alarm. His head ached, his mouth felt dry but he pulled her back to him anyway and she turned into his kisses. The snooze alarm went off while they were making love.

They showered together, Lee marveling at the intimacy, at the perfection of her body, ignoring the chill when it was his turn to wait outside the water. She rained granola into two bowls and splashed milk on top, apologizing, absurdly Lee thought, for not having time to cook. Lee drank several glasses of water, then gratefully gulped the coffee she'd prepared. She poured the rest of hers into a travel mug, apologizing again for not having another, and he left half a cup to get cold on her counter as they hurried out to the car.

"I hate being late," she said as she drove him through downtown and up the hill.

"Me too." Though he wasn't late, he was going to have to sit around in the waiting room for an hour until his appointment at nine.

"Another thing we have in common," she said. He was glad she thought there were lots. He was glad even of this time spent in a car with her way too early in the morning, hung over, going to pay money he didn't have to get his tooth drilled into by someone who wasn't even a real dentist.

"Do you think we should go in together?" he asked as they pulled into the parking lot. "Maybe we should enter separately, since can't you get in trouble for dating a patient?"

"You're not my patient anymore, but, yeah, let's. I'll go first." She looked left and right, furtively, then, laughing, gave him a quick kiss. "Lock the door behind you. And call me when you're done with your appointment." Then she exaggeratedly tiptoed away, like a cartoon spy. Lee grinned until the secrecy reminded him that he hadn't told her about the Coyotes. It didn't matter, he tried to convince himself.

Lee met Valerie for lunch after his morning of drilling and fillings. He had never kissed with a Novocained mouth before; it felt like there was a sponge between him and her, insulating, separating. He tried to tell her this with his numb lisp and for some reason she found it hilarious, couldn't stop laughing.

After squeezing the last of the Cerulean blue acrylic from the tube onto his palette Lee mixed it in with the purple shade he was forming to wash over the sunset-colored background of the canvas he had on the floor. He'd mostly been painting watercolors of his brother or the places his brother loved but those were usually a struggle with the new medium, which wasn't as forgiving of errors as acrylics. Last Thursday was coming up soon so he'd gone back to this big one he'd started before he met Mrs. Tanner.

Lee dipped his brush into the mug of water then placed it on the edge of the small lake of purple paint in the corner of his dinged stained palette. In a wavy line he spread the color over the top of the canvas then tilted it up so the watery paint flowed down in rivulets, smearing dusky trails over the oranges and reds below. He repeated the process in different places, causing trickles of purple to run towards the center from each edge.

When his phone rang Lee was mixing a new, darker color. He saw that it was his mother and answered, tucking the cellphone between his ear and shoulder while he continued squeezing little dollops of paint into the mix.

"Hi, Mom," he said.

"Hello, Lee. How are you?"

"I'm fine."

"And how's Valerie?"

"She's good."

"She seems like a lovely girl. Hold on to that one, ok, Lee?"

"I'll certainly try, Mom. Anyway, how are you?"

"Not good, that's why I called. I'm going to fly back to Georgia to stay with my parents for a while. I need a break from all this, from every damned thing reminding me of Paul. Besides, it's been a long time since I've seen them." They'd wanted to come out but claimed they weren't healthy enough to travel cross-country.

"Is Dad going with you?"

"He wouldn't want to. He wouldn't give up his searches on the coast even though they're hopeless. And he needs to keep the store open, too."

"Are you sure it's a good idea to leave him alone, Mom?"

"I know this is going to sound cruel, but part of the reason I need to go is to get a break from your father. He's being impossible, won't stop blaming me for giving up on Paul, won't stop obsessing over our supposed need to go back and find him. He won't admit that we've done everything we can and he keeps going to the coast all the time. I'll only be gone a week or two. It might be good for him, giving him time to work through things, forcing him to focus on the store. But I was wondering if you could see him a few times, call him, make sure he's ok?"

It seemed like a terrible, cruel, crazy idea to Lee. How could she leave him? Of course he was being difficult, he'd lost his son. "Is there any way I can convince you not to do this, Mom? I'm not sure Dad can handle all this by himself." Would telling her about the Coyotes change anything? No, it changed nothing, just led to more questions without answers. It would just make things worse, as it had for Lee.

"I already have the ticket. I'm sorry, Lee, but this is something I need to do."

After he'd hung up, Lee added a little more black to the color he was mixing. The paint had partially dried because he'd forgotten about both it and the brush in his hand while listening to his mother. Now he went to work making gloom seep into the painting from all four corners. He'd thought about painting a coyote as the centerpiece, but that would hurt too much. Instead, he knew now, he was going to add the boot his father had found, floating mysteriously in the painting's dark center.

THIRTY

Lee was pedaling up Alberta towards where Elly had told him she would set up his artwork. There were a good number of people already out strolling down the street, which was lined with vendors. He found Elly's grin from the blanket on the ground where she sat surrounded by his paintings.

"Thank you so much for doing this for me," he said.

"You're welcome. And I even sold one already."

"That's great. Which one?"

"The big one with the boot."

The boot had been huge, its shoelaces untied and twisting throughout the canvas. He'd worked on that throughout the week, emptied several tubes of paint on it, going back again and again to add details during breaks from several smaller pieces he'd also done in the past few days. He'd thought it was one of his best. It was definitely better than most of the watercolors, only three of which he'd decided to bring: slightly abstracted landscapes of places he'd camped with Paul. The portrait he'd kept for himself.

"How much did you get?" Lee asked.

"Two hundred fifty."

"What?"

"You heard me."

"Jesus, seriously? That's amazing. Who to?" The most he'd ever made on a painting was fifty and if he'd been feeling particularly bold he might have asked seventy-five or a hundred for that one, expecting to be bargained down.

"Some lady. She looked like her purse was worth more than that so I thought I might as well ask for a lot. Maybe I should have tried for more."

"Are you kidding? That's great. You can have half as my salesperson."

"I'm not taking anything. All I did was sit here, you did all the work. That painting was great and art supplies aren't cheap. Well, except the ones I got you from Mrs. Tanner."

"At least let me buy you a drink. Lots of drinks."

"That I'll accept, but not today. I have overnight shifts starting at eight out in Beaverton. I'll be gone until Monday."

"And you spent some of your last hours of freedom helping me out? You're an amazing friend, Elly. Thank you."

"You're welcome. Besides, it was fun watching all the people go by. There are lots of cute girls here."

"I know. And another will be joining us soon; Valerie's going to meet me here in a bit."

"Now that was a good find, Lee. I really liked her, what little I got to see of her. Kind of quiet but that could have just been the circumstances, meeting everyone all at once. That was pretty brave of her, just being there, actually. So, yeah, congratulations, dude, she's great. And hot."

"Thanks. It's kind of a shame that boot painting is gone, actually. I thought that was one of my best and wanted her to see it. She's never seen any of my stuff except the Dragon Pig artwork, which I'm not that proud of."

"Well I'm sure she'll be impressed."

"Wait," Lee said, the thought suddenly coming to him. "You didn't buy the painting yourself because you felt bad for me, did you?"

"Do you think I have that kind of money?"

"Sometimes you do. Like when you get an extra ninety-six hours of work or however much you're doing over the weekend."

"Well, true. But it's not like you wouldn't notice if it went up in my room and it's too good to hide away. No, I really sold it. Though when I do get this paycheck I might buy one of the smaller ones from you, or commission one. You'd do a pair of breasts floating in the aether for me, right?"

"Um."

"Kidding, man. No, you really sold it. Congrats."

He wrapped her in a hug.

"And you said she was just your housemate," he heard Valerie say in a mock-outraged tone.

Lee let go of Elly and went to hug Valerie, giving her a quick but deep kiss. It was a good thing Elly looked like a lesbian, though he didn't think Valerie was the jealous type. "How was school?" he asked.

"Not great. I had to do a filling that was really tricky and I needed some help from one of the professors, which is always a bit embarrassing."

"I can't believe you want to make a living torturing people like that," Lee said with a smile.

"The lady wasn't in much pain, nothing like what you went through. That's extremely rare. And we're helping people, ultimately."

"It's true," Elly said. "You should have seen what my teeth looked like when I was a kid, before braces. She's saving us from looking like we're British."

"Good to see you again, Elly," Valerie said.

"Good to see you too. And impressive that you remembered my name after meeting a hundred people in twenty minutes. But anyway, enough of this chitchat. You have to admire your boyfriend's artwork; he says you've never seen it."

"It's true," Valerie said, and walked past them to look at the canvases spread on the ground and leaned up against the wall. Silently she stared at one for maybe thirty seconds or a minute then moved on to the next. Lee wanted badly to know what she was thinking but was glad she spent the time to really consider each one. He really wanted her to like them, wished they were better, wished that the boot were still here.

After she'd gone through each of his paintings wordlessly, Lee couldn't take it any more. "So, what do you think?" he said.

"They're great. I'm impressed," she replied.

"Really?"

She turned to smile at him and he was pretty sure he believed her. "Yeah. Especially these watercolors. There's a lot of life and energy to them. I like the abstract ones too, but they, and I don't want to sound mean, but they're all a little similar, a little bit formulaic or something. Though they're technically good and on their own each is pretty interesting."

"I know what you're saying, I think. That was a phase, and one I might be done with. The best of the series, and maybe the last, was a really big one of the boot I told you about that my father found. I just finished it yesterday and Elly already sold it. I wish you could have seen that one."

"How much are you selling these for?"

"She sold the boot for two-fifty, which was amazing even if it was the biggest one here. Usually they go for fifty, tops."

"That's all? It seems like they could be a lot more. You're selling yourself short, Lee."

"That's nice of you to say, but if you hadn't noticed I'm pedaling my art on the sidewalk at Last Thursday, not in some ritzy gallery in the Pearl."

"Maybe that's the problem, maybe you need to think bigger."

"You know any art dealers?"

"Nope. For that you're on your own. But this stuff is good. I really like it." She gave him a kiss to prove it.

"So this is the place," Lee said, gesturing at his house, seeing it through her eyes: the peeling paint, the weeds growing amongst the shaggy dying grass in the front yard, the PBR cans on the porch. They'd come here after wandering up and down Alberta, admiring other people's art, stopping a few times to listen to music.

"It's a great old house," she said. "It's just a shame your landlord doesn't take better care of it."

"Yeah, but if he did I probably wouldn't be able to afford the place."

"How much is your rent?"

"Two-sixty for my room."

"Seriously? That's ridiculous. I pay more than twice that and my place is tiny."

"Yeah well, you don't have to share it and your neighborhood is nicer. Your apartment is beautiful, too. And you haven't seen the inside here."

"Well, let's."

Lee was glad he'd cleaned up a little, guessing that she might come back with him. He was even more glad that the stench from the beer brewing disaster in the basement was finally gone. Doug was in the living room reading a music magazine, Modest Mouse blaring from the speakers. "This is my housemate Doug, Doug, this is Valerie," Lee said.

Doug smiled, nodded and said something like nice to meet you that was lost in the music. Valerie did the same and they moved on. Lee gave her the tour. They went from the living room with its beat up couches and spotted, worn carpeting into the kitchen with the surprisingly nice gas stove and fewer than usual dirty dishes piled in the sink, skipping the basement and garage which were filled with junk. Up the stairs they passed the closed doors of his housemates' rooms then peeked into the bathroom with its soapstained shower curtain. Lee's room was the finale. Pausing before the door he said, "It's not that nice."

"I don't mind."

They entered. Lee hated his room at that moment. The ugly teal carpeting, the mattress on a boxspring on the floor, his battered dresser. Most of the free space was taken up by canvases on spread news-paper and by painting supplies. "I'm sorry it's so crappy and that there's nowhere to sit. Do you want to go back to the living room?" He wished her place wasn't so fancy in comparison, that she didn't have real furniture, a real apartment with hardwood floors. She smiled but maybe her eyes were scrunched a little, showing a little concern.

"It's fine," she said. "It's not the place, it's the person, right? And we can sit on the bed." Then, laughing, she wrapped her arms around him and dragged Lee downward in a tangle of limbs and kisses.

Lee woke once in the middle of the night. He realized that he hadn't thought about the Coyotes much all day, distracted by work and Elly and Valerie, but that he had just dreamed of them, or, rather, dreamed of a coyote that he knew somehow was Paul. It was a shaggy, powerful beast, ripping a salmon apart with its jagged teeth then lapping at the blood and scales on the shiny floor of a supermarket beneath high fluorescent lights.

THIRTY-ONE

Lee heard a honk as he was finishing the liquor store's closing paperwork. Out on the street a few minutes later he didn't see his mom's car so figured it hadn't been for him. He turned to lock the door and when he looked back he saw his brother's Wagoneer pull around the corner. His mouth went dry and his heartbeat accelerated. Then it pulled closer and Lee saw his mom behind the wheel. She smiled at him and he walked, a little unsteadily, up to the car and let himself in. The passenger seat sunk down, used to his weight.

"Jesus, Mom, that was like seeing a ghost. And where's Dad?"

"Sorry, I should have told you on the phone," she said as she pulled the car back into traffic. "Your father is being impossible, refused to come, refused to talk to me basically since I told him I was going back home. I'm really worried. Could you go see him soon? You can drive there, we're leaving this car with you."

Lee didn't know which facet of that to tackle first. "I can't pay for insurance or gas."

"I hadn't thought of that. Maybe we can help you out soon, and your brother's insurance should still be valid. But, anyway, you're going to have to keep it for a little while since there's no other way to get it back without your father here."

"What if Paul comes back?"

"You too, Lee? If he comes back you can give the car back to him. It's easy."

"And what about the house? What did you decide to do about that?"

"Paul had paid the last month's rent as part of his deposit, which took care of September. We're going to pay for October and move his stuff out when I get back. We'll keep everything important, of course. There's room in the attic if we clear out some junk, and in his room. But it doesn't make sense to leave the house sitting there forever, paying for all that space that no one's using."

Lee let his head sink to his chest and closed his eyes. They really were letting Paul go.

"I know this is hard, Lee, it's hard on all of us. But if you think about it you'll realize it's the only thing that makes sense."

"What does Dad have to say about it?" Lee asked.

"What do you think he says? He says it's a terrible idea, that I'm giving up and don't love our son enough. He's cruel about it, though he doesn't mean to be." She drummed her fingers on the steering wheel nervously.

Lee didn't want to take either of their sides and didn't think either of them was being fair or reasonable. Not that he could figure out what the right response was, if there even was any right response.

They were completely silent for the rest of the ride. The only times Lee had been to the airport were their few visits to the same grandparents his mom was flying to now. When they arrived Lee pulled over and his mom grabbed two huge bags from the trunk. He didn't say anything but his heart sank. She shouldn't need that if she was just planning on staying a week or two, should she? But she wouldn't, couldn't leave his father for much longer than that, right? Lee couldn't recall how much she'd brought the last time they'd gone there, years ago. It had all been merged with his dad's stuff, anyway.

He hugged her hard and wished her a good trip. She told him to take care of himself, to say hi to Valerie for her. She didn't mention his father or brother again, nor did he. Lee didn't know what to say, how to tell his mom that he thought she was being heartless by leaving. She gave him a kiss on the cheek then walked away, pushing through the glass doors and vanishing. Lee stood there for a moment then went around and sat in the driver's seat of his brother's car, which he'd never done before. He turned the keys in the ignition and drove for the first time in over a year. Pulling into the circling traffic going round the airport, he headed for home.

The phone had trilled several times and Lee was preparing the message he'd leave in his mind when his father picked up. "Hello?" he said, his voice sounding weary and ancient.

"Hi, Dad, it's me. How are you doing?"

"I can't believe your mother would give up on Paul and leave us."

"She's just going for a week or two and she hasn't given up. Or maybe she has, I don't know. But she'll come back."

"You've given up too."

"I haven't. Paul could still come home. But we need to recognize that it's more likely that he won't and that we're not going to find him at the coast. Then if he does come back, think how happy we're going to be." It sounded weak even to Lee. He didn't say anything about the Coyotes. It was irrelevant, just like Tony'd said. Each of the million things that Lee had imagined could have happened to Paul before hearing about the group was still possible. It changed nothing. Except it changed who Paul was, or had been, and so it changed everything.

"It's giving up no matter how rational you or your mom make it sound." Lee's mother was right, he was cruel.

"I'm sorry you feel that way, Dad."

"I'm sorry too."

"Is there anything I can do to help?"

"I don't know. You're not going to search at the coast with me."

That was right. Lee felt physically sick at the idea of wandering in those woods again. "I'd rather not."

"Of course. Maybe I'll come visit you if I can get someone to watch the store. Since your mom didn't think anything of leaving me to run it alone. Maybe that would be best."

"That would be great. Or if you want me to meet you there I could find a way."

"You could drive your brother's car," his dad said bitterly. "I know your mom left it with you."

"If it makes you feel any better I'm not going to drive it. I can't even afford gas and definitely won't be able to afford insurance when Paul's expires."

"That doesn't make me feel any better, Lee. Why would it?"

"Anyway, just tell me when you can come, or if you can't maybe I can take a bus down to Eugene on a day off from work and meet you there."

"Fine."

"I'm so sorry Dad, but everything's going to be ok. Mom'll be back and we'll get through this. We'll both be here for you. And I'm here for you now, whenever you need me, whenever you want to call."

"Well thank you for that at least. I do love you, son, very much."

"And I love you, Dad."

"Goodbye."

Lee dropped the phone onto the mattress next to him then threw himself face forward onto the bed and gave a brief, strangled shout into his pillow. There was just too much pain and he didn't see how it could ever stop.

THIRTY-TWO

"I can't believe this," Bas mumbled as he worked at fitting the new crown, a small flash of gold, onto the stump that remained of Lee's tooth. Lee didn't respond, as he'd been drowsily recollecting the lovely weekend he'd had with Valerie, her explicit plan to take his mind off things. Dinner and a movie with Patrick and Cindy last night, a lovely fun lively laughing date, everyone getting along perfectly. Back to her place, sex before drifting off to sleep in her arms. A delicious breakfast, eggs Florentine, the Hollandaise made from scratch. Watching a movie as rain tapped down outside her windows, making love again on the couch. The vegetable stew she cooked for dinner, him doing the dishes after while she stood behind him kissing his neck playfully. Throughout the appointment he'd kept Valerie's smiling face in his mind.

But when Bas said, "I can't believe they screwed it up again," Lee came out of his daze into the world of the fluorescent lights high overhead, the sound of drills and the vast room full of people dragged out of bed too early to get charged exorbitant sums to be tormented. He wanted to ask Bas what was up but the dental dam was draped across his teeth, drool leaking out onto the bib, and his mouth was numb from the repeated shots of Novocain. He managed an inquisitive grunt.

"Those idiots at the lab screwed up the crown again. I know the impression was right; I did it twice, just to be sure. Well I guess the only thing to do is to try again, though I hate leaving that root canal unfinished for so long. We'll put another temporary in. It's amazing that they keep staying in, actually. You're doing really well with that, Lee. Usually people forget and have some gum or caramel and they pop right out."

Lee tried to grin at the good news. He'd bought more time before he'd have to pay four hundred dollars for a lump of gold to stick in the back of his mouth. He hoped they'd keep messing up, over and over again. The temporary seemed to be just fine. In fact, he'd probably miss running his tongue over it when it was gone.

"They messed up my crown again," Lee said to Valerie, who he'd met at a Thai place near OHSU for lunch. "It's a good thing for me, but really, what kind of shoddy operation are you running here?"

"Crafting an exact crown is tough. It has to be perfect down to the millimeter. Two failures in a row is rare, but it can happen, especially with the student-run lab we use."

"So it's not Bas' fault?"

"Probably not, and it wasn't mine either when I did the initial impression."

"I didn't say it was."

"Yeah, but you were probably thinking it. I know I would have."

He hadn't. "I'm sure you did a great job."

"I'm pretty sure I did. I always try to. I think some of the students treat their patients as test subjects, as guinea pigs to learn on, but I really try my best to understand them. I want to see them as people first, people with real problems, people in pain. Even though I'm just a student I want to help as much as I possibly can."

"So you just saw me as a person you were trying to help?"

"A distractingly attractive person I was trying to help."

"Aw, thanks. Anyway, like I said, it's good news for me."

"You don't want the temporary crown in there forever."

"I don't see why not."

"I could tell you."

"No thanks. I'm sure they'll get it right eventually. Until then, why make me worry about it, right?"

Just then their Tom Kha Gai soup arrived. Nothing sticky or hard, nothing that would rip the temporary crown from his mouth. It was true, he had been careful.

THIRTY-THREE

Lee felt his phone vibrate against his thigh as he rode home from work, rain seeping into the crack between his gloves and the sleeves of his jacket, soaking into his jeans and running down his legs into his socks. It was probably Valerie calling to tell him when he should meet her and her friends with whom she'd gone to get an early dinner while he was at work.

When he got home Lee stripped out of his soggy clothes, leaving them in a pile on the floor and rubbed himself down with a towel. Picking his phone from his jeans pocket he saw that it was his mom who'd called. He hadn't heard from her since he'd taken her to the airport a week and a day ago. He put on some clothes then listened to the message.

"Lee, this is your mom. I need to talk to you so could you please call me back as soon as you get this? I love you." That was it. It didn't seem like it could possibly be good news or she would have said what it was. He briefly considered ignoring it, pretending he didn't get the message until after his date with Valerie, but he couldn't do that.

"Thank you for calling me back so soon," his mom said, having picked up on the first ring. "Lee, this is going to make me sound cruel, but I don't think I have any choice. I can't come back now, or anytime soon."

"What are you talking about? How long? Have you told Dad yet?"

"No. I wanted to talk to you first, make sure you could go out there and be with him, before I called him. My mom had a little fall this morning, nothing serious, but it was a scare and it made me realize that I should take care of them longer. And I'm not sure if I can handle it yet, can handle being there right now."

"You can't do this, Mom. Dad can't take it. You leaving for a week was hard enough."

"You don't understand what it's like, Lee. I've tried to call him every single day since I came here and every time he either hangs up on me or yells at me for abandoning our son, calls me terrible names. There's no way he's going to forgive me for abandoning Paul, for having that stupid thing out at the cape, for not giving up my life to go to the coast over and over again."

Had his dad really said that? Was he really that bad? Probably. But Lee said, "You're all Dad has, he can't handle this without you."

"And you. You can be on his side."

"What are you going to do?"

"I'm going to stay here. Not forever, just until I figure some things out. My parents need me to help take care of them. And I've always missed Georgia, missed the heat, hated the constant cold drizzling rain in Oregon. It will be good for me to be here a while."

"You're leaving Dad because of the rain?"

"No, no, of course not. And I'm not leaving him. I'm just not coming back right now."

"I can't believe this, Mom."

"Maybe with time things can get better but right now it's too hard for me to be there, too hard for your dad and for me. I can't even imagine coming back right now. Let's talk about something else for a while, ok, while this sinks in? How are you doing? How's Valerie?"

"You're leaving my dad and you want to talk about me?"

"I already told you I'm not leaving him. Please, Lee, let's change the subject."

"Fine. Valerie's great. I'm doing fabulous. Everything's peachy. Really, Mom, are you serious about this?"

"I am. And your father, can you go there tonight? I'm going to call him as soon as I get off the phone with you."

"I have a date."

"Then maybe you can go tomorrow. You're off work, right? But I think it would be best if you went tonight."

"Can't you do this some other time? Think about it more, give yourself time to cool off? It's not like you knew exactly when you were going to come back anyway, so why call him now?"

"Every time he looks at me he'll remember Paul and feel betrayed all over again. I have thought about this, I've done nothing but, Lee. I love you both and I don't want to hurt you or him, but this is what I need to do. We all need more time. I'm going to call him a few hours after I hang up. I hope you can go there to help him."

"Christ, Mom."

"I love you, Lee."

"Please..."

"Goodbye." And she hung up.

Lee stood there holding the phone limply down by his side. His mom wasn't coming back. Soon she'd be calling his dad, he would hear the news and yell or break down crying or rush out to the coast or... Lee didn't know, couldn't judge what his father would do. He wished this would all go away, that he could ignore it and go on with what was left of his life, that his mom wasn't doing this.

The answering machine picked up on the first ring. "Valerie. My mom called me to say that she's not coming back right away and she doesn't know when she is. I don't even know if she is. I don't know how my Dad's going to take it either, but I'm going to drive out there to be with him tonight. I'm sorry, I really did want to meet your friends. We'll have to reschedule for sometime soon. Apologize to them for me, ok? Call me back when you get this." He hung up, hoping she'd understand.

Lee whispered a little apology to Paul and got into his car. He wasn't sure it was legal to use Paul's insurance and he didn't have enough money to refill the tank. He pulled off the curb anyway and headed back towards his family's home. Or what used to be.

When he pulled into the driveway Lee saw his father, jacketless in the rain, illuminated starkly by the headlights. He threw something into the cab of the truck and slammed the door. Lee wished his father didn't have to see him in his brother's car but it was too late now. He was looking up, shielding his eyes against the light and walking towards him.

Lee got out of the car. Rain pattered onto his head. "Hi, Dad," he said.

"Did your mother tell you that she was abandoning me along with Paul? Abandoning you, too?"

"She called me. That's why I'm here."

"We'll take your brother's car. It's good that you brought it, it's right. We're going to find him now, I can feel it. I'm sure."

"What are you talking about, Dad?"

"Your brother, we're going to find him. The fact that you're here now in his car means you're not choosing to abandon him like your mother is, though I wasn't sure at first."

"Dad, it's cold and raining, it's ten at night, it'd be crazy to go now. We can go in the morning when there's light if you really want to." He wanted to say that his brother wasn't at the coast, that he was on the run, an eco-terrorist, but he didn't believe that himself any more, if he ever had.

"No. We're going to find him now. We're taking his car. That's why you have it, that's why you're here. And if you're not going with me I'm going alone."

"Dad..." Lee trailed off, having no idea what to say. "Ok. Just put on a jacket, Dad."

"There's one in my bag." Lee's father got a duffel bag out of the truck, threw it into the back of Paul's car then got in the passenger seat. He seemed calm, purposeful and sane. He smiled at Lee, who didn't see any trace of the tears that were in his eyes in his fathers'. But going out to the coast in the pouring rain late on a Saturday night wasn't sane, how his father had been talking wasn't sane. Still, what choice did he have? Lee backed up the car and headed towards the coast.

"Where exactly are we going?" Lee asked after a few minutes of silent driving.

"We're going to park the car where your brother parked it and then we're going to walk to where he walked."

The car would get stuck in the mud. The gully was probably a stream now that the rains had started. It was pouring, it was cold and this was insane. And yet, somehow, his dad's plan seemed right, seemed sensible. As sensible as anything could be in this world where in the past month and a half his brother had disappeared, his mom was maybe leaving his dad, he had run out of money, found out his teeth were ruined and met an amazing girl.

Right when he thought about her Lee's phone buzzed and it was Valerie. He let it ring through to voicemail. He couldn't talk to her now, couldn't possibly explain what they were doing.

They finally came to the familiar road south of Cape Lookout. Lee slowed to a crawl, splashing down into huge puddles, rain pounding on the windshield at the same rate the wipers pushed it away, the headlights illuminating flashes of tangled trees through the streaks of falling water.

"Are we going to be able to find the place in the dark and all this rain?" Lee asked. "It all looks the same to me."

"I'll know when we're there," Lee's dad said in a soft voice.

They hadn't talked much on the ride out here but Lee had kept glancing over at his father and at some point the purpose seemed to have drained from him. Now he was fidgeting and looked miserable.

"This is it," Lee'd dad said and, as Lee pressed down on the brakes, he knew it was. The trees, seemingly indistinguishable from all the others, were the right trees. "But, Lee, wait. I, I don't know what I was doing. This was all so hard and I felt like we had to come out here but now I don't know. It's pouring down rain, it's the middle of the night. Maybe we should just go back home."

"Is that what you want to do, Dad?"

"I'm not sure. I can't believe your brother vanished, that your mom isn't coming back, that it's so easy for her, and maybe for you, to give up hope that we might find him."

"It's not easy, Dad. It's so hard. But maybe it is easier, maybe we're trying to stop the hurt and the questions that keep us up all night and maybe that's the easier way. But it seemed right, it still seems right. And I really don't think it's possible that he could be here and be ok."

"I know. I know he couldn't. But I keep feeling called back to this place, never stronger than tonight. Maybe he is here, his body. Maybe that's what I need to find, just so I can have some peace. Because it would be easier. But I don't want to find his body, I want to find him. And there are so many ways he could still be alive somewhere. So many."

"I know."

"Your mother is probably right. I probably do need to give up, at least on this place. Do you think she'd come back if I stopped coming here?"

"I don't know, Dad." He didn't think anything was going to change his mom's mind easily once she'd made it up, if she'd made it up. "I don't know if that alone would change anything."

"No. I don't either. Your mom is very stubborn, just like me. I don't know what I'm going to do without her, Lee. Without her and without Paul."

"She'll come back soon. I can't believe she won't."

"I probably deserve it if she doesn't. I've been kind of crazy, I've been impossible to live with. I can't control myself, I get so mad, so frustrated that we're not doing anything, that there's nothing we can do. I just wish she would come back. I could be better. It's just been so, so hard."

"I know."

"But she just gives up and you give up and try to forget and go about your lives. But I don't see how to do that, how to forget. So I come here and I search, because it's a way of remembering, a way of not giving up. And because I feel drawn to this place so strongly, like tonight. Don't you feel it, feel anything, here where your brother disappeared?" The passion had returned to his father's voice and his eyes shone again.

"Maybe... Maybe you're right, maybe bringing us out here tonight is exactly the right thing to do." Lee did feel something. It could be his father's returning excitement, or maybe it was just this horrible place, but perhaps there was a reason they were here tonight. So Lee turned Paul's car off the road into the gully up which he'd driven, which now flowed with a burbling muddy stream of water. Lee stopped exactly where Paul had parked this car. They opened the doors and Lee stepped out of the driver's seat, planting his feet where Paul had put his back on that fateful day he'd stepped out of this very car and vanished from their world.

Their jackets didn't help for long. The rain lashed down from above and from the sides, whipped by wind, joined by blowing leaves. They stood where Paul had stood. Lee tried to think. Where would his brother have gone, why would he have parked exactly here? But there were millions of possibilities, ones he'd already thought through a million times. And it hadn't been raining then, it had been a lovely weekend in August. So, so long ago. Lee turned in a circle looking into the trees and the darkness, trying to feel his brother's presence through all that time, to feel which way he would have gone. Then he stared at the car, wondering if it was going to get stuck in the mud on the way out, what they'd do if it did.

"This way," his dad said suddenly, and took off away from the road into the forest. Lee followed. His dad must feel something he didn't.

It was dark but his father had thought to bring a big Maglite that cast a powerful beam of illumination. Lee walked slightly behind him, stepping over puddles and patches that looked especially muddy. His shoes were soon soaked through despite his efforts, his jeans clinging to his legs, rain running down his face like tears. They were headed, Lee thought, towards the ocean, but he wasn't sure, had no idea really where they were or how to get back. But he didn't question his father, just followed, wordlessly trudging after the stabbing beam of brightness as it pushed through the woods.

Eventually time seemed to melt away, and the discomfort. The fact that he was thoroughly soaked didn't bother him and he didn't feel the cold. It felt like he'd always been here walking through this forest, and that it made perfect sense that he was.

Then Lee stopped because his father had. Standing still he heard the crashing of waves, which he realized he'd already been hearing without noticing, somewhere below his conscious mind, like the beating of his heart. The flashlight beam pierced the air before them, illuminating mist and falling rain. Then his father swept it down and Lee saw an end to the land, the cone of light falling down forever and fading away into dark. And there, illuminated by their own phosphorescent glow, the waves crashed. The endless blackness of the sea merged with the formless misty eternity of the sky somewhere out at the invisible horizon.

Was his brother lost in that endless sea? Had he been out hiking like they had, leaving his car, looking for a good place to camp, for a logging truck to blow up, for a way down to the beach, and had he not seen the edge and walked off into the air?

Lee felt himself crying, his tears lost in the world of water around him. And then he heard, yanking him into alertness, a scream of pain, of rage and of loss. He looked over and was startled to find that it was coming from his father whose mouth was opening again for another cry. Totally aware now, of the rain, the cold, the beating of his own heart and the suck of icy air he took into his lungs, Lee screamed too. For his lost brother, for his brother disappearing in this endless, uncertain, cruel way. For his mother, for his father's pain. He screamed and it merged with his father's calls, piercing like the light through the mist and fog and down, down into that endless cold water. Rain fell into his open mouth. He swallowed and it tasted clean, pure. Lee screamed once more as did his father, in unison, in agonized harmony. And then, together, they turned their backs on the sea and started walking inland. He again fell in behind his father and trusted him to take them back to the car. He did so unerringly.

They lay towels from his dad's bag on the seats but didn't try to dry themselves. That was hopeless. Lee wondered at how prepared his dad was, at what else was in the bag he'd brought, but didn't say anything. His father had been out here before who knew how many times, how many nights.

The car purred to life. The wheels spun and chugged at the mud then caught and they lurched forward, bumping down the gully, scraping onto the road.

"Thank you, Dad. I think that really helped."

"Yes. Maybe."

"Have you been doing that, going to that place? The screaming, is that what you've been coming out here for?"

"No. That was the first time. I didn't know I was going there, didn't know the ocean was so close."

"Do you think that was the place?"

"I don't know. No, I don't think so. I don't think I can believe he died in that place, in any place. I think he's somewhere else, still ok somehow. But I don't know. I did feel so powerfully drawn there. Maybe it was."

"I don't know either."

And then his father somehow laughed, bitterly, but it was laughter nonetheless. "Of course not. No one knows anything. You'll stay at the house tonight, right Lee? In your old room?"

"Sure I will, Dad."

"Thank you."

"No, Dad. Thank you." And, soaking in the hot air that was pouring forward onto him, Lee guided his lost brother's car towards home.

THIRTY-FOUR

Lee woke disoriented, wondering why he wasn't in his or Valerie's bed. Then he remembered and realized he'd spent more time in this bed than either of those. Looking at his cellphone he saw that it was late, after ten. He was wearing clean, dry clothes. The wet ones had been peeled off onto the floor of the bathroom before a long, hot shower he'd taken last night.

Down the hall his parents' bed was empty with the sheets pulled tight and the blanket spread neatly over them. There was coffee in the maker in the kitchen, the warmer light on. After pouring himself a cup and spooning in sugar from the brown ceramic jar, Lee went down the stairs to find his father leaning behind the counter of the empty store, his own steaming mug of coffee in his hand.

"Morning, Son."

"Morning."

"You sleep ok?"

"Yeah. Late, obviously. I needed it. How are you doing?"

"Ok I guess. Better. I still can't believe any of this."

"Me neither. I can't believe we didn't get lost in the woods or the car didn't get stuck driving up that stream."

"That too. That too."

Lee came up and gave his dad a hug, remembering the scream that had come out of his frail frame the night before. They held each other for a minute then Lee pulled back.

Lee's father brushed at a tear then said, "Actually, I'm glad you're up. I have a few errands to run and I was wondering, since you're out here, if you'd mind watching the store for a little while?"

"No, that's fine."

"I'll pay you for your time, of course."

"You don't have to do that."

"I want to. You remember how to run things? Not much has changed."

"I sure do."

"Well, then. Good." His father patted him on the back. "Good."

Once his father had left Lee walked around the store inspecting everything. It seemed almost entirely the same: toilet paper, cereal, a little section of fresh produce, a refrigerator case with cheese, deli meats, soda and beer. Rope, cat litter, stationary. Hundreds of items, everything simple you might need, all lit by the strong morning light pouring through large windows, catching lazily drifting dust in mid-flight.

He'd helped out here throughout his childhood, putting away shipments, calling people to let them know their orders had come in, manning the counter when he'd been old enough. As a kid his favorite part was stamping things with the price gun, making blam blam noises every time he marked a box of Kleenex at $1.49. They'd gotten a second price gun for Christmas one year so he and Paul could have productive battles.

Tony had horsed around with them in the store sometimes. He lived in the town, he was a mile away. But talking to Tony again would accomplish nothing other than getting Lee worked up. And he needed to breathe now, to remember the release of the scream last night, anticipate seeing Valerie soon and try not to think about Paul or any of that Coyote shit.

The door opened and Lee walked back behind the counter. It was made of aged, scarred wood and was shorter than the polished black plastic one he was so used to standing behind at the liquor store. Mr. Waithers glanced up at him, down to the list in his hand, then back up to Lee, a surprised smile on his face. "Well, if it isn't Lee Garrett! It's good of you being here, helping out your mom and dad." His wide shiny face grew more sober then and he said, "I'm so sorry about your brother."

"Thank you, Mr. Waithers." He was probably in his sixties, a short roundish man sporting a gleaming bald head with a purple splotch like Gorbachev's, Paul used to say, though Lee only barely remembered seeing Gorbachev on TV. Mostly he knew his image from a picture in a history book. Mr. Waithers grew hops, though his son and two daughters, several years older than Lee but still sort-of friends, did most of the work on the place now.

When Mr. Waithers came back with a box of Apple Jacks, a half gallon of milk, a packet of salami, a jar of mayonnaise and a bottle of Advil he said, "It really is good of you to help out, Lee. It was hard when the store was closed, hard for everyone here imagining what your parents and you were going through. And of course we all knew Paul. He was such a good kid, was doing so well for himself. It's a real tragedy what happened."

Lee lowered his head and nodded. Mr. Waithers patted him on the shoulder then left without another word.

Lee's father returned a few hours later and hauled in boxes of produce from some surrounding farms, rolls of cash register tape and a few other things he'd picked up in Eugene. "Get much business?" he asked.

"Four customers, about a hundred dollars," Lee said. "Mrs. Petterson bought a lot."

"She always does. That's not too bad, especially since we've been closed some Sundays, making it hard for people to know when we're going to be around. No one wants to waste the gas on a trip into town to find out there's no one here."

"That's true, Dad."

"Lee, you wouldn't want to work here in the store more would you? If, if your mother really is gone for a while, I'd need the help. Just a day or two a week since I know you're busy with your other job, with your life. Whatever you can do."

"Of course I will, as much as I can. It'll be good to spend more time with you."

"I'll pay you well. One and a half times what you make at the liquor store, how 'bout?"

"You don't have to do that. You can just pay me whatever you pay any of the other kids you get to cover for you."

"Won't hear of it. You're an expert in the field."

"I guess so."

"Thank you, Lee," his dad said, holding out his hand. Lee shook it, hard. "Now, Mr. Expert, would you rather man the register or put all this stuff away?"

After a microwaved dinner of frozen chicken, potatoes and peas, each separate in their little plastic compartments, Lee's dad handed him a small stack of twenties. Doing the calculations Lee saw that he'd been paid for eight hours of work at $15 dollars an hour without anything taken out for taxes, of course. He'd only worked maybe six hours and one and a half times what he made at the liquor store was $13.50. He didn't argue for now since it would help with the crown which was supposed to come back from the lab again soon and with all the fillings he was getting in the meanwhile, but he vowed that next time he'd make sure his father didn't overpay him.

After packing up the few things he'd brought with him he gave his dad a long hug at the door and asked him to call if he needed anything or needed to talk, promising he'd be back soon. Lee waved good-bye and got into Paul's car. At some point on the way back or soon after he'd have to get gas, eating into his new money. As he pulled out he looked back and saw his dad standing in the doorway. They waved. Lee couldn't believe how alone his father looked, how small. But he'd seemed better today, more in control too, so Lee hit the gas and pulled away. He knew he'd be back soon.

THIRTY-FIVE

Valerie looked lovely in the dress he'd seen her in at the Dragon Pig show, the grayish yellow one with its simple lines that somehow brought out the greens in her eyes. Lee, coming out of his house to greet her, felt a little under-dressed as he often did, though he was in one of the two button down shirts he had, each of which Valerie must have seen at least twice by this point. He needed to go to Goodwill.

He kissed her outside her car and said, "Long time no see,"

"Yeah," she said. It had been a while, almost a week. All of his days recently had been spent working with his dad or at the liquor store and she'd been busy too. The continued absence from her was hard but, two weeks after their scream, his dad was still fragile and truly needed him. His mom's continued silence was hard too, but Lee couldn't gather the courage to call her to find out what she'd decided. He and his dad didn't talk about her. It was as if she'd also vanished.

"I hope you don't mind spending part of our first night together in a week with my friends," Lee said.

"We could call and cancel if you wanted to do something else, though Patrick was pretty insistent."

"No, I like your friends. It'll be fun."

He kissed her again on the cheek. "You look gorgeous," he said.

"Thanks." She didn't say anything about how he looked. Glancing down at the tiny wrinkles that covered his shirt he wished he owned an iron.

They spotted Patrick and Cindy standing in the crowd outside Saburo's, the tiny shoebox of a sushi restaurant that was Cindy's favorite place to eat in Portland. There was always a huge line here on Friday and Saturday nights but that never stopped Cindy and Patrick, who thought of the crazy wait as a positive part of the experience somehow. At least they'd offered to show up early to put their names on the list. When she saw them Cindy's mouth burst upward into a huge grin and she threw her arms around first Lee then Valerie. "We're getting married!" she squealed.

"I know," Lee said, laughing. "You've been engaged for over a year." He knew that wasn't what she'd meant.

"No, silly, we set a date. A really really soon date! December 18th."

"Congratulations!" Lee said.

"That is really soon," Valerie added. "Where are you going to have it?"

"At the little church back in your guys' home town," Cindy said. "It's so cute."

Patrick put in, "We spent all this time planning some huge thing and worrying about the thousands of details and thinking about how expensive it was going to be and so we kept pushing it back and back but then we decided, screw this, we're just going to do it. It'll bring all our families together for Christmas instead of having to decide who to visit and it's going to be really small, easy and great."

"And it's finally going to happen," Cindy added.

"That's awesome," Lee said.

"Plus, in the middle of the winter it'll make our honeymoon to the Caribbean even nicer, leaving you guys behind in the freezing rain," Cindy said with a laugh.

"Well I'm certainly jealous," Valerie said.

"And you two are some of the first we're telling other than our families," Patrick said. "So, consider yourselves invited."

Just then the hostess, a wrinkled tiny adorable Japanese lady, yelled "Cindy," off the clipboard in her hands. They went in and were shown to a table towards the back of the small, crowded and very noisy restaurant.

"What are you two drinking?" Valerie asked. "We have to celebrate. And we're buying, of course."

They ordered two expensive bottles of sake for the table though Lee knew that neither Valerie nor he liked it much. Ah well, they weren't the ones getting married.

After the last hugs of congratulations and promises that they'd spend more time together soon, Lee and Valerie walked away from his friends towards their car, rain drizzling down on a black umbrella Valerie had thrust into the sky.

"I can't believe you guys ate that raw fish. That's disgusting," she said with a laugh.

"I mostly ate the cucumber rolls and veggie tempura with you," he said.

"Yeah, but I saw you put that eel or whatever it was into your mouth, and those California rolls. I don't know if I can kiss you after that."

"Aw, come on, one fishy kiss," he said, puckering his lips.

"I said no," she replied, pushing him playfully.

They reached her car and slipped inside. "Hey, Valerie?" he asked.

"What?"

"Would you mind going back to my place so I can take my car, my brother's car, to my Dad's place tomorrow morning? Or we could pick up the car and go to your house tonight, if you want."

"You're going out to your Dad's again? Haven't you been out there two times already this week?"

"He needs me, Valerie. And besides, I need the money for my damned teeth."

"It just feels like I don't have a boyfriend these past few weeks. You're always there and when you're not we're only getting a few hours together and then one of us has to slip away to work in the morning. It seems like a month since I've spent a whole day with you and I've only been going out with you for a month and a half."

"I'm sorry. I've been busy. You have, too." He felt guilty.

"I know. It just sucks is all. And now you're going to leave me again early in the morning, or I'm going to have to sleep on your mattress on the floor with your housemates overhearing us having sex and then get up early myself when you leave."

"You can come with me if you want."

"No, I don't want to go work at your father's store on my day off. Your father seems like a nice man but he's so sad. I love that you're trying to help him, but... But I don't know. I'm being selfish. And your friends are getting married and assuming we'll come together to their wedding like a perfect couple in two months when we haven't even been going out for two months."

"Valerie, please..."

"I know how hard things are for you. You lost your goddamned brother, your parents are maybe breaking up, you have all these money problems. I just don't know if, with all that, you have time for a relationship, if I'm being greedy trying to get you for myself when you have so many other things to work through."

Lee felt panic rising in his chest. "No! No, you're not being greedy, I am. You're what's allowing me to handle everything else without going insane! You've helped me so much. Valerie, please. I'm sorry. Let's go away next weekend. I'll get the time off work, my Dad will be ok without me for one Sunday. If you can take Monday off we can go for three days. Ok? Just you and me?"

"You can't afford to take time off work and you need to help your dad. We don't need to do that. I'm sorry."

"No. We're going to go. You're right, I have been neglecting you, but we're going to make this work. Ok, Valerie?"

"Ok. That's a good idea, Lee. Thanks." He leaned over to kiss her and she didn't complain about his fishy breath this time.

Lee and his dad were eating a quiet dinner on the couch, the TV droning softly in front of them, when the phone rang shrilly. Lee picked it up, expecting to answer a question like whether they had asparagus, but at the first syllable he recognized his mom's voice. "Hello, Lee," she said. "I'm so glad you're there with your father."

He hadn't spoken to her since that conversation more than two weeks ago when she'd announced that she didn't know when she was returning. What could he possibly say to her? "Hi, Mom," he said.

"Is he there?" she asked.

"Yes," Lee said. He saw that his dad was staring at him, a scared, hungry look on his face. He must have heard Lee say "Mom." "Do you want to talk to him?" Lee asked.

"I want to talk to you first," she said.

"What do you want to talk about?"

"How is he, is he any better?"

"He's right here. He's listening to us."

"Oh. Then I guess give him the phone, Lee."

"Do you know when you're coming back?"

"Not yet."

Trying to keep his expression neutral, Lee held the receiver out towards his dad. "It's Mom," he said, unnecessarily. "Do you want me to go upstairs?"

"No, you can stay. Anything she says involves you, too." His father took the phone from him, but stared at it a few seconds before saying anything.

His dad, Lee thought, had mostly been handling things well, had been more or less cheerful when Lee had been around helping in the store, not talking about anything but business and Lee's life. But his eyes were always shadowed and Lee noticed his hands trembling and his gaze far away from time to time. Still, Lee thought, he was better.

"Hello," his dad said quietly into the white phone, sounding tired, wrapping the spiraled cord around his wrist.

Lee couldn't hear what his mom was saying, then his dad replied, "I really wish you'd come back. I'm sorry I was acting so crazy. I can be better." Another pause and then, "Lee and I went to the coast together, to where Paul had been, and we screamed into the night. It made things better, I think. It was a great release and I wish you had been there too, had healed with us."

Had he healed, were they healing? Maybe, maybe a little, though everything still seemed so chaotic and painful. So raw. Lee slipped towards his room. He didn't want to eavesdrop. But from there he didn't hear any yelling or raised voices. And that was a very good sign.

THIRTY-SIX

Lee was scooting out from behind the liquor store counter to lock the door and close for the night when Joseph burst through with his new coat, already almost as dirty and frayed as the previous one, flapping around him.

"Hi, Joseph," Lee said. "We're just about closed so could you make it quick?"

"I'm not here to buy anything, Lee. I finally have news about your brother!"

Lee's heart leapt. "What do you mean?" he asked. There was a grin on Joseph's face. Lee tried to tell himself that there was no way this guy could have found something that all the rangers and police had missed, but he felt a wild hope rushing through him. He tried to squash it down.

Joseph put his hands on the counter and leaned in close towards Lee. "My friend Eddie met this lady on the Greyhound going north from here who said she saw someone who looked just like you said your brother looked, but with a beard, in the redwoods in California! And he had the big orange backpack, so it must be him! It was towards the end of August or maybe the beginning of September."

That was nothing, Lee told himself, a third-hand account of a sighting of someone who could be anyone. But in his mind he had a clear image of Paul with a scraggly new beard walking well off the road in the redwood forest, lost amongst the immense trees, disappearing into a thickening fog.

"Do you know anything else?" Lee asked. "Can I talk to this lady?"

"I don't know. I heard from Eddie who just got back into town and ran to find you. But you can ask Eddie. Come on, we'll go get him. Isn't this exciting?" Joseph asked.

Lee saw his brother turn back then, in the mental image of him in the redwoods, turn back, smile and gesture for him to follow. Exciting wasn't the right word. Lee felt hope, exhilaration, but also fear and dread, like he was teetering on the edge of a large cliff with an endless fall below.

They found Eddie right where Joseph had said they would, sitting on a bench in Waterfront Park, the strip of green grass and trees now turned brilliant oranges and reds that ran along the Willamette River. He was a thin dark-skinned man, maybe forty or fifty with a lined and cracked angular face, bundled in several jackets and sweaters. Next to his bench was a shopping cart filled with blankets, bottles and cans. There was the faint smell of old beer around him, presumably from the cart. He gazed with a fixed stare over the slow moving river toward the east side of the city, an industrial zone by the water with trees and houses beyond. Mount Hood's jagged pyramid could be seen towering over it all on clear days, but now the sky was smothered in gray.

Eddie's eyes didn't move until they stood in front of him and Joseph said, "Eddie, this is Lee. Lee, Eddie." Lee leaned over, offering his hand. Eddie shook it jerkily.

"Eddie, tell him about his brother."

"Weeell," Eddie said, "I was on my way to see my mother in Tacoma. She hasn't been doing good, you see. Joseph here helped a lot with the bus fare." His voice was scratchy, drawling. Joseph nodded and Eddie continued. "So, Joseph's been asking forever about your brother that disappeared and said to me to ask too, as part of the payment for helpin' me out."

"Really?" Lee asked Joseph, amazed. "That's so great of you."

"I said I'd try to find him, didn't I?"

"He asks everyone about it," Eddie said.

Lee reached over and patted Joseph's arm, not knowing what to say or how to thank him.

"So anyways, I get to talking to the lady next to me, this pretty lady, maybe thirty, name's Patty. She said she'd been staying in Eureka for a while and that she's been moving north for the winter, aiming for Alaska by the summer but takin' her time, takin' most of a year, I guess. Anyway. Especially since she'd been by the coast, even if not the right part, I asked if she'd ever seen any tall skinny kid with black hair, blue eyes, big ears and a big orange backpack named Paul Garrett. She said maybe, that she'd been hiking in the redwoods one day and across a valley she said she saw a tall good lookin' kid with a giant orange backpack, but with a scruffy beard. She wouldn't have remembered it, she said, but the kid, when he saw her, scurried off behind some trees and vanished. Like he was hiding from her, or from someone."

"And?" Lee asked. "Did she chase after him, did she see him again?"

"No, man," Eddie answered. "She finished her hike and never really thought about it, I guess, until I asked her. But she thought it could definitely be him."

"When was this?"

"She wasn't exactly sure, see. She was in Eureka from about the middle of August to the middle of September but she thinks it was probably right about the beginning of September. And it was on a trail near some town called Orick, she said, but didn't know which trail, she'd been doing a lot of hiking. She wasn't really too clear on any of the details. It seemed like maybe she'd done some serious drugs at some point and didn't have it entirely together," Eddie said.

"Why didn't you tell me that in the first place? What do you mean?"

"I don't know, she was just, kind of, you know, spacey. I mean, who goes north for the winter, right, man? It's weird."

"Fine. Anyway, do you know how to get in touch with her? I need to ask her some more questions."

"Sorry, she didn't really say where she was going. I don't think she knew, actually. She mentioned Seattle and Olympia. And I never really caught her last name either. I didn't think it was important since it was here in Oregon your brother was supposed to be lost and since there could be tons of kids with orange

backpacks out in the woods, but Joseph got all excited, saying he was sure it was the right guy."

"Could you describe her, at least?" Lee asked.

"Sure. She was maybe my height, a little less,
five-five or five-six, had long hay-colored hair, a little
nose and a great big smile with a few crooked teeth.
Yellowy greeny eyes, I think. Wearing a yellow dress
when I saw her, kind of a hippie thing, and sandals.
With a giant purse with purple flowers on it. Not really dressed to be going north, if you ask me, though
it was kind of a nice day at the time. This was two
and a half weeks ago, about. I've been back for a couple days but just ran into Joseph here."

It was Paul, Lee knew, even as another part of
him tried to tell himself that the story was too unreli-
able, a drugged hippie telling a homeless man about
someone seen across a valley in the woods. It could
have been anyone, anything, and either of them could
have made up the story completely. But in his mind
he could clearly see Paul in the redwoods.

"I don't have much money, but is there anything
I can do to repay you? Either of you?" Lee asked.

"They're taking all his money to work on his bad
teeth," Joseph explained. Then he said, "You don't
have to give anything to me. I'm just helping out a
friend."

"Me too," Eddie said. "Just helping out my friend
who helped me out." He nodded at Joseph.

Lee pulled out his wallet anyway. There were
only sixteen dollars in there, which would be almost
insulting to offer. "Maybe my dad could give you a
reward," he said. Though his dad still hadn't paid him
for his last week's work.

"How about this?" Eddie said. "If you find your brother then you can give me something. Right now all I did was ask a few questions. It could lead nowhere, right?"

"Ok," Lee said. "But will you take this anyway, for now?" He offered fifteen dollars to Eddie.

"I guess I won't say no," he said, and took the bills. "Thank you."

"No, thank you. Thank you so much. Both of you."

Eddie's story was all Lee could think about as he walked over to the MAX and rode it through fareless square to where he'd parked across the river then got in his brother's car and headed towards his dad's. He didn't see anything around him, running on autopilot, the same thoughts churning endlessly through his head, his heart beating fast, his palms sweaty. Could it have really been his brother that the lady had seen? The timing was right, more or less. Paul had grown a beard, he was off the trail, he didn't want to be seen. He was south of where his car had been abandoned by maybe eight hours driving, by days or weeks of walking. It probably wasn't him, it was probably just some other hiker with an orange backpack who had just kept on his trail as it turned, not run away. Almost certainly it was. But what if it were Paul? What would that mean?

It would mean Paul hadn't fallen into the ocean or been murdered or kidnapped or lost his memory. It meant that he wanted to disappear, to vanish into the wilderness. That he had done something with the Coyotes whether Tony knew it or not and was a fugitive, on the run. That's what really made Lee believe: the Coyotes. That group gave Paul a reason to be there, to be running away. Or maybe he was planning something, had yet to commit the act? Maybe he wanted to be underground, disappeared, so he could strike in secret.

A car honked and Lee realized he was still stopped at a light downtown that had turned green. He didn't even know why he was downtown, headed, more or less, for Valerie's place. He should be on the highway. He waved an apology and aimed himself again for his father's.

Maybe it wasn't eco-terrorism. Maybe Paul had never gotten over Jenny, maybe she'd broken him when she'd stopped seeing him secretly and started dating that new guy. Maybe he owed someone shady, someone dangerous, a lot of money. Or had a gambling problem Lee didn't know about, or drugs, or made a bad investment. Maybe he'd been cheating on someone's wife and they threatened to kill him. Maybe he'd overdosed on acid or gone insane.

Or maybe he'd just grown tired of life and its problems and letdowns, of traffic and internet popups and commercials and concrete and waiting at traffic lights and the war in Iraq and oil changes and credit card bills and bad dates. Of the strip malls and giant churches that Lee was passing now as he cruised south on I-5. Paul had always been happiest in the wilderness, hiking with no sign of civilization around on high mountains or in dense old-growth forests, rushing down rivers, holding out his hands to warm them by a fire on the beach. He'd talked about hiking the Pacific Crest Trail down the entire west coast, long backpacking trips in Central America or walking across Spain, if he just had the time and the money. Maybe he couldn't wait anymore, maybe he couldn't take it any more. Maybe it was a combination of some or all of those things.

Lee hadn't believed that his brother would leave without telling him, without telling his family, would just leave everything behind. But what if that was what you needed to do to get away from everything, if any remaining ties would draw you back, would make you weak, would cause you to fail? Could his brother hide his car on the coast and start walking? To blow up logging trucks or just to escape? Could Lee? If Valerie left him, if his mom never came back, if his teeth sucked away all his money and he couldn't afford to paint, if all those things and everything else added up? Maybe. Maybe he could believe his brother had done it.

If he had chosen to disappear should Lee leave him alone? Should he give up his search and live with the image of his brother waving back at him from within the redwoods? But he knew he couldn't do that. He had to know, to see. He'd keep his brother's secret, wouldn't let the world in on it, wouldn't let the police know if he'd done something. He would let Paul complete his escape. But Lee needed to know for himself.

Should he go up to Seattle or Olympia and try to find the lady who'd maybe seen Paul? Seattle was where he and Valerie had been talking about going this coming weekend, there or Crater Lake, though they hadn't made any final plans yet. But even if by some miracle he could find her, that lady wouldn't know much more, if she knew anything at all. No, he needed to go to the redwoods, follow Paul there to look for a trace, a story, a fragment or a clue. He clenched his hands on the steering wheel in determination.

If he told his dad they'd turn the car south and drive to California through the night. But could Lee do that to his father, who seemed calmer now, more accepting? He couldn't. He couldn't ruin the tenuous equilibrium his dad was reaching, plunge him back into doubt, despair and frantic, obsessive searches. Couldn't make his dad feel the empty rushing inside he himself felt now, this void opening up.

Lee's dad came out of the house to greet him as Lee pulled up and Lee remembered finding him here out in the rain the night they'd gone to the coast and screamed. Lee had thought that'd been powerful in putting this behind him, in mourning, in closing over the wound. And now the scab was ripped off. He'd been wrong, his mother had been wrong. His dad had been right, his brother was goddamned alive! Alive. He hadn't died at the coast, he was an eco-terrorist on the run. Maybe.

Lee got out of the car and gave his dad a hard, fierce hug. "What's wrong?" his dad asked him.

God, he felt a surging need to tell, to get an ally again in this new chapter of the endless search. But he didn't know anything, didn't want to open his father's healing wounds. Until he knew, if he could ever know. So he said, "Nothing's wrong. Valerie and I got into a little fight, but we patched it up and we're going away together this weekend. So I'm not going to be able to help out on Sunday. You'll be ok without me, right?"

"Of course. I appreciate your being here, I don't know what I'd do without you, but one day off is fine. You're here now and you'll be here the week after, right? Where are you going?"

"We haven't decided yet. We talked about Seattle or Vancouver, or maybe Crater Lake if the weather's going to be good, but I was just thinking on the drive up here that maybe we could go down to Northern California to see the redwoods."

"It's beautiful down there. Do you remember the trip we took? You were really young."

"I, I think so." Lee hadn't even stopped to consider why he had such a clear picture of the redwoods in his mind to place his brother in. He guessed he'd just assumed they'd taken a camping trip there together some summer. But that wasn't it, the images were much older, murkier. And now he placed Paul, much younger, ahead of him on a narrow dirt trail, gesturing Lee onward as he took toddling awkward steps after his older brother who seemed so tall and important, who seemed to glow in a stray beam of sunlight that caused his hair to gleam like obsidian. He was everything Lee wanted to be. And then Lee was scooped up into his mother's or father's arms and tilted back to see the huge reddish trees rising straight and proud, jutting forever upward into a green and golden sky.

"It was a wonderful trip. We spent a week car camping, taking hikes and driving among those giant trees, going to the coast, to Eureka, winding up and down that gorgeous twisty road along the ocean.

You, your brother, your mom and I, all so happy..." Lee saw that there were tears in his father's eyes and hugged him again. "It's ok, I'm fine," his dad said.

Lee wished he were, too.

"Tony, did Paul or the Coyotes ever talk about the redwoods in Northern California or a town called Orick?" When he'd left his dad's store Lee'd tracked Tony down in the town's only bar, practically dragging him away from his friends to talk in a booth in an empty corner.

"Why?" Tony asked, his voice low, looking around to see if anyone could hear them. "I told you, that stuff doesn't have anything to do with anything, it doesn't lead anywhere."

"Just tell me if you ever talked about the redwoods!"

"The redwoods? Fuck, sure, I guess we talked about how utterly tragic it was that they were still being logged, those huge ancient beautiful trees, and how that fucked up the habitat for the salmon in California, but we talked about a lot of things, a lot of places. There's no end to the environmental disasters in the world. But, Lee, why are you asking? Did you hear anything about Paul?"

It was clear from his face that Tony didn't know anything more. He hadn't been hiding anything and he didn't need to know about this, Lee decided. "It's nothing important; he'd just called someone there before he disappeared and I wondered if it meant anything. Probably it doesn't. I'm sorry to bother you," Lee said hurriedly. But Paul had talked about the redwoods and the salmon. He had a reason to be there. He was there, planning something, ready to act or on the run. And Lee would follow and find him.

"Are you sure it's nothing?" Tony asked. "What if Paul..."

"Don't worry about it," Lee said. "Thanks for your time. I'll let you get back to your friends." And then he was gone.

THIRTY-SEVEN

Lee breathed in deeply to steady himself then asked, "Hey, have you ever been to the giant redwoods in Northern California?" He lay next to Valerie in bed, her head resting on his shoulder, her hair tickling his mouth. He'd decided that he couldn't tell her why he wanted to go there, couldn't risk her thinking it was crazy or obsessive and saying no.

"No. Why?"

"I was thinking we could go there for our long weekend. I went when I was a kid and it was amazing. And California's probably sunnier than Washington or Oregon this time of year."

"Well, we did say we needed to go camping sometime, right?" she asked, sitting up. "And it would be silly coming to this part of the world and never seeing the redwoods. Yeah, I like that idea. I'm so glad I have you to show me all the beautiful spots around the northwest, Lee." She reached over, took his head in her hands and kissed him.

Not telling her tasted like bile in his mouth. But what if she thought he was insane for wanting to go search there, what if she said no, that it didn't make sense, that she didn't want to ruin her vacation on a far-fetched story? He'd agonized over this constantly, vacillating back and forth. He could tell her when they got there if he needed to, if there was anything to do there other than hike around and hope.

There was a knock at Lee's door. He dropped his paintbrush into the cup, green spreading from it in eddies throughout the clear water, diffusing, dying it a uniform green in a matter of seconds. "Come in," he said, hoping it was Elly.

It was. She walked in with a smile. "How ya' doing?" she asked.

"Ok, I guess," he lied. "How are you? I haven't seen you in forever."

"Yeah, work's been crazy, I've practically been living in Gresham: Mrs. Tanner and this grumpy old guy. But the pay's good."

"Thank Mrs. Tanner again for me. Her watercolors are really helping. Tell her I'll come see her sometime soon when I have a few pieces I'm really proud of to show her."

"I will, she'll enjoy that. Anyway, you and Valerie have plans for Halloween weekend? I know of like five parties happening within twenty blocks of here, it's crazy."

"Oh, shit, I'd kinda forgotten Halloween's coming up. Valerie and I are going down to Northern California this weekend to see the redwoods." He'd looked up Orick, and it was right on the edge of the Redwood National and State Parks, tons of green space on the map around it, miles and miles.

"That'll be great, I've always wanted to go down there. You can tell me whether it's worth the trip. Though it would be much better to have a girlfriend to go with. You were supposed to hook me up with some hot friend of Valerie's, remember?"

"Still working on that. I haven't even really met her friends yet. I keep having to cancel."

"Well find one for me, man. I'm getting desperate. It's been weeks since Steph and I finally ended our thing." She laughed. "But, yeah, going on a road trip's way better than some stupid parties. Halloween night's Monday, anyway. You going to be back by then, do you think?"

"We should get back into town that night."

"Well, see, it'll work out. We'll give candy to kids or egg houses or something."

"Sounds like a plan."

"What're you working on?" she asked, gesturing at the canvas spread out on newspapers. Watercolor redwoods made up the background, a blank white space where his brother would go filled the middle. "Those trees are looking great."

"Nothing," he said. Then, in a rush, "Fuck, no, it's not nothing, it's Paul walking into the redwoods, or it's going to be. But you can't tell this to anyone, it's a secret. Ok?"

She nodded, her eyes wide, and he spurted out the tale of Joseph and Eddie and Patty and the man in the woods with the orange backpack. In his rush he told her about the Coyotes too and worried for a second about breaking his promise, but it was too late and Elly would never tell anyone anyway. It felt so good to tell it, all of it; it had been so hard to keep the excitement and agony and questions inside with his father and with Valerie.

"Wow," Elly said when he was done. "I have no idea if that was him, but you've got to go check it out, don't you? Just to see the spot? But you should have told Valerie, man. I understand not telling your dad, he's really fragile, but you should have told your girlfriend everything."

"I know. I just needed to go see, couldn't stand it if she said no. I'll tell her when we get there and I'll apologize. She'll understand, She needs to, right?"

"I think so. She knows how hard losing your brother is on you. You really do have to tell her, though, and sooner rather than later."

"I will," Lee said. "Anyway, thanks for listening to all my problems. Thanks for everything you've done these past few months."

"No problem. I can't believe that shit. Do you really think your brother could have just decided to leave like that and vanished without telling anyone? Be out in the redwoods right now, plotting to blow up a logging operation?"

"I don't know. That's why I have to go there. To find out."

"Well," she said, leaning in to give him a hug. "Good luck."

"Will you stay, keep me company while I paint?"

"Of course, buddy. Of course."

Lee went back to his canvas, putting down his memory of Paul in the redwoods, but not Paul as a kid, Paul as man, Paul now with a beard. Something didn't seem quite right about it, but he couldn't figure out what. He kept working, determined.

THIRTY-EIGHT

Valerie opened her door. Behind her camping stuff was spread haphazardly on the floor and on the couch. After a kiss, she said, "I wasn't sure if we were going to be camping since there was a chance of rain in the forecast and then I didn't know what I should bring..."

"It's fine, there's no hurry," he said even though there was. It was already dark out and he wanted to get pretty far south before they stopped for the night. "Let's just pack your camping stuff in case the weather's good, we don't have to use it, and then we can head out."

"It's nice having you pick me up for a change."

"No problem." He'd never mentioned to her that he didn't have his own insurance. They could have taken her car but it felt more right to look for Paul in his. "Anyway, let's get you packed up. It's not like the redwoods will wait forever."

"They won't?"

"Ok, fine, they will, or close enough to it. But we only have three and a half days and it's a long drive."

"I think this'll be great, just you and me and some big trees. I'm excited."

"Yeah, me too." He still hadn't told her.

They passed the turnoff for his hometown about nine o'clock and Lee didn't say anything. They'd have a free place to stay there without driving all night but the point was that he was spending too much time with his father and not enough with Valerie. So far the drive down flat wide I-5, which he'd done so many times the past few weeks, had been nice. It had been good to be driving while Valerie fiddled with her iPod to play the Shins and Bob Dylan through his brother's car's CD player. She'd been resting her hand on his thigh and chatting softly about how good it was to be with him, what they'd do that weekend, how her classes had been going and the music, about nothing much at all. He kept turning and seeing her gentle face lit by the slow strobe of passing street-lights. It made him glow with contentment until he remembered that he was lying to her about the reason they were going to the redwoods. He just didn't think she would have gone, wouldn't have thought it was healthy or reasonable. And it's not like there was anything he could do once he was there. There probably wouldn't be any trace of Paul left. Mounting a search or asking questions wouldn't accomplish anything. If his brother wanted to be gone, he'd be gone. He could be in Mexico by now. Lee just wanted to see the place, that was all, he told himself. And maybe when the time was right he'd tell Valerie. Tell her that he just needed to look, just needed to be there. With her, holding her hand.

"When do you want to stop?" she asked.

"Roseburg is a bit past halfway. That's where I was originally thinking, though it's a little later than I was planning."

"Sorry."

"No problem. Anyway, I'm not tired and this is easy driving as long as you're ok."

"I'm great. And I can take over any time you want me to."

"I'll let you know."

"Hey, did you know we're going to be coming back on Halloween? It's on Monday. I hadn't realized, somehow, until earlier today."

"Yeah, Elly told me. There were a bunch of parties this weekend, but this will be better, right?"

"Of course. And maybe we can do something on Monday night when we get back into town. Though I don't have a costume."

"Me neither. Maybe we can come up with something on our trip."

"In the redwoods? What are we going to be, sticks?"

"You're right, it's dumb."

"Maybe we'll pass a store or something. And you'd make a great stick, a skinny guy like you." She leaned over and kissed him on his cheek. A truck rumbled past going in the other direction, then another, their headlights briefly illuminating the interior of the car then leaving it seemingly darker then before. They continued to drive south, the direction his brother had taken, maybe, when he'd escaped from his life.

"This is nice," Lee said, stretching out on the crisp sheets of the queen-sized bed in their clean, generic, small motel room. "Come here, sugar momma." She'd paid, she was paying for everything. Joking about it made it a little better.

Smiling, Valerie came over from where she was going through her suitcase, jumped onto the bed, bounced once then flopped down beside him. "Yeah, this place isn't so bad, is it?" she asked. They'd driven around Roseburg at ten thirty at night, stopping at the first neon vacancy sign that had glowed out of the quiet darkness.

"Not at all."

"And it's nice being away together, no obligations, no one but you," she said, kissing him. "Now let's mess up this neatly made bed."

"Let's," he said, kissing her back. And he wished she did have him to herself. But in his head Paul vanished into the redwoods just a few hours south and west of here. He wished he could tell her. Maybe he would, but not now. Now, he needed to concentrate on this gorgeous girl undressing in front of him, this girl that had kept him sane through all of this. He pulled her to him and, for a while, forgot about his brother.

"Ooh, House of Mystery at the Oregon Vortex!" Valerie said, pointing to a sign on the side of the highway. "Sixty miles!"

"I think that's past where we turn off towards the coast," Lee said.

"Aww, really? It sounds like fun."

"It does?"

"Sure. I love cheesy roadside attractions."

"I don't think I've ever been to one."

"Seriously?"

"Seriously. My parents would never stop at that stuff, neither would my brother and I."

"Well then we definitely have to go. I've never been to a mysterious vortex before. Mystery spot, yes, vortex no."

"You can check the map and if it's not too far out of the way we can stop. I guess we're not in much of a hurry, we'll have all tomorrow to hike around in the redwoods and whatever."

"Aw, thanks, honey," she said, her voice dripping with friendly mockery.

It looked like it was going to be a half hour out of their way, past Grant's Pass towards which they were rising now, the views out the windows of sweeping hills covered with trees and granite peaks in the distance, patches of snow scattered here and there. "Why not?" Lee said, so he kept on I-5, ignoring the sign that pointed to where his brother had been. He could wait, he told himself. He'd get there soon enough.

THIRTY-NINE

A rustic sign, slats of worn dark wood painted with orange writing, announced that they had arrived: "OREGON VORTEX, LOCATION OF THE HOUSE OF MYSTERY."

"Nice," Valerie said, and he agreed.

They parked in a dirt lot and walked back towards the little wooden structures at the entrance. A smiling girl who looked about eighteen, with pigtails from which wisps of blond hair struggled to escape, took Valerie's money. "It's a quiet day," she said, "so you two will get a personalized tour. You got great weather for it too, for the end of October." She pointed up. The sky was dotted here and there with clouds, but some sunlight filtered down, splashing between the golden, red and orange leaves that hung on the trees and lay rotting in piles on the ground. Lee saw on the sign that the place closed for the winter in two days, on the 31st.

The girl continued, "Things are usually boring this time of year until Halloween. We get a lot of weirdos then."

"That would be fun," Valerie said. "Going to this spooky place on Halloween."

"Ah, here's Mary now," the girl said, gesturing up the hill towards where a middle aged woman, her brown and gray hair in a bun, approached. She was dressed in a thick Oregon Vortex sweatshirt and faded jeans. Her widely smiling face was wrinkled and tough.

"Welcome," she boomed out, trotting down the hill towards them. "Nice to have some visitors on this fabulous fall day. I'm Mary." She held out her hand. Valerie shook first then Lee. "A pleasure to meet you. Where are you two coming from today?"

"Portland," Lee said. "We're heading towards the Redwood National Park but made a detour to stop here."

"Well you won't regret it. First time to the House of Mystery?"

They nodded.

"Prepare to be amazed, then," she said with a little laugh. "Now if you'll follow me..."

She turned and headed up a path. Around them were trees, none of which seemed very old. Sunlight made the fall colors of the deciduous ones glow while the evergreens stood tall, straight and sober amongst them.

"So," Mary said as she walked. "We'll start with a little history." She proceeded to tell them how Native Americans avoided the area, how the trees didn't grow straight and animals wouldn't enter. The house they were going to visit was built in 1890 for mining. Later it had fallen off its foundation and been abandoned. A scientist had supposedly studied the vortex for years before deciding the world wasn't ready for the knowledge of the place and burning his notes. There were various theories: time slowing, magnetic fields and spheres, strange forces exiting from the center of the earth.

And then they came to the house, a crazily tilting peaked-roof structure made of time-bleached wood. In front of it was a seemingly level concrete platform. Mary said, "Alright, usually we do this with two members of the audience but since the audience only has two members I'll have to participate. Which of you will be my first volunteer?" Valerie raised her hand, smiling. "Alright, Valerie," Mary said. "Stand here and I'll go over there. Now Lee, pay attention to our heights relative to each other."

Mary seemed maybe a few inches taller than Valerie, who stood at one end of the little platform, Mary at the other. Then they switched places. Valerie seemed to shrink, Mary to grow, so that when she got to the other end Valerie seemed a foot shorter. It was probably just the dramatically tilting structure behind them that caused the optical illusion, Lee thought.

Next it was his turn. Even looking forward it seemed as if Mary grew when he walked past her, that he was looking levelly at her instead of down like before they'd switched places. Valerie oohed. Lee had been making a point to look straight ahead, not at the house behind him. Maybe the platform wasn't actually level. Maybe that was it. But he felt the beginnings of a queasiness in his stomach.

They went into the House of Mystery. It was an open structure with rough wooden beams supporting the ceiling, the floor slanting away downward. Walking across upright was a struggle, like you were drunk, and the feeling of unease deep in his stomach increased, his body telling him that things weren't right. Mary brought out a level, demonstrated a ping pong ball appearing to roll uphill, a broom balancing at a bizarre angle. She showed them photographs of people switching places outside, then the same photographs with the background removed. The people still appeared to be different heights in the before and after pictures without the slanting house behind them to skew perceptions.

Within the structure heights changed, balance was thrown off kilter. The world was out of sync. Everything seemed wrong.

Valerie was having fun, laughing, struggling up and down the floor while asking Mary questions about the various theories. Lee leaned against a wall as his girlfriend shrank and grew, as the world swayed around him. Nothing made sense, nothing was right. He felt, he realized, exactly how he'd felt when he first started really believing, with sickened gut, that his brother was gone. "I, I need to go," he said weakly and pushed his way back across the floor, stumbling and almost falling once, out the door and past the platform. Still he felt like he might vomit. He kept going down the path, making his way to the road where he leaned against a tree, taking each breath deeply, letting it out in a rush, breathing in again, trying to calm his stomach and his mind. Everything was fine, he told himself, it was just an optical illusion, everything was real and solid. But of course everything wasn't fine.

Valerie came hurrying down the path after him. "Are you ok, Lee?" she asked, putting her hand on his shoulder.

"I don't know. I felt sick. Now maybe I'm a little better but I couldn't take that again, can't go back there."

Mary was hurrying down the hill now, too. "Sometimes the vortex really affects people, especially people that are prone to sea-sickness. I'm sorry. But you're out of it now so you should be ok soon."

Lee wasn't sure he'd ever be ok. "Valerie, I have to tell you something," he said.

"What?" she asked.

"I had another reason for bringing us here. Someone, this guy Joseph who comes into my store, he introduced me to his friend who saw someone who looked like my brother in the redwoods where we're headed. And Paul had started a group called the Coyotes that was talking about doing some radical environmental things and maybe that's why he was here, if he was, though I swore not to tell anyone about that. I should have told you everything anyway. I'm so sorry. I just needed... I'm sorry."

"You should have told me," she agreed, her face going hard, any emotion hidden.

"I know."

"Who thought he saw your brother? How sure was he?"

"He was some homeless guy who talked to a lady he doesn't know how to get ahold of. She saw a guy in an orange backpack who looked like my brother off the trail, running away. I don't know, obviously it's iffy, but I had to come, had see if I found anything, felt anything. And Paul had talked with these Coyotes about the redwoods... I'm sorry. And now, I don't know, this place..."

"I would have come. I know you haven't worked through this, how could you have? Though I don't know that chasing after third-hand stories is helpful. And what is this about Coyotes?"

"A friend of Paul's told me they'd formed a group and talked about environmental actions but that it was just talk, that they hadn't done anything, that Paul wouldn't have done anything by himself, but I don't know. Paul was going to tell me about it the weekend he disappeared, if I'd been with him."

"God damn it, Lee, I really, really wish you would have told me about all this. And that makes two things you weren't telling me, two lies."

"I did tell you. Just later than I should have. I'm so sorry." He felt miserable.

"Right. Because the stupid vortex made you sick. Were you going to tell me otherwise?"

"I was."

"Let's leave. I need to think. We need to talk, alone."

Lee looked away from her face, from trying to read how angry, how disappointed or how under-standing she was. Mary had backed away to the ticket booth, giving them space to fight.

"Thank you for the tour," Valerie said to her as they walked past.

"I'm sorry it upset you," she said, to Lee or to both of them, he wasn't sure. "We can give you some of your money back if you want, since you had to leave early."

"That's fine," Valerie said, and kept walking. She slammed the door when she got back in the car. Lee took several more deep breaths, but his stomach was still churning, Valerie's anger making it worse. So he leaned in the window and asked if she could drive. Without a word she scooted over and he got into the passenger seat, closing the door softly behind him.

She started the car and drove back the way they had come.

For maybe ten minutes, as they wound their way down the little road beside a stream that led to the highway, Valerie was silent. Lee kept his head down, cupped in his hands, breathing deeply, trying not to vomit. Occasionally he would say, "I'm sorry" without looking up. He was. He was sorry he had lied, that he was sick, that his brother had disappeared, that his teeth were falling apart. Sorry that he didn't have any money, that his mom still hadn't come back, that Valerie was mad at him, that he was such an asshole. He was sorry this was his life.

When they got to the wide stretch of I-5 she headed back north. Towards home and towards the turnoff that led to where his brother had been seen. As soon as they merged onto the highway she started talking. "God damn it, Lee, you shouldn't have lied to me!" She sucked in a breath, paused her speech, gathering herself together. Lee squeezed his head tighter with his hands but didn't look up at her, didn't say anything. "You shouldn't have lied to me and it's so damned hard being your girlfriend now when you're going through so much." She said this slowly, measuredly, though there was obviously pain in the way she controlled her voice, pain and anger. "Even on this trip, which was supposed to be about us, I'm second place. I don't blame you for wanting to come here. If it were my brother I would have done the same thing. But I would have told you. And I want to help, wish I could help you. But I can't be there for you when you go down to the redwoods. I'm too angry, I'm feeling too betrayed. You do need to go, though, to see if there's anything to see, to work through whatever you can, do what you can to find Paul or to realize that you won't find him. I can't keep you from that."

She breathed out heavily. Lee felt her words bouncing back and forth in the vast black space that was his mind, that was his world. His tongue ran endlessly over the roughness of the temporary crown. She remained silent, the only noise the hum of the car and the rushing highway sounds. The sounds of his world rushing to a crashing end.

Slowly he pulled his head up and winced at the sunlight that poured into the windows and lit with a glow the tears on Valerie's cheeks. She was so beautiful, even with red eyes and tears and her mouth a thin straight line, her jaw set firmly as if bracing for a punch.

"I'm sorry," he said. Was that all he could say? It was all he felt, it was everything, but he had to say more and tell the truth, had to try harder. He had to keep her. "I'm so sorry, I shouldn't have lied to you. I wish I'd never heard about this, that we'd just gone to Seattle. But I, I couldn't let Paul go. But I'll try. Stay with me. Valerie, I need you. We'll turn around, go to Ashland instead, or to Crater Lake, we're not too far from there. We'll do something, anything else. I don't have to go there. Please?"

"Lee, you and I both know that you have to go to the redwoods even if there's nothing to find there, even if your brother was never there and there's no way to prove if he was or wasn't. And I know I can't go with you, can't spend what was supposed to be our weekend there. I wish I could, but I just can't."

"I don't have to go. Or I can go some other time, we can go anywhere you want, we can go back home."

"You know it would tear at you if we didn't go now, that you couldn't handle it."

It was true, he realized. He did need to go there or he'd feel this nausea, this vertigo, for the rest of his life. He needed to keep following his brother until things were, somehow, resolved. He wished she could come with him, could be by his side. But she said she couldn't and it wasn't, he realized, fair to her to drag her down into the black hole that was his life right now. So he said, "Maybe you're right. But, Valerie, I need you. I love you."

"God damn it, Lee, I love you too. Or I did before this shit. But I fucking wish it weren't so hard. I wish I'd met you before this or way afterwards so that I wouldn't have to sort out who you are from what happened to you."

She loved him. It was the first time she'd said it. Or she had loved him and he'd thrown it away. "And you can't come with me?"

"I can't. I, I think maybe what we should do is you should drop me off at a hotel somewhere, I'll do some thinking and try to calm down. You go down to the redwoods and do whatever it is you need to do there and then you can come back and pick me up and we can see what happens. Or I'll find a bus back. If I can forgive you we'll work on what we need to do to make sure you don't lie to me ever again, to make this relationship work. If it can still work."

"Ok," he said. Maybe to follow his brother he did need to be alone. But she would be there when he came back. Maybe. "And you think things can be ok when I get back to you? You can forgive me?"

"I truly don't know, Lee. I wish I did."

They drove north in silence. Valerie kept her eyes ahead on the road and soon turned off the highway when they saw a sign advertised lodging. They circled around for a while until they found, a ways out of a small town, a series of cabins under tall trees along the swift Rogue River. The same damned river where his brother had caught the salmon, though that had been miles and miles from here. The place looked romantic; he wished he didn't have to leave.

They got out of the car and stood facing each other in the parking lot. Valerie said, "I think this place looks good. At least I won't be stuck in some crappy chain motel while I wait for you. And I do have to wait for you. You have to go there. You wouldn't have lied to me if you didn't. God, I wish you hadn't lied to me, Lee. I could have been there for you. But I'll be fine here, I can hike or read by the river and I can try to work through all this shit you've left me with and figure out a direction forward."

"Are you sure?"

"I'm sure. You should go."

"You'll be ok without a car?"

"It's not ideal, but I'll make do. Now get out of here, Lee. Go to the damned redwoods."

Crying, he leaned forward, wrapping his arms around her, and sobbed into her shoulder. She held him loosely. He let her go, stepped back. "I love you," he said. "I'll be back soon."

"Don't come back until you've worked through whatever it is you have to work through down there, Lee. Don't make all this shit be for nothing."

"I promise."

"Good. I'll give you a call when I've figured things out, if I can, and then you can come and get me. Or else maybe I'll see if there's a Greyhound that will take me back home, depending on what I decide. Now leave." There were tears in her eyes too. She yanked her backpack from the trunk, slung it over her shoulders and staggered towards a large wooden lodge with a reception sign. She didn't turn and look back. Lee felt weak, drained. His tongue played with the false crown.

Lee got back in the car. When she hadn't come out in fifteen minutes he headed for the turnoff for 199 to Crescent City. The turnoff they should have taken earlier in the day if they hadn't gone to the Oregon Vortex, if he hadn't told her he'd lied. They would be in the redwoods together, still together. Still lying.

He followed the sun west as it dipped lower in the sky, as afternoon turned to evening. The road wound down out of the mountains towards the coast. There were sweeping vistas, endless stretches of forests, cliffs falling away to rushing rapids below, but

Lee didn't really register them as more than brief impressions, lost as he was in his own head. He crossed from Oregon into California, told the border agent that he didn't have any fruits or vegetables. He kept driving. And then, near the coast, he entered the redwoods.

FORTY

The road wound through dense forests of towering ruddy trees, their branches slender and green-tufted high above, cutting off the light like in Lee's memory of Paul. There was a sense of silence and stillness even as he was driving through. According to the map he was in Jedediah Smith Redwoods State Park, the northernmost of the string of redwood parks in which his brother had been seen. Orick was maybe fifty miles further south.

Lee kept driving and merged onto 101. It was the same coastal road he and his parents had driven up and down so many times back in Oregon, searching, searching. And here he was again, searching. As he made his way through Crescent City he spotted the Pacific Ocean, the sun leaking reddish through a thick layer of clouds above it, its waters dark and unsettled.

Lee's stomach rumbled and he realized that he hadn't eaten anything since breakfast, the memory of which was a bright little gem in his mind now: laughing with Valerie, sunlight entering through the window of the little diner they'd found a few blocks from their hotel, cheersing with mismatched coffee mugs. It seemed a decade ago, a thousand miles away. It was so precious now though it had seemed like nothing at the time. He decided he wouldn't eat, at least not now. He'd subsist on only that glowing breakfast with Valerie for as long as he could.

As he left the city the road curved alongside cliffs overlooking stretches of beach, rolling hills, rocks and trees. It was the same as the Oregon Coast where they'd spent so much time, or almost the same. Paul hadn't escaped yet when he made it here, if he made it here. It was beautiful, though, in the sunset, the colors washed to gentle pastels. Just like the coast where Paul's car was found was beautiful. There was a sign for Damnation Creek Trail. There were lots of signs, that one didn't mean anything.

It was mostly dark now, not too many other cars on the road, their brights blinding for a second before flicking off. The trees were black around him as was the moonless, starless sky above, but a blue light faintly infused everything. He rose up onto a bridge over the Klamath River. On the other side, off the road, lit from below, a massive Paul Bunyan at least forty feet tall appeared, waving, leaning on an ax. A giant Blue Ox, coming up only to the lumberjack's knees, stood by his side. They looked menacing in the faint light, like they were racing forward or running from something behind them in the dark forest. A sign Lee saw just then read "TREES OF MYSTERY." A shudder ran through his entire body and he felt bile rise in his throat. Lee pressed down on the accelerator and sped onward.

Another road sign passed, just a blurred green glimpse out of the corner of his eye. Lee thought about slamming on the brakes, going back to make sure, but he really didn't want to know. Didn't want the sign to have said, "Lost Man Creek Rd." He wondered if he was going crazy or if the world was.

The trees cleared and the road ran beside, then over, a dark stream. Soon Lee was passing through Orick, which consisted of a few buildings off the side of the highway, mostly unlit, a couple vacancy signs from inns and motels and then, before he knew it, there was darkness again and he was through the town. He turned around on a road that led to what looked like a farmhouse, its windows glowing cozily from the darkness, then headed back north slowly, crawling through town. He could stay at one of those inns, that's probably where he and Valerie would have stayed, but he kept going. There had been a sign with the tent that symbolized a campsite a little north of town, he thought. Near that other one, the one whose name he must have misread. He didn't think it would rain and he certainly wasn't going to find his brother in a motel. Or find any sign of his brother. Find whatever the hell it was he was looking for, whatever it was that he'd maybe thrown away his relationship with Valerie for. But maybe she could forgive him. Maybe she would call.

He came to the turnoff back over the stream and a few miles into the woods. Bald Hills Road. He'd been wrong, there wasn't a campsite sign, just ones for trails: Ladybird Johnson Grove, Redwood Creek Trail, Redwood Creek Overlook. After pulling over to the side of the road he took out his driving map on which he saw that the road ran through the heart of a green park. Starting the car again he turned onto it and headed forward. He passed a giant lumberyard, huge stacks of boards piled high, and thought, no wonder the hills were bald. He barked out a bitter laugh. Maybe it was a logging operation feeding this lumberyard that Paul was planning on destroying.

There was a turnoff right away for the Redwood Creek Trail but he kept going. Trees were suddenly all around the car, sensed more than seen to the sides, illuminated ahead on the twists of the road as it rose into the hills, quiet sentinels. He drove slowly as the road wound steeply up.

There was a little parking lot for the Lady Bird Johnson Grove Trail. He slowed, stopped the car on the shoulder. Could this be the hike on which the lady had seen his brother? It was only a few miles outside of Orick, it could be. But so could a hundred other trails. Did it feel right? Lady Bird, did that mean anything? The place seemed as good as any to start. This road maybe even felt a little familiar from their childhood trip here, though really he had no idea. It was dark, maybe he just wanted it to be the same.

There was a no overnight parking sign and a no camping sign so he kept driving, staring down into the underbrush illuminated starkly by his brights. The road came to the top of a rise then tilted back down. And, there! A little wash where the canopy overhead must be complete because the ferns and bushes that had been covering the ground were gone, leaving just the widely spaced trunks of huge redwoods to interrupt the needle-blanketed ground.

Slowly Lee turned Paul's car off the road. There was a large bounce, the wheels kicked at mud and then he was bumping slowly down the hill, weaving between trees, feeling each lurch in his gut. When he'd been going for maybe five long minutes Lee stopped the car, turning the wheels and engaging the parking break. Looking back up the way he came he didn't see the road, didn't see anything.

Not sure he was hidden, Lee got out his flashlight and walked back up. The air was chilly, the night filled with rustles and whooshes: wind in the branches far above, Lee thought. Needles crunched underfoot and his shoes occasionally sank into deep patches of mud. He was back on the road in a few minutes. Swinging the beam of the flashlight back and forth down the hill he didn't see an answering gleam of metal. Perfect.

Lee walked back towards the car, planning on getting out his pack and finding someplace flat further down the hillside to set up his tent. Then a cold drop landed on his check, another on his bare head, then more and more, thick icy drops of rain pattering down all around him, working their way through the trees.

The water brought Lee to alertness. What the hell was he doing? He was in the middle of the woods in the middle of the night and he was alone. He wanted to find his brother who might have been here or might not have been, might not have even been anywhere near here. And he'd been half thinking he'd just crash off into the woods in the dark, leaving Paul's car hidden behind just like Paul had. What could he see in the dark, what could he find? Did he think he would bump into his brother, stumble on where he was sleeping curled inside a burned out tree? Lee remembered suddenly his brother leaping from a hiding spot in the fire-charred heart of a redwood when they were here as kids, screaming boo, both of them breaking into uncontrollable laughter. Their mom had told Paul sternly not to go ahead out of her sight again.

If he set up his tent in this downpour it would get soaked inside and out. So he pulled his sleeping bag from his pack and spread it out in the back of Paul's car. He stripped naked, hung his already damp clothes over the front seats then slipped into the bag, pulling it shut around him, shuddering. Everything was wrong. Valerie was gone. Maybe in the morning, maybe then he could make sense of things again. Now, though, he needed to sleep.

But sleep didn't come. Thoughts rushed through his head as his body turned and twisted, trying to get comfortable, trying to stretch out, trying not to fall off the narrow seat. His feet banged again and again into the car door as he extended his legs and again and again in his mind he saw Valerie, tears in her lovely eyes, deciding she couldn't be with him, cursing him for lying and saying she couldn't forgive him, that he was too damaged to love. Saw Paul jumping from inside the redwood, saw the adult Paul waving and walking into the trees. Paul dressed as Paul Bunyan, Paul Bunyan looking like Paul, massive, crashing through the forest. His dad screaming in the rain at the dark waters below. His mom walking away from him in the airport. Valerie, that first day he saw her, that half smile as she stood there, so pretty in her baggy dental student smock, Valerie glimpsed across the club. Valerie's hand in his as they watched the swifts spiral. Valerie saying she loved him, or had. A coyote snapping its jaws into cold rushing water, a salmon flicking past just out of reach. His brother ahead of him on some hike in the woods somewhere, looking back with a smile, and Lee trying to catch up and failing.

FORTY-ONE

There was faint light in the air. Lee didn't remember sleeping. There'd been hours and hours, it seemed, of turning and obsessive thoughts, but maybe he'd slept, maybe some of that had been dreams. It didn't matter. Now it was dawn. The ground was damp, steaming fog rose from the trees and the needle-strewn earth. Now it was time to find his brother.

Lee was hungry. He was naked. There was some food in his pack, trail mix, a few granola bars. The plan had been to buy food if they decided to camp. He wanted eggs, sausage, a sandwich, a steak, rice, anything. His stomach was a void, sucking him inward. But he wouldn't even eat the granola, he wouldn't eat anything. He'd subsist on the sunlight and memories, he'd fast. His brother was hungry too.

After putting on a dry change of clothes he stuffed his sleeping bag into its sack then pushed it into his green backpack, a hand-me-down from Paul. He hoisted the pack onto his shoulders, adjusted the straps, tightening and loosening until the weight rode on his hips, until it felt right.

He started downhill into the trees for ten steps then turned and headed back. Patty had seen his brother from the path. He'd start there.

After backtracking up to the road Lee walked alongside it. Birds called, darting from branch to branch. There was fog, glowing white with light that filtered down from above, swirling in eddies among the thick trunks of the trees, hiding their tops in the mist. On the ground was a carpet of giant ferns, a shocking green, an infinite complexity of leaves.

Ahead Lee saw a sleek wooden pedestrian bridge arcing over the road that he hadn't noticed in the dark last night. It went from the parking lot to the trailhead. It was the start. Lee crossed the road to the lot. There were no cars. He headed across the bridge, his steps clanking on the wood, his hand running lightly along its smooth rail. On the other side there was a little informational kiosk with booklets that promised to educate him all about the redwoods' ecosystem. He didn't take one, he wasn't here to learn. The trail was, it said, an easy one mile loop. But maybe it intersected other trails, trails that twisted on forever all the way back to the Oregon coast.

The fog was already burning off, or maybe it was that he was above it now, maybe it still clustered thickly in the valleys below. The trail was wide, soft packed dirt littered here and there with plaques and benches. The trees were huge, gorgeous. A few were burned out, little caves eaten into their trunk, the edges a charcoal black though the redwood still lived tall above. Some were big enough for a child to hide in but Lee didn't think this was the place, the exact place, of his memories.

Lee walked slowly, imagining he was Patty walking here, imagining he was his brother. Wisps of fog drifted occasionally in the air. Patches and tatters of sunlight lit the sides of trees, bringing out the red in their bark, fell on the sparkling diamond drops on the leaves of ferns and glowed in the dark green boughs of redwoods dizzyingly high above.

He didn't know what he was doing, didn't know what he hoped to find. His stomach growled and the pack dug into his shoulders. And then Lee stopped still. Between the trees right here there was space, openness. And beyond that another ridge, the base of redwoods away across a valley. And a glimpse of movement, something hurrying away. A deer, maybe. Or maybe it was just a branch blowing in the wind. Lee could clearly see Patty standing here, where he stood now, seeing across this valley to that ridge, glimpsing his brother there, his orange pack visible between the trees, his face, scraggily bearded, seeing her and then turning, running away. He'd be instantly lost in the jigsaw maze of trees that blocked sight, that only revealed that other ridge here, just here.

Lee walked off the path, stepping over ferns, pushing a larger branch of a bush out of his way. He lost his view of the ridge immediately but knew it was there, ahead. Soon the trail and the road were lost behind him, forgotten. The ground tilted down away sharply, trees, shrubs, plants, life everywhere growing. He broke through.

The hill fell steeply down, the lowest branches of redwoods that grew on the bottom at eye level now. The ground was mostly clear, the canopy thick above his head. He slowed, carefully edging downward. Now below he saw a thick clump of green vegetation: skinny trees with interlocked branches dripping with moss, the remnants of brilliant fall leaves clinging here and there, thick brush and an occasional glimpse of a stream, black at this distance.

He'd have to cross somehow, but first he had to get down there. He worked his way across the face of the hill to a gully and headed down that, crossing from side to side, zigzagging downward, stepping over the little trickles of water that flowed down with him. His mind was blank, lost in the puzzle of moving forward. Soon things leveled out. He pushed a tree branch out of his way, stepped over a clump of ferns and found himself on the stony banks of a small dark stream laced with white ripples.

Suddenly he wondered, could this be Lost Man Creek? But there was no road in sight and anyway, he must have read the sign wrong. Loman Creek Rd., Mossman Creek. And even if it was, it wouldn't mean anything, it was a coincidence. It would have been named after someone lost hundreds of years ago.

To cross Lee would have to leap. It would be easy except he had the backpack weighing him down. Briefly he considered throwing it across, but what if he missed and everything got soaked? Instead he turned, following the stream, regaining ground he'd lost moving away from the ridge that was his goal when he'd gone to the gully. After a little twist around a clump of what Lee thought were alders the stream flattened out, spreading to a pool lined by smooth, wet shining rocks. It narrowed to a little rushing channel at the other end. Lee stepped over.

The hill going up from this side, the ridge he needed to climb, was steep, steeper than what he'd come down. But going up was easier, less dangerous. Lee wound between the whitish ghostly trunks of the trees that grew here where the sun broke through the endless canopy of redwoods at the stream and its rocky banks. In fact, he noticed now, a little light fell a ways upstream, gleaming on the water, turning it to translucent gold. Looking up Lee saw little cracks of the sky for the first time in what seemed like hours, blue with wisps of white. Then he was through the alders into the soft needly ground of the redwoods again, climbing, sometimes on his hands and knees, besides the trees that soared effortlessly up this hillside into the sky. The sky of their interlocked branches, a brown and green ceiling. But there was light up there now, sunshine playing above in the boughs, darting down in broken spears. Sunshine up where he was going, up there where his brother had been.

It seemed like the top was just ahead, right after another steep scramble. The going had been agonizingly slow, having to backtrack to avoid thick clumps of vegetation or impossible rises. But this he thought he could do. His goal was right there.

Lee rushed up the steep hillside, his hands in front of him for purchase on the soft damp earth. There was a lurch, his feet flew from beneath him. A thud rattled his chest as he hit the ground and then he tumbled, scrambling as he slid downward, arms hindered by his pack grasping but there was nothing there except dirt that tore through his fingers. A thud resounded through his body as his leg hit something hard. He twisted to the side and stopped, resting against the unfeeling trunk, gnarled and rough, of an enormous redwood.

Lee lay there panting, the forest still, everything still. And then the pain seeped into his consciousness. His leg. His palms. His ribs. Slowly, cautiously, he stretched his body, moved his limbs, still lying on the wet ground. His palms, when he held them up to his face, were covered in earth and seeping through that here and there was dark blood. He breathed deeply and there was some tightness in his chest, but nothing shooting, just an ache. His knee was what really worried him, the twinge of pain there when he straightened it, a little line of fire running somewhere just under the cap. He slipped out of his pack, leaned it against the tree then slowly tried to rise. His hands stung when he placed them back in the dirt and pushed himself up, stung again when he pressed one against the strangely soft bark of the tree that had stopped his fall so solidly. When he was up, he slowly put more and more weight off his right leg and the tree onto the left. It ached burningly but he could stand. Lee took a few cautious steps. He could walk, though each step jolted pain up his leg and towards his heart.

Lee wished he could make a walking stick but the ground was clear, the branches far, far above. He knew he should stop, rest, put Neosporin on his cuts and wrap something around his knee. But fuck it, he'd embrace the pain. Embrace the hunger, the loneliness and the exhaustion. How else could he find his brother? And the top, the ridge, was just up there, mocking him, calling him. He leaned down, sweeping the backpack up and onto his shoulders. Another twinge of fire erupted in his knee. Slowly and steadily this time, digging his torn hands into the dirt and pulling on the trunks of the redwoods, he made his way back up to where he'd fallen and, half crawling, continued up the rest of the way.

Finally he made it to the top. The ground seemed to slope away in front of him though it rose still to his right. Seemed to, but who knew, it was impossible to see anything clearly through the trees. Was he at the spot he'd seen from the other side of the valley? He couldn't see back now, didn't know how he could have seen through this thicket of endless giants, how a sightline could have opened. Maybe he'd imagined it. Or maybe it was further up, maybe with height would come vision. There was no way he was going to get above these trees, but what could he do but walk? So he turned to his right and continued upward, the slope easy now. His knee hurt, his hands hurt, his mind and soul hurt. With his tongue he rubbed at the rough edge of his fake tooth. He kept walking.

Lee stopped. There! There was the view, the opposite ridge back the way he'd come, some gap between hundreds of trees. It was a line of sight, a connection. Was it the same one? It had to be. He was here, he'd reached his goal. Lee looked around. Redwood trunks. A few scattered ferns. There was no more light overhead; clouds must have moved in again. There were no footprints, no signs of a campfire, no scrap of trash. His brother wouldn't leave any trash, any sign. He would blend into the wilderness. Of course. His brother had always picked up litter they'd found on trails, had packed everything out with him. Lee had known this, it wasn't a surprise. He'd known all along there was nothing to find if he got here. And here he was. Maybe. There were hundreds of trails near here, thousands of miles of them, and most probably had a place where one ridge viewed another through the trees. The trail he'd been on probably had multiple and he wasn't even sure this was the same; he couldn't see a path over there, couldn't see one anywhere. All he could see was trees, trees everywhere. Redwoods, covering the hills, obscuring the world.

Lee threw himself to the ground, unbuckled the pack and let it fall away from him. He lay there on his back, staring upwards as the trees bent inward towards a point an infinite distance above, converging in the heavens overhead. He lay there feeling pain. There was nothing to find. The rising trees dizzied him so he closed his eyes.

When Lee's eyes opened next the light had changed. He must have slept but he had no idea how long. It was still light but what if he'd slept a whole day, what if it was the next morning? That would make it Halloween. He was groggy but didn't know if it was due to too much sleep or too little. His knee throbbed with each beat of his heart, the pain swelling then retracting.

Lee looked around. There were trees everywhere. He couldn't tell where the sun was. Maybe he'd only slept a minute and it was still lost in clouds.

The ground sloped away in three directions, rose in one. That was the way he'd been going, he thought. Suddenly he wasn't sure, wasn't sure which way he'd been headed, where he'd come from or how to get back. It was hard to think through the fog in his head, fog burst with every breath by the lightning of pain from his knee. Lee felt rising panic, the taste of metal on his tongue.

He thought he knew which way was back but he wasn't sure. And even if he was, he couldn't just turn around and go back the way he'd come, could he? The thought of stumbling down that hill then climbing back up the other side, his knee throbbing, maybe sprained, torn or broken, exhausted, starving, the pack weighing him down, looking for that path, searching for his brother's car... It didn't seem possible. He wouldn't make it. It was too hard, too far. He couldn't cross the stream, he wouldn't even get there. He would fall where he'd fallen before and break something else. He would die in these woods, lost forever. And if he'd slept a few hours, which was most likely, it would get dark soon and then there'd be no hope. The ghosts of this forest would take him, or animals or exhaustion and hunger.

Even if he could somehow make it to the car, a dream that didn't seem possible, could he get in and drive back to pick up an angry Valerie who may or may not forgive him, return to life in Portland without his mom or his brother? Go back to scraping up money to pay for them to drill holes in his teeth? It didn't seem real. These trees, the ground under his feet, the pain: that was reality, wasn't it? He didn't know. He just knew he couldn't go back. Maybe if he went forward he'd find something, someone to help him, some way to safety. Or he'd find Paul.

So Lee rose and struggled to get his pack on. And he continued ahead, away, downhill towards what he thought was north. Maybe the next ridge was the one. Or maybe he'd find the creek named for his brother, named for him.

The hill sloped gently down between the endless trees, some of the easiest terrain he'd encountered yet, but he went slowly, limping, trying to keep the weight off his leg. The pack dug into his shoulders. He was somewhere beyond hunger but his mouth was bone dry and he'd long ago drained his Nalgene, though he didn't remember when he'd had the last sip. Soon it was apparent that the light was dimming imperceptibly, that night was falling. At midnight it would be, probably, Halloween, time of the spirits, ghosts and lost men. He'd join them if he didn't find some way out.

Night came on quickly, the shadows of the enormous trees darkening, subsuming everything as the dim light faded from the air. Lee wasn't sure which direction he was headed or where he was going. Clumps of trees and fallen branches got in his way and he had to go around, trying to stay on course, whatever that was. He kept moving though his knee screamed. And then, so soon, it was dark. The trees were still visible, silhouettes in the bluish air, but the ground at his feet was pooled in shadow. Lee stopped.

He put his backpack on the ground and dug his hand down into it, feeling blindly for his flashlight.

Sleeping bag, clothes, cooking utensils and stove but nothing to cook, deodorant, a toothbrush. No flashlight. Shit, fuck! No flashlight. In a rushed panic he upended his bag, dumped it on the ground and started digging frantically through everything. He needed the flashlight or else he'd be lost. Lost like his brother in the dark, never found, disappeared, a mystery, his body rotting amongst the redwoods.

Or lost like his brother, traveling the backroads, escaping his life and all the shit in it, escaping civilization and all his pain, hiking in the woods, heading south. Suddenly famished, forgetting about his fast, Lee tore into his bag of trail mix then devoured the granola bars. He was still starving when he finished and he rooted around in his pack though he knew there was nothing to find.

If he was going to follow his brother into the woods he needed to eat more. But he didn't fucking know what he was doing out here, couldn't go catch a salmon with a sharpened stick or eat wild berries or mushrooms, hunt squirrels or deer. He was worthless, he was doomed. And would his brother do any better? Paul had spent more time outdoors than he had but he wasn't a survivalist. He'd brought dehydrated backpacking dinners and Cliff bars when he went camping and that salmon was one of the few fish Lee had ever seen him catch.

Paul was dead. Lee realized it finally, suddenly, like a weight settling onto his shoulders. He was living what might have happened if his brother had tried to escape and he couldn't survive a few miles off the highway for a day. He was lost. His brother wasn't so different from him that he could have made it hundreds of miles south without using his credit cards, without making a call, without leaving a trace. His brother was human, not some Coyote superhero eco-terrorist. His brother was dead somewhere back in Oregon, on the coast, maybe playing at being an eco-terrorist, practicing. Maybe he'd slipped like Lee had slipped but there was no redwood there to stop him, just an endless fall to the unsettled waters and jagged rocks below, the icy foaming surf. Maybe he'd find Paul's ghost here near Lost Man Creek but he wouldn't find Paul.

Lee would follow him and his parents would lose both their sons to the wilderness. It was night, his knee was stiffening with pain, he had no food, no light. He was lost. And he couldn't find the goddamn flashlight, had forgotten it back at the car like a motherfucking idiot. The car that was hidden off the road and wouldn't be found. He would die too and that would be easier. It would be right.

And then Lee felt a buzz jolt through his body. He looked wide eyed, bewildered, into the darkness. The trunks of trees were just a shade blacker than the air around them, no stars, no moon. He was seeing the world outside his head for what seemed like the first time in ages. This was where he was, and the buzz had been his phone. He pulled it out, amazed that he got a signal here, amazed that it still had batteries. When he flipped it open its bluish light spilled into the world, illuminating it, bathing his hands matted with dirt and blood, his possessions scattered on the ground along with redwood needles and an arc of gnarled mushrooms growing from the earth nearby. Lee blinked, focused on the screen. It told him he had six missed calls, six voicemails. Two from his dad, one from his mom. Patrick. Elly. The most recent was from Valerie.

There was only a sliver of battery life left. He decided he wouldn't listen to the messages now, saving the power for the phone's faint light. And then in his head there was a gap, a sudden change, an emptiness. Lee's tongue ran over the stump of his missing tooth. Pressed between his lips was something hard, something alien.

The knowledge of what had happened filled him, somehow, with calm. He'd been worrying the temporary crown with his tongue, running it over and over the spot that didn't feel right, and it had come loose. Carefully he pulled it out of his mouth with two fingers and felt it, tiny and hard. He ran his tongue gingerly over the rough remnants of his tooth, what was left after the ravages of the root canal. The void felt bigger than his head, bigger than the world, bigger even than the darkness. But there was no pain.

Lee put the fake tooth carefully in his pocket. Then, by the eerie blue glow of his phone screen, he found the soft lump of his sleeping bag. He pulled it out, spread it on the ground and climbed inside. A rock dug into his back, so he felt around again, found his pad and flopped in his bag on top of it. He flipped his phone closed and the darkness was complete. Insulated from the air and from the ground he lay on his back staring upward, seeing nothing, seeing the hole in his head. It wasn't really that big. It was just the size of the tiny bit of resin he'd pulled from his mouth. And it could be fixed, with work. Valerie had called and he needed to pick her up in the morning.

Lee heard now, somewhere, the faint soothing rushing sounds of flowing water. He would sleep. In the morning, in the light, he would find the creek and limpingly follow its flow, dropping his pack if he needed to, until it reached a road, a town or the ocean. He could make it. He could find his way back.

ACKNOWLEDGMENTS

There are so many people to thank I don't think I can possibly get to them all. Here's a try, though. Much gratitude to:

- The People's Ink and all its members, especially the five other authors who are releasing their books with mine. This wonderful group gave me the push and the support I needed to publish this novel.

- Everyone who backed the People's Ink Kickstarter, with special thanks to our biggest donors: Lottie Ingalls, Brenda Pope and Frank and Alice Streng. You're making it possible for our books to reach a much wider audience than they otherwise could have.

- All the friends and workshoppers who have critiqued and edited versions of Fillings over the years. With your help I have made this a vastly better novel than I could have on my own.

- Greg Jensen, who supplied me with the perfect title. Elin McLain, you made the cover of this book look great; Joshua Talbert, you made me look good on the back. The last minute copy-edit from Travis McGuire was invaluable. Rich Pope, this novel never would have seen the light of day if it weren't for your inspiration and tireless work.

- The wonderful coffee shops of Southeast Portland, especially Albina Press, Cellar Door, Ford Food and

Drink, Oblique Coffee Roasters and Rocking Frog Café. They have given me welcoming spaces in which to write and delicious caffeine to fuel me.

- Last but far from least I need to thank my family (Mom, Dad and Lindsay especially), all the friends I haven't mentioned yet and the wonderful Melissa Streng. Without all of your love, support and encouragement, writing, editing and publishing this book would never have been possible.